BREAKING POINT

BREAKING POINT

Riva Pomerantz

TARGUM/FELDHEIM

This is a work of fiction. The characters are imaginary; any resemblance to real people, living or dead, is unintentional.

First published 2004
Copyright © 2004 by Riva Pomerantz
ISBN 1-56871-333-9

Published by:
TARGUM PRESS, INC.
22700 W. Eleven Mile Rd., Southfield, MI 48034
E-mail: targum@netvision.net.il
Fax: 888-298-9992
www.targum.com

Distributed by:
FELDHEIM PUBLISHERS
208 Airport Executive Park, Nanuet, NY 10954

Printing plates "Frank," Jerusalem

Printed in Israel

To my husband Joel
For everything.

To Bracha Raiza, Dovid Yosef,
and Akiva Nachman
You light up my life.

Acknowledgments

The Ribbono shel Olam, my Creator, has endowed me with the ability to write this book. I am unable to fully express the depth of my *hakaras hatov* for His constant, infinite goodness.

My appreciation goes to my parents, Ron Henig and Debby Henig, who have always encouraged me to be creative and to write. Their inner strength and self-sacrifice is truly inspiring. I thank my wonderful siblings for cheering me on through the publication of this book.

My grandparents, Paul and Roberta Tobias, have always believed in me. They are a real *berachah* to our family.

My in-laws, Larry and Phylis Pomerantz, are more than I could have ever asked for. Their caring and kindness know no limits, and they are a huge blessing to us.

I want to thank Rabbi Doniel Neustadt, who has always given generously of his time, advice, and endless wisdom — in this project, and in so many others.

Thank you to R' Yitzchok Feldheim, who carefully reviewed the manuscript and offered incisive *he'aros*. It is a pleasure to work for Feldheim Publishers, and I value the entire Feldheim family.

Thanks to Rabbi Shmuel Waldman, author of the excellent work *Beyond a Reasonable Doubt*, who took the time to review this manuscript and offer his insightful suggestions.

Rabbi Moshe Speiser, who runs the Kav Baruch Hotline, has also offered invaluable insights and advice, and I have endeavored to incorporate some of his effective techniques in this book.

A special thanks to the Targum team for their expertise in publishing this book. My gratitude goes to Miriam Zakon for her input and to Diane Liff for her beautiful cover. A big *yasher koach* to Chaya Baila Gavant — your editing talents are astounding.

My kids are too young to know exactly what "writing a book" means, but they have endured their fair share of watching me type on the computer, though I have tried to balance my parenting with my writing as best I could. Thanks, guys!

My wonderful husband has taught me so much, supported me through myriad projects, and has always been there for me. He is my cheerleader, my best critic, and my role model.

Thanks to the many people who contributed to this book, both directly and indirectly. I feel certain that I must have overlooked thanking key people in these acknowledgments. If you are one of them, please know that I do, indeed, appreciate you.

R. P.

Note to the Reader

Dear Reader,

I beg you to forgive my audacity at undertaking the writing of so sensitive a book. My intention is to bring to mind a tremendous challenge that has come to the forefront of our lives. Increasingly, *frum* teenagers are becoming disenchanted with their way of life and testing the forbidden waters to varying degrees. This issue has been addressed by a number of *gedolei Yisrael*, and valuable guidance is being offered to both parents and children. My goal in writing this book is simply to provide some experience, strength, and hope to anyone with whom this topic may strike a chord.

In this novel, I have tried to portray a completely fictitious family who is struggling with their son "going off the *derech*." I have taken great pains to avoid finger-pointing, judging, labeling, and stereotyping. It is my fervent hope that whoever you are, dear reader, you are not in any way offended by my attempt to highlight an issue of extreme sensitivity and deep emotion.

I do not pretend to be an expert on child-rearing, on *hashkafah*, or on dealing with teenagers "on the fringe." On the contrary. I can only offer my variegated life experiences, my exposure to many teenagers as a teacher and mentor, and the extensive resources I have researched and assimilated. Due to the sensitivity of the subject, a number of Torah authorities have reviewed this manuscript and made their corrections.

In the back of the book, I have compiled a list of resources and suggested readings, which you may find helpful.

May we all be *zocheh* to tremendous *siyatta diShmaya* in every area of our lives.

B'vrachah,
Riva Pomerantz
September 2004

Prologue

They say it's best to start at the beginning, even though beginnings are the hardest. But how does one define the beginning when the beginning seems undefinable?

He was a perfect baby, as his mother never used to tire of telling everyone. Hardly cried, gained steadily, rarely got sick. She was quick to show pictures then too — of a chubby, beautiful little boy holding rattles, tearing apart books. There was something in those clear blue eyes, though. A determination, a curiosity, that gave some sort of indication, perhaps, of the mystery behind the metamorphosis from perfect baby to troublesome teen. But then again, it's hard to know. It's always so hard to know.

She has more pictures, too. A toddler digging in the sandbox. A young boy playing baseball, wearing a too-big cap over one eye. There are also family portraits: two parents smiling, embracing three children grinning at the photographer's pet parrot. Then four children, five, and then six — parents still smiling, but looking less young, less fresh; some of the children more reluctant to smile. He is there too, in that family portrait, but he is not one of the smilers. He has his hands in the pockets of his — no, they are not jeans, but close — and those defiant eyes stare at the photographer, or maybe through him, with the casual air of one who spurns authority. His father's hand rests lightly on his shoulder, but the gesture is awkward and may have been the photographer's doing. This is usually the point when his mother stops showing the pictures.

One

The first blush of dawn seeped through the cracks in the curtains, daubing splashes of light on Ephraim Faber's silhouette. He moved quietly so as not to disturb his wife, washed his hands in the basin next to the bed, and began to dress. But Dina had awakened and was watching her husband through half-closed, languid eyes. She was permitted another precious half-hour of sleep, but she lay in bed, observing Ephraim's careful movements, watching him comb his black hair, put his pens in the pocket of his crisply ironed white shirt. She smiled. He was such a wonderful husband. It was hard to believe they had stood together under the *chuppah* eighteen years ago — it seemed like just yesterday. She felt herself a very fortunate woman.

Ephraim caught her eye as he inspected himself in the dresser mirror.

"Up so soon? Go back to sleep, Dina'le — you need your rest. You have a busy day."

"Thank you. I'll drift off."

"What did you say you were going to do again today?"

"Take the kids shopping for winter clothes."

"Right. I left you money in your wallet."

"Thank you. What are your plans for the day?"

"Didn't I tell you? We're making a *siyum* together with the other class. The boys are so excited — the yeshivah ordered donuts for them.”

“Sounds exciting to me!”

“Should I bring one home for you?”

Dina smiled. “Nah, I’m on a diet.”

“As they say in French — give me a break! You don’t need no diets, Dina.” He knotted his tie methodically. “Do the children need a lot of things?”

“Well, Yosef said that he and Chanan must have an electric saw, or we will be forever responsible for stunting their promising career as architects.”

Ephraim laughed out loud at the antics of the ten- and nine-year-old who were constantly scheming, dreaming, and otherwise getting into trouble.

“And Chavie is pretty predictable, actually. She told me that since she’s almost in ‘the *parashah*,’ she’ll need a few suits. And she decided that she can’t have her hair cut by Malky down the block anymore — only the salon will do for her now, at $40 a haircut.”

Ephraim smiled, but he was not pleased.

“What will be with that daughter of ours? I wonder if she dreams about clothes and jewellery all night — her head is so full of it. *Nu, nu* — at least she learns a little *ruchniyus* in school every now and then, no?”

“Of course. And she’s a tremendous *ba’alas chesed*, don’t forget that. They asked her to be head of the *Chesed* Committee this year.”

“Good. Maybe it’ll knock some *tachlis* into her. Go through her closet and see if she really needs anything, but be firm with her, Dina. I don’t know where she gets this pettiness from — certainly not from you.”

Dina smiled inwardly and blushed. “It’s just a stage, Ephraim — there’s no need to be harsh with her. She’ll grow out of it and when you see the son-in-law she’ll bring us, *b’ezras Hashem*, you won’t have even one word to say about Chavie’s wardrobe!”

“Amen!”

He gathered some papers from the dresser.

"I notice that Shira is becoming clothes conscious, too. She wants me to buy a certain pin that 'all the girls in her class have' to put on her uniform shirt. *Baruch Hashem* for uniforms, or every day would be a new battle." Seven-year-old Shira had recently become very much aware of the differences between their financial situation and that of some of her friends. Although she was well-liked and a class leader, she had started complaining about all the things her peers had that she didn't. It bothered Dina very much, but she wasn't sure how to deal with it, and Ephraim would surely be angered by it.

"*Oy*, do I hate this 'all the girls have it,' Dina. There's no end. '*Yesh lo mei'ah, rotzeh masayim*' — you give in on one thing, and she immediately wants something else. Don't even let it start. We're a Torah family and we don't have the money for these things. And besides, who needs brooches when we're preparing for the Olam HaEmes — they don't have any of this junk over there, you know."

"I know, but it's very hard to explain to a seven-year-old."

"You don't need any big explanations, Dina. Just say, 'You don't need this and the Torah says it's not the best thing for you, so you're not getting it' and finished."

"You're right, Ephraim."

He glanced at his watch. "*Oy* — I'm late for davening."

"You'd better hurry, then. Oh — Avrumie also said he needs some new clothes."

"Really?" Ephraim was surprised. "Avrumie never took much of an interest in what he wore."

"Maybe it's peer pressure, but he gave me a whole list of things he absolutely couldn't be without."

Ephraim frowned. "I'm not sure we should cater to every whim of his. Let him spend his time thinking about learning, not about *narishkeiten*. Besides, it's expensive."

Dina nodded. "Sima's also complaining that the girls laugh at her clothes. She feels like she doesn't fit in. Do you think we should splurge and buy her a whole new wardrobe?"

"Are you being serious, Dina? Of course not! If she's feeling that way it's because she has poor self-esteem. We have to correct the problem at the source, not the manifestations of the problem. Why is she feeling insecure?"

Dina didn't know what to say. Why did Sima feel insecure? Probably because she was just a little too bumbling, a little too slow, not "with it" enough to make it with her classmates. How had her personality developed that way?

"I don't know. What do you think, Ephraim?"

"Well, I never really noticed that Sima had problems fitting in. She seems okay at home."

"I guess so," said Dina, not in the mood to continue the conversation further.

"Please don't let the children pressure you into spending more than you feel you should, Dina. It's not proper *chinuch*."

Dina nodded again. He was right.

"I look around these days and I'm shocked by what I see — these kids who drive to school in their brand new Lexuses, wearing the latest styles. It ruins them — it simply ruins the kids."

Dina sighed in agreement and closed her eyes to catch another few minutes of leisure.

Two

vrume'le, supper's ready, please come down!"
A faint voice wafted down from the attic. "Start
without me."

Dina stood at the staircase undecided, her hand poised on her slender hip, a frown on her face. Family supper time was a sacred ceremony, not to be missed. And yet, was this a molehill waiting to become a mountain? Ephraim was not home that night to tell her what to do. She turned away and went into the kitchen.

"We won't wait for Avrumie," she said resolutely to the children at the table and turned to cut the food on the baby's high-chair tray. This was not the first blatant breach of the day. Her morning had been heralded in with the sight of her *bechor* in the washroom shaving, head uncovered.

"I don't wear *kippah*s in the washroom, Mom — I hold it's not right to bring something holy into a bathroom," he had laughed when she said something. She didn't find it funny. Not the deliberate choice of "*kippah*" over "yarmulke," not her new title, and not his attempt at playful humor. And she had told him so, in no uncertain terms. In retrospect perhaps she'd come down a little too hard, but then again, wasn't she the mother? Wasn't she the one entrusted with the responsibility of raising this child to become a *ben Torah*, an *ehrliche Yid*? To walk around without a yarmulke! And what had his reaction been? Sulking, hostile acquiescence of a sort. He'd stalked out of the washroom without looking at her, shaver and all, to resume shaving in his own room. But he'd reappeared with the black velvet yarmulke perched on his head, albeit at a jaunty angle, and for a minute she thought it looked smaller than she'd ever remembered it, but surely it was her imagination.

The day had gotten consistently worse when Avrumie had brought over his friend Menachem. Menachem and Avrumie had become friends only recently, although they had been living in the same neighborhood for years. Dina was decidedly not in favor of Menachem. Tall, lanky, with an odd taste in clothes and a carefully cultured two-days' beard growth on his handsome face, Menachem was not her "type." She could not pin him down for any specific wrongdoing, a fact which Avrumie was quick to point out. He was always polite, in a mocking sort of way, and he complimented her cooking, but a mother could see past that, couldn't she? When Menachem came over, he and Avrumie would disappear into the attic, from which strains of loud music could be heard the rest of the evening. Loud Jewish music, at least, though in Dina's mind it was as Jewish as she was Catholic. It was not the kind of music she ever bought for the family.

A plate clattered to the floor, shocking Dina out of her thoughts. Supper was over, and she'd day-dreamed right through it. Cries of "It wasn't me!" (Chanan), "Yoseeeeeeef!" (Shira), "I can't believe it — you got spaghetti sauce on my brand new blouse!" (Chavie), erupted. Dina sighed.

"Was that your plate, Yosef?" she asked her mischievous nine-year-old. He smiled guiltily.

"It slipped."

"I'm afraid you have a big clean-up job, Yosef," she said sternly and handed him a towel. Sixteen-year-old Chavie flounced out of the kitchen to rub Stainstick into her blouse. Another day, another supper, another mess.

"Sima, let me see your homework," Dina said to her awkward *bas mitzvah*, and she sighed again.

Three

Dina peeled the potatoes, humming to herself. She loved cooking for Shabbos. For her it was both a release and a labor of love. What would she make this week? She liked trying out new recipes while incorporating the things her family liked best. Of course, there would be the golden chicken soup with *kneidlach* — what would Shabbos be without chicken soup, prepared exactly as her own mother had made it, and her mother before her, for generations? "*Shabbos kodesh yom chemdaso*," she sang softly. She had never been much of a singer, but she liked to sing a bit when she was in a good mood and alone in the kitchen, her own domain.

She processed the potatoes — they would make a delicious potato kugel, fried to a crusty brown on the outside, but soft and tantalizing inside. When the kugel was done she would prepare the chicken. The chicken always took careful deliberation and much flipping through her cookbooks to find something traditional, yet different, that she would enjoy preparing as much as the family would enjoy eating.

Some of her friends were aghast at her deviation from the usual roast chicken routine. Once she had been telling one of her friends about a great recipe she had for Hawaiian chicken with coconut milk in it, and there had been a pregnant pause. "Did you say coconut milk?" Esther had asked, shocked. Dina had laughed. "I sure did," she asserted. "I wait six hours, though, before putting the milk on the chicken!" She laughed gaily. She just couldn't resist. Esther had laughed too, after Dina had explained exactly what coconut milk was.

Sometimes Dina second-guessed herself. Was she really a "deviator"? Was she not *frum* enough? She wanted so badly to fit into the mold, but did Hawaiian chicken really make her stand out? She dressed the right way, spoke the right way, did the correct amount of *chesed*, attended the requisite *shiurim* — didn't she? And yet, when Esther stared at her in disbelief, she felt uncomfortable. Perhaps she wasn't doing enough to fit in. Dina's parents had been plenty *frum*, but they just hadn't measured up to the standard of today's *frumkeit*. Her mother wore things like leopard-print shirts; her father wore a knitted yarmulke. Sometimes these things seemed so petty and childish to her, and yet at other times, she viewed them as very vital. *Belonging* was the byword. She had had enough of being an outsider as a child and young adult. The *frum* community was very insular and safe, fenced in by black hats and white shirts. This was the path she and Ephraim had chosen, and she was very happy they had.

She would make an apple pie for dessert, she decided, deftly braiding the challah dough that had risen on the counter. She loved the feel of the dough springing back beneath her fingers. One day she would teach Chavie how to bake challos, but for now she could not bear to share the beloved preparations for Shabbos.

She'd like to think it was because she loved Shabbos so much, but the thought didn't sit so well with her conscience. She knew, deep down, that she relished the praise, the compliments, the requests for seconds. Was it such a terrible thing? she wondered. There were worse. She took out a small pastry brush and painted the challos with beaten egg. They would rise for another hour and then enter the oven to be baked to a heavenly, amber crisp. She began peeling the apples, her hands moving rhythmically in downward strokes of the peeler.

Tomorrow she and the children would clean the house until it shone. There would be the regular grumblings and groanings about who would have to clean the washroom and who would have to wash the floor, but Dina would strive to impress upon them the beauty of Shabbos and how wonderful it was to prepare for it. Then Ephraim would come home and give them a little speech about listening to their mother and finding enjoyment in doing mitzvos. Dina made a mental note to check if they had enough *chrain* in the fridge to serve with the fish Friday night and for *shalosh seudos*. On Shabbos morning they would have the traditional "*ein mit tzibul*" — egg salad with fried onions, with liver for anyone who wanted. Then they would eat the savory *cholent*, which had been bubbling enticingly on the *blech* for nearly twenty-four hours, and sing *zemiros* together. Shabbos was the only real family time, what with Ephraim so busy, and all the children with their different schedules. Dina smiled to herself in anticipation.

Four

"*A gutten Shabbos*," Ephraim greeted his wife as he and the boys entered the front vestibule, closing the door behind them in a gust of cold air.

"*Gut Shabbos*," Dina replied, smiling. She had had a chance to lie down on the couch after *licht bensching* and she felt refreshed and happy, smiling in her almost-new robe that she had bought recently. She helped the boys hang up their jackets in the closet. Ephraim sat down in his chair at the head of the table to begin singing "*Shalom Aleichem*" in his melodious voice.

"Dovidel, Chanan, Yosef — come sing with me!" he called to the boys.

Dina suddenly realized that someone was missing.

"Where's Avrumie?" she asked Ephraim, worry creeping into her voice.

He looked up at her and stopped singing.

"You're right — we didn't see Avrumie in shul. He must have davened somewhere else. He'll be here any minute. When did he leave the house? I didn't even see him around here today."

Dina's thoughts raced. Avrumie had done his required jobs, complaining and kvetching as he polished the silver and tore the toilet paper. Then he had disappeared into his room, announcing that he was taking a shower, and that was the last she'd seen of him. Had he gone to shul at all? Could he still be up in his room? She hoped against all hope that he was not. That would be...she didn't even want to think about the repercussions such an act would have.

Just then the door swung open and Avrumie stood, framed in the doorway. All eyes turned to him and he blushed.

"Good Shabbos — why's everyone staring at me?" he said self-consciously.

"*A gutten Shabbos*, Avrume'le," Ephraim said. "We were just wondering where you were."

"I davened...somewhere else," he said lamely. "Sorry I'm late."

Ephraim didn't press the point.

"Take off your coat and come sing with us," he said. "Now where were we? *Bo'achem leshalom*...."

Dina eyed Avrumie. He was wearing his new olive suit that he had begged her to buy, much against her will. The condition was that he always wear his hat with it, a promise he made under duress. She had noticed lately that he was "forgetting" his hat at home, complaining that it made his forehead sweat, it was another thing to remember to bring home with him, etc. Dina could not allow him to abandon his hat-wearing. It was too big a breach, with far too serious connotations. Thank God he had agreed to wear it! He looked handsome, though, his blue eyes complimented by the dark green, as he stood in the living room next to his chair.

Dina took her place at the table and watched Ephraim *bensch* the children. He took such pride in them, showed such obvious love. After the *berachah*, he kissed each one on the head and smiled. Dina noticed that Avrumie didn't smile back and escaped his father's kiss. The two hadn't been on good terms lately, but it was probably just a stage. Ephraim was very busy, and Avrumie was struggling with his own private problems. It bothered her to see the coldness Avrumie displayed toward his father, and how sometimes he seemed to goad his father into losing his temper. Surely it would pass, Dina reassured herself every time Ephraim replied sarcastically or disapprovingly to Avrumie's barbed comments.

Ephraim filled his *becher* and began reciting Kiddush, and Dina allowed herself to melt into the relaxation and sanctity of Shabbos.

It happened after she had brought out the plate of kugel and the chicken, which, after careful thought, was sweet and sour. Her first warning was one of Avrumie's sly looks and the little smile in the corner of his mouth.

"Abba, I have a question," he announced with a quiet determination.

"*Nu*, Avrumie?" Ephraim looked pleased. Dina looked anxious. The children stopped their bickering.

"Why does Hashem need us to daven to Him? What does He care if we daven to Him or not? Is He so egotistical that He needs us to constantly praise Him and say how wonderful He is?"

Dina's heart sank. Why did he have to do this in front of the other children? She looked at Ephraim's face. It was tight with disappointment, anger, and a certain element of fear. The children were quiet, confused. Ephraim looked at Avrumie, then looked down at the chicken on his plate. He let his breath out in a loud hiss and his voice was loud, foreboding.

"Avrumie, I'm very surprised that at your age you ask such a question. Haven't you been davening now for almost thirteen years? Haven't you seen the beauty of the *tefillos*? You learned about davening in kindergarten — it should be Shira asking this question, not my eldest son. I am very shocked to hear you speak about the Ribbono shel Olam in such a way — I will not have such a lack of *yiras Shomayim* at my table. Avrumie, I'm sorry to say this, but I must have you leave the room. I cannot have such behavior which borders on *apikorsus* at my Shabbos table."

A stunned silence reigned. The children lowered their eyes to their plates. Dina, after recovering from the harshness of Ephraim's words, attempted, under her breath, to convince him to retract his order. He shook his head sharply. Avrumie would have to leave. Dina glanced at Avrumie. He was pale, but had a triumphant look on his face. Dina knew he had baited his father and had anticipated the outcome. *But why, Avrumie?* she thought. *Why?* Then he got up abruptly and walked slowly out of the room. The warm, pleasant glow of Shabbos had disappeared. Silverware clinked as the children ate quietly. Ephraim sat with a look of pain on his face and would not finish his food.

"Ima, I'd like to speak to you in the kitchen, please," Ephraim said, and she followed him out of earshot of the rest of the family.

"I just can't believe it," he almost shouted. "In front of the children, those *taiyere*, innocent children, he has to ask a question that makes him sound like an *apikores*. A question that a two-year-old can answer, my seventeen-year-old son pretends he doesn't know. Is he trying to make a fool out of his father? 'Abba, I have a question,' he asks, like the *chacham* in the Haggadah, and he turns out to be the *rasha*. I had to send him out of the room — I can't let the rest of the children see such a disgraceful thing be left alone. And such a chutzpah! If he had really wanted to know the answer, he would have come to me privately. I think that it was best that I put an end to it this way. The children will see that these questions are not proper, and they will see that their father is not to be made fun of in public. They won't learn from the silly questions of a troublesome teenager. It's so hard to raise *temimusdik* kids in today's *velt*. We have to fight it, Dina. We have to fight it."

"You're right, Ephraim," Dina murmured, although the only thing she felt like fighting right then were her tears.

Ephraim seemed to have calmed down somewhat, but he continued to pace the narrow kitchen, his brow furrowed, his mouth set in a grim line.

"Come, Dina," he said finally. "It's time for *zemiros*."

They did not see Avrumie the rest of the evening. He must have *bensched* upstairs in his room (*If he had bensched at all*, thought Dina, in the innermost recesses of her mind). The family tried to sing *zemiros*, tried to carry on a light conversation, but for the most part, they failed miserably. The table was cleared and dessert put out.

"Who has something to say on the parashah?" Ephraim asked, mustering an inviting tone. No one offered.

"Shira, what did you learn this week?"

He had chosen his prey cleverly. Shira could not resist an opportunity to be listened to, and she launched into a complicated *d'var Torah* which no one really felt like hearing.

"Very good, Shira. Ima, do we have a treat for Shira?"

"Of course," Dina said woodenly, getting up from her seat. They had made it a tradition to give the children sweets when they said *divrei Torah* at the Shabbos table, and Dina had a whole stockpile in a high kitchen cabinet.

The promise of a treat inspired Yosef to remember something he had learned, and then the family *bensched* and broke up into their individual pursuits. Dina stretched out on the couch and glanced through the pages of a novel Esther had lent her. Ephraim retired to his study where he was probably sitting and agonizing over the devastating scene he had just witnessed. He normally would learn with the boys, but tonight that would have to wait. Chavie left to her friend's house, offering a subdued *"Gut Shabbos"* before she walked out the door. Dovid, Dina saw with pride, was sitting in the living room at his *shtender*, learning. He was listless, though, unenthusiastic. Chanan and Yosef were playing a *berachos* game on the dining room floor. Sima was nowhere to be seen, and Shira was reading the latest book in a popular series for children about a third grade class and the challenges they faced. *It would do her good*, Dina thought scornfully. Shira's class was rife with politics and cliques, and unfortunately her beloved daughter was at the helm of many a problem. Bracha was sleeping peacefully, perhaps the only one not reeling from The Scene.

The pages of the book swam before Dina's eyes, and her thoughts turned to her eldest son. She could almost feel Avrumie hurting, smarting from the blow his father had dealt him. But it had been Avrumie's doing — why had he set his father up like that? What had gotten into him? He knew Abba's views and *hashkafos* all too well, that was for sure. She wanted so badly to go upstairs to his room and comfort him somehow, but she knew it was out of the question. If Ephraim found out, he would be upset with her, and probably Avrumie was in no mood for her company. So this was what *tza'ar gidul banim* was all about.

And what of the family? How did they view the scene, and the little changes that had surfaced in their brother? Dina reviewed in her mind the different reactions of the children, those unbelievable little antennae who registered every slight jolt as though it were a seismic quake. She thought of Chavie, only a year younger than Avrumie. Outgoing, vivacious, clever, pretty — "a real catch," Dina could hear her friends saying a few years down the line. Either Chavie was pretending or she really didn't notice any changes in her brother. Her social life was full enough that it was possible she hadn't been home at the right (or wrong) times to register that there was anything amiss. She did not like change, though; peer pressure was the story of her life. If any waves would be made, she would not be the most adept at dealing with them.

Then there was fourteen-year-old Dovid. Quiet, studious, and extremely responsible and bright, Dovid was her secret favorite. He resembled his mother so much, emotionally and physically, though he would have been grateful for a larger build, especially in the playground. Dovid sensed what was going on — indeed, how could he not notice a change in Avrumie — he worshiped him as only a younger brother could.

"Ima," he had said to her the other day when the two were alone in the kitchen, "I noticed that Avrumie wears green pants now, instead of black." Dina hadn't known what to say. How did she answer such a statement without putting down Avrumie but not condoning his behavior?

"Avrumie needed a little change," she had told Dovid. "Avrumie's going through a difficult time right now, and he needs a little space. *Baruch Hashem*, Dovidel, you are making us very proud in yeshivah." And then she had spoken to him about his wonderful report card, and the conversation was over. But how much longer would it be before Dovid's admiration of Avrumie won him over to his new "stage"?

Sima came next. Twelve, shy, and awkward, she was too often excluded, both in school and at home. Immature in some ways and yet too mature in others, Sima was somewhat of a social outcast, and she suffered greatly from it. At home, she was aloof and quiet, taken advantage of, teased and provoked. It was hard to know what was going on in Sima's head, behind the big glasses and the bangs perpetually in her eyes. Sima probably exchanged an average of ten words a day with Avrumie at best, mostly trying to avoid him and his verbal attacks on her.

Chanan and Yosef were not at all interested in anyone in the family but themselves. They were best friends, a phenomenon Dina spoke of proudly to her friends and guests. They were always together, except when reluctantly separated into grades a year apart at school. They had been nicknamed "the twins" and were always to be found intently working at some "project." They had a treehouse, a fort, a hammock, and a secret office in which they planned their next activities. Chanan was the thinker and Yosef was the doer, and their report cards showed as much.

"What will be with your marks, Yose'le," Ephraim had asked his nine-year-old, shaking his head at the rebbe's comments.

Yosef had smiled, that bright, engaging smile. "I'm going to be a builder, Abba, and build huge bridges and skyscrapers. It doesn't really matter if I get one little *gimmel* in Chumash, does it?"

Ephraim had shaken his head, resisting the charm. "I'm afraid one little *gimmel* does matter, Yosef. If you want to be a builder, build *divrei Torah*, build *p'shatim*. Bridges and skyscrapers can collapse with one little earthquake or explosion, but Torah lasts forever."

Yosef had been momentarily stunned, but soon resumed the sketches he was working on for the swimming pool he and Chanan were preparing to build. Ephraim had shaken his head and given Dina a wry smile. She had shrugged her shoulders.

Shira was seven, and occupied an unenviable niche in the family. She was excluded by her older brothers and considered it beneath her dignity to play with Bracha, who she disdainfully referred to as "the baby." Whatever she lacked in popularity within the family, though, she made up for in school. She was a natural leader, and her circle of friends extended even to the older grades. It was Shira who, when she'd left her schoolbag on the city bus, had commandeered two classmates into boarding each returning bus and searching it for the precious bag. Her self-assuredness landed her in trouble sometimes with teachers admonishing her for her chutzpah and adults obeying her crisp orders with disbelief. She was also quick to annoy her siblings, perhaps as a silent backlash for the lack of attention she suffered at home. She had noticed Avrumie's behavior and took various opportunities to comment on it.

"Avrumie's hair looks like a girl's," she had taunted as her brother stood at the mirror, combing his bangs into a sticky creation. He had scared her away with a menacing fist, but not before she had sing-songed her remark a couple more times.

Bracha was the baby in the family, adored and spoiled by all. She was, indeed, a *berachah*, as Dina tried to remind herself when the one-year-old emptied the kitchen cupboards and rubbed peanut butter into her hair. Just today she had gotten into the chocolate cake Dina had baked for Shabbos and eaten a huge piece, squishing the rest of it between her fingers.

Avrumie loved Bracha. He loved to swoop her up in his arms, high into the air, and hear her giggle with terrified delight. He was usually amenable to feeding her and once he had even changed her diaper, though he had sworn his mother to secrecy on that deed. When she saw Avrumie in a particularly bad mood, Dina tried to coax him into taking care of the baby, on some pretext or another, to help him soften up. Dina would quietly observe her son. The sight of tough Avrumie, with his sleeves rolled up to show his developing muscles, tickling and stroking his blond little sister, would bring a lump to her throat. *You were once that happy, laughing baby*, thought Dina. *What happened?*

Five

Ephraim closed the door of his study and sat down heavily in his chair. His mind was reeling, his heart pounding. What had happened? He replayed in his mind the entire scene, beginning with Avrumie's casual question, right down to his last angry word. Had he reacted correctly? He didn't know. All his life Ephraim had been taught that one's actions must be governed by *yiras Shomayim*. He had always striven to follow this directive, however difficult it was. He had a regular *mussar seder* every day and listened to inspiring tapes in the car on his way to and from school. His training as a rebbe, he thought, would help him in raising children. A rebbe cannot scream or he will lose control of the class and all that he taught will go out the window. He was very careful in the classroom to control his voice. Why, then, did he have such difficulty controlling it at home?

He knew the answer very clearly. His *talmidim*, although considered his children in the merit of his teaching them Torah, were still *talmidim*. Avrumie, though, was his son. Any misdemeanor on Avrumie's part hit home much harder than a prank or rude comment from a student. But wasn't he justified in reproaching Avrumie for poor behavior and improper questions? Who was responsible for raising his son to be a proper Jew if not him? And there are certain times where anger is justified, he remembered. A little voice inside him reminded him that only outward displays of anger are permitted when necessary. He acquiesced to his conscience in shame: his anger had been deeply felt. Why? Because deep down Ephraim took Avrumie's rebellion as a personal attack on himself; as a pointed finger at his own faults and inconsistencies.

Avrumie had been baiting him frequently in the last few months. Every time he was faced with one of his son's challenges, Ephraim felt his back go up and the words come sharply to his mouth. He wished he could view Avrumie as just another *chutzpahdik talmid* and tell him off calmly and carefully, but that was impossible. The boy standing before him was a measure of his own success as a parent and, ultimately, as an *eved Hashem*. What did that say about himself?

He tried so hard, he thought, leaning on his *shtender*. He tried encouraging Avrumie, talking to him in learning, calling him names of greatness: "My tzaddik, my *ben Torah*." To no avail. Not only did they not help, but they seemed to actually hinder. His intent was for Avrumie to know that his father had very high hopes for him; that Ephraim hadn't given up on his son, no matter how rebellious a streak he had in him. Surely in this Ephraim was right. Although Avrumie clearly resented the expressions, to stop referring to him as a *ben Torah* or a *talmid chacham* would just cause Avrumie to think his father had lowered his standards. That would be a tragedy.

And yet, the question gnawed at Ephraim: Why did Avrumie resent being called a *ben Torah*? Hadn't he, Ephraim, inculcated him with an appreciation of Torah beyond any doubt? Didn't he see his father learning all afternoon and evening and teaching Torah in the morning? Was that not enough to impress upon him how important Torah was? How could Avrumie have missed the boat?

Calm down, he told himself. Avrumie hadn't really missed the boat. He was just going through a difficult stage. Hadn't he himself had some difficulties during his teenage years? He didn't recall doing anything rebellious or heretical, but perhaps he would ask his mother — she would certainly remember, if there was anything to remember. This last thought calmed Ephraim. Avrumie was the same Avrumie whom he had entered into the *bris* and with whom he had walked to shul hand-in-hand. He was still going to yeshivah, still involved in Torah study. No doubt this difficult time would pass, and the old Avrumie would be back, asking to learn with Ephraim at night. Ephraim felt relieved. He picked up his *gemara*, placed it on the *shtender*, and soon lost himself in the age-old words.

Six

Dina slipped into her robe and clogs and made her morning pilgrimage down the hall and into each room to wake its sleeping inhabitants. Some rooms were entered more cheerfully than others, based on their sleepers' waking tendencies. Chavie was first, and Dina entered with some trepidation. She had bought Chavie an alarm clock long ago, but the alarm could be ringing for two days, and Chavie would not have heard it for the world. She approached her sleeping daughter, curled up underneath her floral bedspread that perfectly matched the floral linen and curtains, and even the floral wallpaper, last year's birthday present, and smiled. Chavie looked so small and vulnerable. Dina patted her arm.

"Chava'le, it's morning — time to get up, *sheifele*." Chavie didn't budge.

"Chavie, please get up or you'll be late for school."

A groan emanated from deep within the blanket.

"I know, sweetheart — it's hard to tear yourself out of bed, but you must."

Another groan. Dina pulled her last card.

"If you get up quickly, you get first dibs on the washroom."

Chavie stirred. It took Chavie at least ten minutes to do her hair in the morning, and the big washroom mirror all to herself was a tantalizing prize. Mission accomplished.

Next came Sima and Bracha. The trick was to wake Sima without waking Bracha, so that she would be able to do a little housework before the baby got up. Shira, who also slept with them, was already up and playing a computer game. She was the early riser in the family, and for that Dina was grateful. One less kid to pull out of bed. Bracha lay in her crib, snoring softly. Dina approached the bed and touched a sleeping Sima lightly on the cheek.

"Simi, time to get up, darling," she whispered. Sima pulled the blanket over her head.

"Sima, I know you want to sleep more, but you'll be late for school if you don't hurry." *Hurry* was not a word in Sima's vocabulary. Everything she did took her hours. She needed a good half hour to get dressed, and eating breakfast was out of the question, or she'd never make the bus.

"Please, Sima, be a good girl. I want to see you downstairs, dressed, in five minutes, and I'll put a special treat in your lunch." Sima moved slightly.

"But only if you hurry and get up right now."

She hoped the bribe would work. She did not want to lose her temper with Sima so early in the morning. It would get them both off to a bad start.

Dina walked into the next room. Dovid slept in a single bed near the window, and Chanan and Yosef lay sleeping in the bunkbed. They had only agreed to the bunkbed arrangement if they were allowed to rig up a makeshift intercom system between the top and bottom bunk so they could talk at night. Dina smiled to herself. They had such personalities, those two. She approached Yosef first.

"Yose'le," she said softly.

Yosef opened his eyes, yawned, and grinned sleepily. "Oh, hi, Ima. I was just in middle of the best dream about going to the airport and getting into one of those huge planes and flying to school. All the kids were so jealous!"

"Sounds exciting," said Dina, laughing. "Why don't you —" but Yosef had already climbed up to Chanan and was tickling his unfortunate brother's exposed toes.

"Ahhhhhh — get off, Yosef! Iiiiiima! That's it, Yosef — you'd better watch out!" Okay, Chanan was up. Dina beat a hasty retreat.

Yosef's tactic had killed two birds with one stone. Dovid sat up in bed, rubbing his eyes. "Can you two be quiet for a change?! Waking up to you screaming is worse than — it's worse than any other kind of alarm clock in the world! We should record you on tape and sell the tape to parents who can't wake their kids in the morning. We'd make millions of dollars!"

Chanan threw a pillow at him, and the morning had begun.

Or almost. Dina had one more child to wake, and she approached Avrumie's room uneasily. His door was closed, and she eyed the large "Trespassers Will Be Prosecuted" sign unhappily. This was not going to be easy. She quietly opened the door and walked into the small room.

Avrumie lay asleep in his bed with the covers thrown off him. He was always hot. His walls were covered with a mixture of road signs and pictures — mostly cars. His ceiling was dotted with glow-in-the-dark stars which glowed faintly in the dimness of the room. He had painted his walls black, a move which Dina had strongly discouraged but had been won over by Avrumie's convincing argument that black hid dirt better than white, and that, after all, it was his room — she didn't have to sleep in the depressing gloom.

She would have loved to touch him gently, but lately he had shied away from physical contact. "Don't touch me, Ma," he had said when she had impulsively kissed the top of his head as he bent over to tie Bracha's shoe. So she held back and instead used her best, most caressing voice.

"Avrume'le, sweetheart. It's time to get up." No response.

"Avrumie — it's late already. I woke you last because I know how tired you must be." He had stayed up late reading a book about a famous basketball hero. Dina had flipped through it and hadn't found anything too objectionable, and it was better than the rest of the trash out there, but he would be exhausted today.

"Avrumie, darling, please." He still had not stirred. Dina felt herself losing patience, but she quickly steadied herself.

"Avrumie, I will give you five more minutes of sleep, on the clock, and then I will come and wake you. Okay?"

She didn't wait for a response. She left the room, leaving the door open.

Chavie was in the washroom already, brushing her teeth. Chanan was half-dressed, and Yosef was trying to put his shirt on with his feet. Dovid was dressed and combing his hair. She handed out some cheery remarks and compliments and went downstairs to prepare breakfast. She wasn't feeling so cheery, though. She had the funny feeling that Avrumie was not going to be very accommodating this morning.

"Shira, can you help me put out the bowls, please, honey?"

"Ohhhh, Ima — I did it yesterday. And I'm in the middle of the best part of the game. If I don't get out, I'll break my record. Uchh — I just got out!"

"Shira'le, I believe I asked you to do something," Dina repeated.

Keep the anger out of your voice, Dina, she thought to herself. *Stay calm.*

Shira huffily began to take the dishes out of the cupboard and put them on the table. Dina assembled the cereal boxes and milk and decided to make some orange juice.

"Orange juice for everyone who's ready on time!" she called upstairs. Her ploy was effective: Chanan and Yosef came bounding down the steps. Dovid followed at a more dignified pace. Shira poured herself a glass of juice. Dina looked at her watch. She was one minute past the promised five. She headed for the stairs. Sima was putting on her socks, which was a good sign. Dina headed to the end of the hall and entered Avrumie's open door. He couldn't possibly have slept through all the noise, she decided. He had to be pretending.

Avrumie still lay on his bed. He had turned to face the wall, but he made no movement as she approached him.

"Avrumie," she said as patiently as she could. "It's six minutes — I even gave you an extra minute to sleep. Now it's time to get up, darling. Let me see you get out of bed and I'll leave you alone." Avrumie did not budge.

"Avrumie," she allowed her voice to rise a little. Could he really be sleeping? "Avrumie, I'm getting a little frustrated. All the other children are already up and dressed, and you, my eldest, is lying in bed when you should be going to davening already. What's going on here, Avrumie?" There was no response.

"Avrumie Faber, I do not appreciate being ignored. Please explain to me why you are not getting up this morning," she demanded.

"Iiiiiiiiima!" she heard a shriek from downstairs. "Yosef poured —" there was a loud crash. Avrumie would have to wait, Dina fumed as she ran downstairs. Predictably, there was a broken bowl on the floor and cereal all over the place. There was also a big fight in process which Dina attended to first. When the dust had cleared, Yosef had gone off to school early, sulking a bit, and Chanan had followed him, brushing corn flakes off his shirt. Dovid had smiled good-bye and left for his bus, looking handsome and serious in his hat and jacket. Shira had seen some friends outside and was also leaving early, and Chavie was on her way out.

"Bye, Ima, have a great day," she said, as she dashed a kiss on her mother's cheek. Dina smiled the best smile she could muster and went to clean up the mess. Sima sauntered into the kitchen as she was wiping the splattered milk off the seats of the chairs.

"Well, hello there, Sima," Dina said, a trifle sarcastically. "Everyone else has left already. Where have you been?"

Sima looked at her without speaking.

"Maybe tomorrow morning you can try harder to be ready on time, please?"

"I'll try," said Sima, not very convincingly. Dina let it pass.

"Have a cup of juice, and you're off, dear. Did I sign your homework last night?"

"Yeah."

"You've got your lunch packed?"

"Ummmm — I think so."

"Okay, then take your jacket today. It's pretty chilly outside."

Dina walked Sima to the door, smoothed her ponytail, and kissed her on the cheek.

"Have a great day, dear, and don't forget those multiplication tables that we went over last night!"

Sima smiled uneasily and walked into the sunshine, not looking behind her.

Dina closed the door, squared her shoulders, and slowly walked up the carpeted steps. What was going to be with Avrumie this morning? Soon the baby would wake up and would need to be fed. She had to deal with him now or never. She wished Ephraim were here to help, but he had to leave early in order to daven before class with his regular minyan. It was just as well. Ever since the Shabbos incident, things had been even more strained between Ephraim and Avrumie.

She gave a light knock on Avrumie's open door and walked in. He was lying in bed, on his back, staring up at the ceiling. He didn't look at her as she approached him.

"Well, good morning, Avrumie, I'm glad to see you're up."

"Yup, I'm up," he said.

Well, that was good — at least he was speaking to her. He had once given her the silent treatment in protest of her not buying him a certain outrageously expensive brand-name shirt. Was he angry at her now? Was that why he wasn't getting up?

"What's going on this morning, Avrumie? What happened to getting up on time today?"

"Oh, Ma, you know how it is," he said nonchalantly. "Some days you just don't feel like getting up."

Perhaps it was his too-casual attitude, or maybe his lame excuse, but Dina gave way to her irritation.

"No, actually, I don't know how it is," she said acidly. "I take my responsibilities seriously, and so does everyone else in this family. We all got up this morning even if we didn't really feel like it. What about you?"

Avrumie didn't reply. He continued gazing at the ceiling.

"Avraham Chaim Faber, you will please get up out of bed, get dressed, and get to yeshivah. It is already nine o'clock and you should have been there an hour ago. Discussion over."

She stalked out of his room without a backward glance and went down to the kitchen. Maybe a glass of juice would steady her, she thought as she took a cup from the cabinet. She heard his footsteps creaking upstairs and the washroom door slam shut. He was going to obey her, but he apparently wasn't going to do it pleasantly.

Seven

ina went downstairs to the laundry room and began sorting and folding a mound of clean laundry. As she worked in the pleasant quiet she found her thoughts wandering to a time, not so long ago, when she would never have dreamed Avrumie would wake up late for minyan. When he had been, for all intents and purposes, a disciplined, well-behaved child, at least on the surface.

There had always been something, though, in the flashing blue eyes, that hinted at a defiance that would not be tamed. Sometimes she wondered whether she subconsciously worked to break that rebellious spirit — it irked her to see such mockery and disobedience in her own son. And then again, it was her duty as a mother to raise him to be a humble, obedient *ben Torah*, with a healthy respect for his parents and elders, wasn't it? Besides, she dreaded the "I'm sorry, Mrs. Faber, but Avrumie was asked to leave the class today for chutzpah" calls. They were so embarrassing, so glaringly directed at exposing her failings as a parent, when here she was, trying as best as she could to raise eight children to be *ehrliche Yidden*, which was not an easy task.

Why was it that some children were easier than others? Just the other day, she'd gotten a call from Dovid's rebbe. A "*nachas* call," he had said, expounding on the wonderful virtues of her fourteen-year-old and how he was a "model" for the rest of the class. It had made her day. And at parent-teacher conferences, she had received glowing reports of Chanan, and even praise for mischievous Yosef, whose gaiety melted away even justified anger. And she'd been speaking the other day to her friend Esther who had a girl in Chavie's class who'd been telling her how popular Chavie was. Her own Chavie was a class leader, respected and chased after! It seemed incongruous compared to Dina's own teen-age years, spent hovering shyly at the sidelines, smiling awkwardly for all the world, but hurting deeply inside. At least her children would get what she herself never had. The outgoing, sparkling personalities were definitely passed down from her husband. He was so gregarious, so confident in himself, that people were naturally drawn to him. His *talmidim* flocked to him, building lifelong relationships with him. He was consulted for advice on various matters, well respected in the community. Everyone loved Ephraim Faber. Everyone except one young seventeen-year-old who happened to be his son.

The animosity between Avrumie and his father had become an unavoidable part of life in the Faber household. Ever since the Friday night incident, the friction had escalated. Ephraim, for the most part, seemed somehow oblivious to it. He continued speaking to Avrumie, striking up conversations innocently, then becoming irritated by the lack of response from Avrumie, or at least a lack of the response he had hoped for. And Avrumie seemed to deliberately want to aggravate his father.

"How's yeshivah, *zeeskeit?*" Ephraim had asked his son just the night before.

"School's okay," Avrumie had replied. School? Ephraim had pretended not to notice the subtle connotations of the switch and had instead focused on the adjective.

"Just 'okay,' Avrume'le? Torah is more than okay; Torah is wonderful — right, Avrumie?"

"Right," Avrumie had said sarcastically, and Ephraim had frowned. At this point Dina had tried to offer him a cup of coffee to defuse the potentially explosive situation. But Ephraim would not be stopped. He had slipped into the role that came so naturally to him: the classroom rebbe. Turning to his younger son, who was also in the kitchen at the time, he had said, "Dovidel, tell me, *zeeskeit*. Why is Torah so precious to us?"

Dovid had turned red and mumbled a hasty answer about Torah guiding one's life and helping one serve Hashem, and Ephraim had smiled.

"Yes, boys. Torah is more valuable to us than diamonds and pearls. Torah is our lifeblood. We must always remember that. A day spent learning Torah is not 'okay,' it is wonderful! *Baruch Hashem*, we are all *zocheh* to learn Torah every day, and we must use every spare moment." His lesson delivered, Ephraim had relaxed in his chair and accepted the coffee. Dina managed to change the topic, and the uncomfortable moment had passed. But Avrumie's flushed, stony expression would not dissipate. He left the kitchen as soon as possible, escaping up to his room and slamming the door — a move which had elicited raised eyebrows from his father, but thankfully no comment.

Dina felt torn by Ephraim's attitude towards Avrumie. He was obviously trying to inculcate him with the values he himself had been taught. He had no other reason for the lectures, for the comments. But then again, wasn't there some other way that he could impart them? Every conversation seemed to drive another dagger into his relationship with his son. Avrumie had started to actively avoid speaking to his father. *What is going to be?* Dina thought, with the slightest twinge of fear in her heart. She attacked the laundry with renewed vigor.

Eight

The clock in the hallway chimed, and Dina glanced at her watch. Absorbed as she had been in her thoughts, she had not noticed the morning slip by with only a mound of neatly folded laundry to show for it. *And a seventeen-year-old truant upstairs lazing around*, she thought angrily. Then she felt a surge of panic: why hadn't Bracha woken up yet? She was usually up half an hour ago. Dina took the steps two at a time and practically ran to the baby's room. The scene she saw made her breath catch in her throat.

Avrumie was lying on the carpet, holding Bracha on his chest. The two were nuzzling noses. The baby was laughing and Avrumie was laughing, too, with careless abandon and true pleasure. Dina wished she could retract her steps and leave them alone in their delight, but she had been noticed, and the moment was gone. Instantly, she felt Avrumie stiffen. He did not put Bracha down, though; he just stood up with her balanced carefully in his arms.

"The baby was crying and you didn't hear, so I got her," he said gruffly. She suddenly realized he was embarrassed.

"Thank you, Avrume'le," she said. "I'm sure it was a real treat for Bracha to have her big brother play with her this morning." Then her warning bells started ringing: *Are you condoning his miscreant behavior, Dina?* her conscience shouted at her. *How will he ever learn if you make it all sound okay?* And yet she had seen his expression, his whole body, relax at her comment and at the friendliness in her voice. Maybe there was a way she could talk to him now.

"Avrumie, let me just change the baby for a minute. Can you pass me the wipes, please? They're on her shelf."

Avrumie put Bracha on the changing table and went to bring the wipes. Dina unsnapped the baby's sleeper. She kept her voice even and nonthreatening.

"It's nice to have you around this morning, Avrumie," she said pleasantly. "To what do I owe this extra company?" She laughed, hoping it would soften the question. She felt Avrumie's eyes upon her and she concentrated on changing the wet diaper.

Avrumie looked at his mother. Could this really be Ima speaking like this? So nicely, as though she was really listening to what he had to say? Maybe now was the time to talk to her. Now, as the morning sun streamed in from the open blinds, with a gurgling Bracha to break the ice. But what if it was all a show? What if she was just hiding her distaste for him under a layer of niceness so she could extract information from him and then throw him away? He studied his mother's face, but she would not look at him. What if she would tell Abba? That was all he needed. Suddenly Dina looked up briefly and smiled at him reassuringly. Something in his heart melted.

"Ma," Avrumie began hesitantly, "I've been meaning to talk to you for awhile now."

Dina felt her heart pounding, but she just nodded her head and continued with her task.

"But you have to promise not to tell Abba," Avrumie burst out passionately.

Dina froze. Now was not the time to discuss his relationship with Ephraim, and she couldn't lose him at this point.

"Well, I suppose we could work this out between ourselves and try not to involve Abba," she said, nearly tripping over the words. She hadn't outright promised, but he was satisfied.

"It's school, Ma," Avrumie began. "I just hate it. I really feel it's not the place for me. I...I haven't been getting along so well with the rebbeim. They're just not my type. They don't understand me at all. All they're interested in is the surface of things, not the insides. They don't care who I am; all they care is about how I look. Just the other day, remember I was wearing that striped shirt that I borrowed from Menachem? The one you didn't like so much?" He stole a glance at his mother, but Dina just nodded. "Well, the rebbe came over after class and started ranking me out about wearing a striped shirt. A striped shirt, for goodness sakes! What's wrong with a striped shirt? He tells me it's not yeshivish, that a *ben Torah* representing the yeshivah world has to look a certain way, blah, blah, blah. I just tuned him out after the first few sentences. He sounded exactly like —" Avrumie stopped abruptly, but Dina could read his mind: *exactly like Abba.* She waited for him to continue.

"And once he kicked me out of class for saying something that I've heard other guys say too. Guess what he does to them? Nothing. Guess what he says to them? Nothing. And me he calls rude and *chutzpahdik* and tells to go take a walk. Now if you're trying to teach me the whole day about good *middos*, and how you have to be honest and everything, how am I supposed to listen to you if I see you acting this way?! And how can a rebbe go and embarrass a guy in front of the whole *shiur* as though he's a nothing piece of dirt, and expect to be respected? It really makes me sick. I can't learn in such a place — I feel like it's all hypocrisy. Do you know what I'm saying?" he finished off desperately.

Dina looked away from Avrumie. She could not believe that all this had spilled out of him so quickly, without prodding. It was definitely divine providence that had led her to deal with him this way, with such astonishing results. But now she had to answer him, and she was walking on thin ice. What to say? At that moment, thankfully, Bracha began to whimper, and Dina realized that she must be very hungry.

"Let's continue our conversation downstairs, Avrumie," she said quickly. "I have to feed Bracha'le, okay?"

He nodded and, picking up the baby, followed her downstairs. She fixed a bottle for Bracha and poured a glass of orange juice for Avrumie, which he accepted gratefully. He must be hungry, too. Dina took the baby from him and began to feed her. The silence lengthened and she knew she had to say something. *Please, Hashem*, she prayed mentally. *Put the right words into my mouth*.

"Avrumie," she said quietly, "I really appreciate your sharing all this with me. I couldn't have known how you felt if you hadn't told me."

She saw his face flush a little and knew she was on the right track.

"I see you have some real problems with the yeshivah and the rebbeim and you're really not happy about learning in Zichron Yosef. Of course this is really a shock to me — I hope you understand that. Up until now, aside from a few calls from your rebbe, I didn't really know that you were so unhappy. But what do you want to do now, Avrumie? If the choice was in your hands, what would you choose to do?"

Avrumie sat quietly, sipping his juice. He felt as if a load had fallen off his mind and heart. How long had he been aching with anger and defiance without having anyone to discuss it with? Even Menachem was no help — he just encouraged Avrumie to get away from yeshivah, from his family, and go make a new life for himself. Although it sounded tantalizing, Avrumie realized it was highly impractical and not even something he really wanted. At least, not at this point. But his mother's question was a good one: what did he want to do?

"I don't know," he began. "Maybe there's another yeshivah that I would be more comfortable at. We can do our research. I should be able to get into somewhere else — my record isn't that bad. And I think I could stick it out till the end of the *zeman*. I just want to know that something will change, because this is really making me depressed."

"That's a good suggestion, Avrumie," Dina said approvingly. "Why don't you finish the *zeman* and meanwhile we can look into other yeshivos. I'm sure there's something out there that's more appropriate for you. But Avrumie, you do realize that Abba has to be involved in this. You can't switch yeshivos without him knowing about it — right? He might be a little unhappy...."

Avrumie's face darkened. The mention of his father was enough to destroy all the confidence and closeness he had felt.

"I told you I don't want Abba in on this," he shouted. "Abba doesn't care about me at all. All he cares about is himself. He always has, and he always will. I don't want him involved in this decision. It's his fault that I ended up in Zichron Yosef to begin with. And all the rebbeim, when they yell at me, they say, 'I can't believe this. Ephraim Faber's son would say something like this? I just can't believe it.' You said you wouldn't tell Abba, and now you go and change your mind? I don't want anything to do with Abba. It's like he's not even my father. He's...he's a hypocrite himsefl!"

All of Dina's good intentions and sweet words came tumbling down in a heap around her feet. She was blinded by a rush of anger and a devotion to her husband and the values they had to preserve.

"You will not speak about Abba like that!" she shouted. "He is your father and he loves you and you must honor and respect him. Your father is an amazing person, a wonderful person, and everyone adores him. Except his son who is too selfish and ungrateful to realize how lucky he is. Get to your room, Avrumie, and think about everything you have said. I cannot hear you call your father such despicable names!"

But Avrumie had already turned and bolted out the door, slamming it behind him in his rage and torment. Bracha began to wail. Dina realized she had unconsciously taken the bottle out of the baby's mouth. She put it back in and let her shoulders hang limp. How could their wonderful discussion have ended like that? It was too much to bear. Dina saw the tears even before she felt them. She gave herself up to her despair and let them fall.

Nine

Avrumie felt the cold sunshine on his face as he slammed the door behind him. It had happened. He had let his guard down, had trusted his mother, and she had betrayed him so absolutely, so deeply. He felt as if his heart would break in two. He should have known not to trust her, that she was just putting on a show. He'd been taken in by her friendly tones and her smile. He had thought that maybe it was the parenting book she'd been reading that had changed her so drastically. But she was just being conniving, waiting for him to spill his guts so she could go tattling to Abba on just how much of a disappointment their eldest son was. He was furious with himself for having been so completely taken in; furious with his mother for being such a traitor; furious with his father for being the father he was. Avrumie's feet pounded the sidewalk as he ran aimlessly. Where was he going? He wasn't even sure. Maybe he'd go to the park. It didn't really matter where he went, all that mattered was for him to escape.

He had laid open his heart to his mother, and the realization both surprised and scared him. He had a lot of resentment bottled up inside, and sooner or later he knew he'd explode. He'd been letting off steam in very minor ways, relatively speaking: Mouthing off to the rebbe here and there, not showing up for class occasionally. Nothing big. It helped him assert his defiance, yet covered up the big, festering pool of resentment that was building day by day.

What was it the rebbe had said to him? "Avrumie, if you would only apply yourself, I know you could really fly. You have such a head, Avrumie. And you would make your father so proud!" And the rebbe thought that would inspire him? Make his father proud? That was the last thing on his to-do list, if it was listed at all. Abba would never be proud of his "Avrume'le." He would *shep nachas* from his Dovidel, from Chanan, probably even from Yosef, but never from Avrumie. Avrumie would always be the bane of his existence. And "apply himself"? To what? To the hollow words of the *shmuessen* that left a bad taste in his mouth? To *shiur* where they argued hairline points that had no application at all to real life, back and forth, brutally, for hours on end? How was he supposed to apply himself to such an inane waste of time? *Then again, it doesn't really matter — you're an apikores*, he told himself. Hadn't Abba said so? And in front of everyone, too? Avrumie had known that his father wouldn't give him a straight answer to his deliberately off-color question — in fact, he had relished the fact that he would get his father's goat. But he hadn't expected such a strong reaction. Even Ima had been shocked.

Avrumie kicked at a stone. He had stopped running and was walking along a deserted dirt path he'd discovered awhile ago. Some of the pain had left his chest, excised by the running and furious thoughts, but it was by no means completely gone. He felt alone, very alone. How could he go back home to parents who didn't understand him and who probably even hated him? To siblings who looked down upon him as their father had taught them to and to a yeshivah that he despised? Avrumie sat down on a bench and covered his eyes with his hands. What was he to do? He had never felt so alone in the world.

Ten

Ephraim Faber parked, straightened his tie, and opened the car door. The morning sun welcomed him as he clutched his briefcase and made his way through the swarms of students awaiting the morning bell.

"'Morning, Rebbe!"

He turned around to see Shimon Feder, a former *talmid*, now in eighth grade, smiling at him.

"Good morning, Reb Shimon. How are things with you?" Ephraim asked, smiling kindly.

"*Baruch Hashem*, Rebbe. Of course, I miss Rebbe's class, but Rabbi Rabinowitz is really good."

"What are you learning now?" The two were soon involved in a complicated *braisa* which the eighth grade was working on. *How wonderful it is to be a rebbe*, Ephraim thought as he clarified a point Shimon was grappling with. *To teach Torah to the future roshei yeshivos and melamdim is such a zechus.* He looked at his watch; it was time to hurry to class. He bid Shimon good-bye and strode down the hallway. He had almost reached his classroom when he met the *menahel*.

"Ephraim," said Rabbi Epstein, pausing as if to speak with him.

"*A gut morgin*," replied Ephraim, slightly quizzically. He knew that Uri Epstein did not stand and talk idly in the halls when the morning bell was to ring in half a minute.

"I wanted to speak to you, Ephraim. I know you have to go into class now, but perhaps at recess...?"

Ephraim paused, uncomfortable. He had wanted to spend recess going over the lesson in *parashas hashavua* that he'd be teaching during the second half of the morning. "Of course, of course, *b'li neder*," he said.

"Good. *Hatzlachah!*" The *menahel* turned and walked briskly down the hall. What could he want to speak to him about? Ephraim turned his thoughts to his students, straightened his tie once more, and entered the classroom.

Every morning, as he scanned the faces before him, Ephraim Faber felt a fresh burst of excitement. He loved his job, if you could call it a job. He cherished the opportunity to impart Torah to these young, quick minds. While others spoke about burnout, Ephraim was as eager to teach his class after ten years as he had been his first year teaching. He gave each *talmid* a moment's eye-contact, just as he'd done every day for ten years. He felt it built a rapport with them.

There was Yanky, looking tired, as usual, from staying up too late — a result of overpermissive parents. Ephraim made a mental note to make sure he was still with the rest of the class. In the front row sat Shmuel, his star pupil, though he tried hard not to show it. But the boy was clearly an *iluy* — there was no doubt about it. Next to him was Gershon, a sweet boy but unable to keep up with the material. He'd been held back a grade already, and Ephraim struggled daily to explain the concepts to him three or four times, with doubtful success. He looked at Tuvia, the quintessential class clown — overweight, bright, and bored, by his own doing — and gave him a slight wink. Tuvia's parents had called him the other night thanking him for doing wonders for their son. His marks had improved and he was getting into much less mischief, even in his afternoon classes. Ephraim had felt a burst of pride and he knew all the attention and patience had paid off.

The boys watched him and smiled back. They liked and respected their rebbe. He was kind, he was smart, and he was tolerant. He put a

lot into "his boys," and it showed. Ephraim took one last, lingering look, and pulled out his *gemara* from his briefcase, lying it on the table alongside his grade book.

"Good morning, boys. Open your *gemaras* to *daf ches, amud alef.* Who can tell me Rashi's question that we learned yesterday?" He watched the hands shoot up with happiness and pride.

Eleven

"Enjoy your recess, boys," smiled Rabbi Faber as his class filed out to the playground in an orderly line three hours later. He was very proud of the *seder* that he instructed his boys in: "Always be *mesudar* in actions and appearance, and your thoughts will be *mesudar*," he would tell them. When the last boy had left the classroom, Ephraim gathered up his *sefarim*, snapped up his briefcase, and put it under his chair. Then he headed toward the *menahel*'s office, a small knot of nervousness in his stomach. Rabbi Epstein had asked to meet with him that morning, and he wondered uneasily what the reason for the summons could be.

"Come in," the *menahel* called, after Ephraim rapped lightly on the door. Ephraim walked in and sat opposite Uri Epstein in a big, plush chair.

"Thank you for coming, Reb Ephraim. I know how hard it is for a rebbe to give up his recess preparation time." He smiled.

Ephraim smiled back, surprised.

Rabbi Epstein looked at him for a moment. "I need not tell you that this conversation is in the strictest of confidence."

Ephraim nodded.

"The reason why I asked you to come here was because I wanted to talk about the Tauber boy."

Ephraim's heart sank. Elisha Tauber had only been in the yeshivah for two years, and yet he had a folder an inch thick full of all his misdemeanours and the notes that had been sent home to his parents. His family was almost completely dysfunctional — it was no wonder he behaved as he did. Ephraim had a special place in his heart for Elisha, and always made a special effort with him. The boy had made some progress, it was true, but not as much as everyone had hoped for. In the beginning of the year, the sixth grade rebbe had looked at Ephraim knowingly and said, "Have fun with Tauber — he'll keep you on your toes like you've never seen," and smiled grimly. That had been one of his first introductions to the boy, and the rebbe was not wrong.

"I know that you have always had a good relationship with Elisha," Rabbi Epstein began. "Unfortunately, some of the progress he made seems to be coming undone. I spoke to his parents, of course, but we all know that there is only so much they can do."

He waved his hands dismissively, and Ephraim nodded.

"Right now, he's really on probation. The reason I wanted to speak to you was because I hoped that perhaps you could be more on top of him and give him more of your time in the areas he needs it."

Ephraim looked down at his hands. He always strove to give every one of his *talmidim* exactly what they needed, and he felt a rush of guilt at the *menahel*'s words.

"I should have given him more of my time," he said lamely. "I hadn't noticed that he was slipping."

Rabbi Epstein picked up on Ephraim's distress.

"Reb Ephraim, of course you are a first-class *mechanech*, and Elisha Tauber's behavior is in no way connected to your relationship with him. I know that you have had a positive *hashpa'ah* on him from day one, and I know that you will continue to do your *avodas hakodesh* in every way. I just ask you to be more vigilant with him because of his tendencies towards inappropriate behavior."

Ephraim nodded his head again.

"I will certainly do the best I can," he said in a steadier voice.

The bell rang shrilly, and both men jumped up from their seats.

"Thank you for your time," Rabbi Epstein said warmly, gripping Ephraim's shoulder.

"Not a problem. We should hear of *hatzlachah* soon," said Ephraim, and he turned and walked towards his classroom purposefully.

Twelve

"And who can tell me, girls, the answer to this question?" Mrs. Markowitz turned to the blackboard and wrote in big, chalky letters, "8 x 6 =." Instantly, hands were in the air. She ignored the eager faces and instead pointed to a reluctant one in the back row.

"Sima, please tell me the answer to the equation on the board," she said, trying to keep her voice calm. She knew that Sima would not know the answer, and yet she couldn't very well let her sit in the class without at least trying to give a correct answer.

"Sima?" she repeated. Sima shifted uncomfortably in her seat. Already some of the girls were turning around to look at her. Mrs. Markowitz fixed her glasses and looked hard at the Faber girl.

"Sima, please tell me the honest truth. Did you study your multiplication table last night?"

This time Sima answered her. "Yes," she said softly.

"With your mother?"

"Yes."

"Very good. Then please tell me the answer to the equation on the board. What is 8 x 6?"

Silence.

"I'm waiting for an answer from you, Sima," Mrs. Markowitz demanded, growing stern. There was something about that child that got under her skin.

"Thirty-six?" Sima's answer had been more like a question. She had known it was wrong even as she said it. Sima felt her cheeks burn with the shame of appearing stupid, avoiding the eyes upon her. She knew that the whole class thought she was dumb. In fact, they had made it quite clear to her on different occasions. *But I did my homework*, she thought despairingly.

"No, Sima, that answer is wrong," Mrs. Markowitz declared. "Who can help Sima answer this equation? Yocheved? Forty-eight. Good. That is the correct answer. What is the correct answer, then, Sima?"

"Forty-eight," Sima said miserably.

"I'm glad you're listening, Sima," Mrs. Markowitz said, somewhat approvingly. "Now, girls, who can give me the answer to...."

Now how did Yocheved remember the right answer? Sima wondered. She could sit and memorize for hours on end, only to forget everything she had so carefully learned. Maybe she was stupid. Maybe the girls were right. Everything came hard for her. Well, almost everything. Certain things were easy, like drawing, painting, writing stories. But those weren't the important things. The important things were *chumash* and *navi* and, well, also math and science.

Even the family thought she was dumb, Sima reflected sorrowfully. They all treated her as if she didn't belong. Chavie hardly deigned to speak to her and ignored all of her efforts at being friendly. Sima secretly admired Chavie — who didn't? Sima would lie in bed at night imagining what it was like to be Chavie, loved and looked up to by everyone. The only time Chavie had anything to do with her was when she wanted Sima to take over one of her jobs. And Sima always obliged, hoping against all hope that perhaps she could win her sister over by doing her favors.

Dovid had no time for her, but at least he didn't push her around. Sima felt that they shared a secret kinship due to their mutual social difficulties, but of course, they never spoke about it. When Shira had started teasing her the other day, it was Dovid who came to her defense, and she had sent him silent thanks through grateful eyes.

Chanan and Yosef were nothing to even talk about. They were in their own little universe, and Sima was strictly barred from it. They had hung a "No Girls Allowed" sign on their door which Ima had made them take down, but their motto very clearly resounded from their attitudes.

Shira was very difficult to deal with, and Sima sometimes hated her. With her big mouth and overconfidence she was quick to pick up on her older sister's problems, and equally as quick to point them out. It didn't help matters that Shira brought home consistently good marks and was praised highly for them. Whenever Ima would tell Shira how proud she was of a particularly good test, Sima could almost hear her silent reproach: *And what about you, Sima? You're a lot older than Shira, and you still can't bring home a decent grade?* Of course Ima never said it straight out. When Sima brought home her sixties, Ima would look her paper over and say, "Hmmmmmm. Well, I guess you'll try harder next time, dear." The words hurt like a punch in the stomach. She did try, but it didn't get her anywhere. She could still hear Shira's stinging words echo in her mind, "Try harder, Sim-Sim, and maybe you'll get a really good mark like me!" She had almost hit her right then and there.

Bracha was, of course, a doll, and Sima loved playing with her. Bracha didn't condemn her. Bracha didn't think she was stupid. At least not yet, she warned herself.

Then there was Avrumie, but he didn't really count, did he? Avrumie had absolutely nothing to do with her except when he could comment about how her glasses were slipping down her nose. "Hey, Four Eyes," he would call to her, and she would simultaneously flush in embarrassment and be thrilled that he had at least acknowledged her presence. Avrumie seemed to be having his own problems lately — arguing with Ima and Abba and getting reprimanded a lot. He was probably feeling pretty left out and miserable. Sima sighed. She knew what it felt like.

Thirteen

"I'm hoooooooome!" Shira shouted, as she pushed open the front door.

"Hi, Shiri-Biri," Ima shouted from upstairs. "There are cookies on the table. Take a glass of milk with them."

Shira headed for the kitchen. Why wasn't Ima coming down to greet her like she did every afternoon? Maybe she was in the middle of something. Shira helped herself to a couple of cookies, poured herself some milk, and sat down in her favorite swivelly chair. It had been a good day. No tests, no homework, and she was one of only five girls who had been invited to a very private, elite birthday party at Shoshana Fishbein's house. And what a house that was! The first time Shira had gone over to play there, her eyes had opened so wide, they had almost fallen out right onto the deep, plush carpeting. Shoshana looked like she was rich, too. Even her uniform blouse looked expensive! *What would it be like to have money?* Shira wondered. She began to fantasize: she would buy bags of candy for all her friends, and eat pizza for lunch every day, then go out to restaurants at night for supper. She would wear two gold rings, one on each hand, and a gold necklace on the weekdays, and a special one for Shabbos. They would have a leather sofa in the living room, not like the old, worn green one they had now. She.... Her daydream was interrupted by Sima tripping on her shoelace as she entered the kitchen.

"Sima, you're such a klutz!" declared Shira emphatically.

Sima looked at her and rolled her eyes. "Shira, you have such a big mouth," she retorted.

Shira resorted to a tried and true tactic: "Sticks and stones can break my bones, but words can never hurt me," she sing-songed repeatedly.

"Oh, be quiet," grumbled Sima as she tied her shoelace.

"Wow, Sima — you even know how to do up your own shoelace," Shira said sarcastically. She liked teasing Sima and making fun of her. It made her feel old and important. She knew it hit home, though, and sometimes she felt very sorry. But honestly, Sima was, well, she was so...out of it. At school her friends sometimes said, "Shira, I can't believe you and Sima come from the same family. You two are totally different." "You bet," Shira would say, and laugh.

Ima walked into the kitchen, carrying Bracha. Her face looked pale, and was it Shira's imagination, or were her eyes a little red?

"Hi, *zeeskeit*," she said, kissing Shira on the cheek. "How was your day?"

"Great, Ima," Shira gushed. "I got invited to Shoshana Fishbein's birthday party. Only me and four other girls were invited, and even though it's supposed to be a secret, the whole class knows, and they're so jealous of us!"

"Shira'le," said Ima sternly, "this doesn't sound like a very nice plan. If someone is making a birthday party they should either invite the whole class, or they shouldn't make it at all. And if they're going to make it, it definitely shouldn't become something that causes jealousy in the class. I think I'll have to speak to Mrs. Fishbein about this."

Shira's face fell. Was Ima going to ruin her good fortune and make all her friends upset at her by calling off the party?

"Please, Ima," she begged. "I was just joking — no one really knows about it except us. We're keeping it very secret. Pleeeeeease don't call Shoshana's mother. It would be so embarrassing!"

Dina frowned.

"I'll think about what you said," she told a downcast Shira. Then she turned to Sima. "And how was your day, dear?"

Sima shrugged her shoulders. "Okay."

"Okay?" Dina repeated. "Just 'okay'?"

How could it be any better than "just okay"? thought Sima, but she didn't say a word. Just then Chanan and Yosef burst into the kitchen, chasing each other.

"Boys!" Dina called sharply. "Stop this wildness immediately! If you want to play roughly, go outside please." She certainly was in a snappy mood. Well, after the events of the morning and the disappearance of Avrumie for the entire day, she had a right to be. *Where was that boy*, she fumed. Perhaps he had gone to yeshivah after all, but she knew his back-pack was still upstairs in his room, so it was unlikely. She set to making lasagna for supper. The phone rang, and Shira, ever the curious one, ran to pick it up.

"Hello?"

"Um, who's calling please?"

Dina looked up hopefully. Perhaps it was someone calling about where Avrumie was.

"Ima — is Avrumie home sick?" Shira asked. "Shimshon wants to know why he's not in yeshivah."

Dina's face fell. "Tell him he's not home," she said shortly. Shira re-layed the message and hung up. Shimshon and Avrumie were very close friends — at least they had been a month ago, before Menachem had come on the scene. Shimshon was ideal in Dina's eyes. A *shtark bachur* with a pleasant personality — a good influence on Avrumie. But Avrumie never mentioned his name anymore, and she wondered sadly how many other friends had been abandoned in the space of such a short time.

Shira dawdled at the kitchen table, glancing at her mother.

"Ima?" she asked tentatively.

"Yes, Shira?"

"Ima, is it true that...well, a friend of mine at school said that...." She stopped.

Dina turned around. "Are you trying to ask me something, Shira?" she said, annoyed.

"Oh, forget it!" Shira said huffily, but she didn't leave the kitchen.

"I'm listening, Shira, if you want to tell me something," Dina said, with her best "patient" voice.

Shira looked up and paused.

"Well, my friend said that...that Avrumie's becoming not *frum*." The last words came out in a rush, almost as though they were burning her tongue.

Dina turned sharply and looked at Shira, aghast. Were people really speaking about her son like that? It was happening already. Shira was looking up at her, waiting for a response. Dina looked down at the lasagna noodles.

"Your friend shouldn't be saying such things, Shira, and you definitely shouldn't be listening to them," she said dumbly. How was that for a non-answer?

Fourteen

"**S**o whaddaya think I should do, Mark? Should I go home tonight, or just sleep here? If I don't come home, my parents are gonna be furious. They'll probably track me down here, anyway. What should I do?"

Menachem regarded Avrumie coolly. He had recently started going by his English name, and he thought it was very suave.

"I can't make decisions for you, Abe, but if it were me, there's no way I would go back to that place! How much hurt can a guy take, you know? You're welcome to stay the night — my parents won't mind. You're right about getting in trouble, though, if you don't call home or anything. You know your mother — she's a real worrier."

He was right — Ima was a worrier. She had been known to call out the police when he had stayed in school late, shooting baskets in the gym. She had had all the kids fingerprinted, and she wouldn't open the door to anyone — even the gas man had to show ID. *Maybe it's good for her to worry a bit about me,* Avrumie thought savagely. *It'll make her realize what she did to me. Let Abba worry a little too — that'll be good for him also, if he even cares enough to worry about me.*

"I — I think I'll stay the night," Avrumie said.

"Sure thing," said Menachem. "I'll tell my parents. Whaddaya want to do tonight? I mean, we're not just going to stick around this boring old house, are we?"

Do? Avrumie had never done anything at night, short of playing basketball and taking walks alone. Recently, just to taste the sweetness of rebellion, he had hung out in the mall and read the advertisements for movies playing at the theater, but that was child's play. Menachem was moving in different circles than he. He probably had something in mind other than going for a stroll.

"What did you have in mind?" he asked Menachem.

"Oh, nothing special. Maybe just hang out at the Hall for a bit, check out the action."

Avrumie flinched. What would his parents say if they found out he was going to a pool hall hangout? Avrumie Faber, son of Ephraim Faber, the master rebbe, hanging out with unsavories in a smoke-filled pool hall? Something inside him shuddered and exploded with sweet revenge and rebellion.

"Sounds great, Mark," he said, with real enthusiasm. "Let's go!"

Fifteen

"Yosef and Chanan, into pajamas this minute," Dina yelled. "Sima, brush your teeth — what's taking you so long?! Shira, I want to see you in pajamas too. I don't know where your nightgown is — where did you leave it when you took it off this morning?! Chavie, come change the baby, please. Yes, I know you have to make an important phone call, but *kibbud eim* comes first, at least in my book. Sima — do you have three mouths to brush?! Get out of the washroom already. Chavie, the baby's stretchie is in her crib. Yoooosef — get off that windowsill this instant and into your own bed. No, Chanan, you can't have an ant farm — get into bed right now. Dovid — fifteen more minutes!"

Dina had given up on maintaining control of her anger and her voice. Tonight was going to be a scene straight out of the "Don'ts" of the parenting books, and she just didn't have the energy to fight it. Half her mind was intent on getting the kids to bed, and the other half was a jumble of madness, fury, and fear. Where was Avrumie? It was already nine o'clock — where could the boy be? He hadn't even taken his jacket with him when he ran out. Shira's innocent question raced through her mind like a lumbering eighteen-wheeler, with the same impact. She could not bear to believe that people were talking about her. Sitting in their nice, quiet, peaceful homes and discussing how she and Ephraim could not raise their children properly; shaking their heads at Avrumie's downward descent to who knew what.

Her whole life she had dreamed of having children and raising them to be perfect *ovdei Hashem*. In seminary, she had sat in class drinking in the lessons, the *mussar*, inwardly preparing herself for the job of becoming wife and mother and excelling at both. When she had met Ephraim she had known her dream was within reach. He too was devoted to *avodas Hashem*, and constantly strove to work on himself. Ironically, Avraham had been his choice of a name when their first son was born. "He should serve Hashem like Avraham Avinu," Ephraim had fervently declared. *"My friend said that…that Avrumie's becoming not frum…."* It reverberated through her mind and gave her no peace.

She rapped on the washroom door.

"Who's in there?" she shouted.

A timid voice emanated. "Sima."

"Well, get out! What are you doing in there for so long? Why is everything with you a whole production? How are you ever going to get anything done if every single little thing takes you hours to do? I told you to get into bed ten minutes ago and you're still in the washroom?!" There, she had given in to her rage and left a trail of destruction in her wake. But Dina could not hold herself in check.

"Chavie — don't leave the dirty diaper here in the room — throw it in the garbage. That's what we have garbage cans for. What are you waiting for; someone to throw it out for you? What am I raising here — a princess?!" Chavie gave her a horrified look and ran out of the room.

Look at what you're doing, Dina — stop it! Stop it! But she couldn't. Images of Avrumie's face, filled with hatred and despair, pricked her like thorns.

"You ask me to read you a book now, Chanan? Now that it's fifteen minutes since I told you to get into bed? No way, Jose, young man. You should have thought of that before. Good night." She turned off their light. She heard a small voice behind her. It was Yosef.

"You didn't kiss us good night, Ima."

Her heart melted.

"You're right, *boychik*," she said, as she came into their room and kissed them both. Then she went into her own room, fell on the bed, and began to cry.

Sixteen

Ephraim turned the key in the lock and let himself in the front door. The lights downstairs were off — Dina must have gone to sleep. He felt bone-tired and had a splitting headache. He would drink a tea and then go to bed himself. He had just flicked the light on in the kitchen and put the kettle on the stove when he heard padded footsteps coming down the stairs. His wife entered the kitchen, her face pale and haggard.

"What is it, Dina?" He felt the fear rise inside him, seeing the despondency on her face.

"Avrumie ran away, and he hasn't come home yet," she said very quietly.

She had been crying, he noticed — her eyes were red-rimmed and swollen.

"What happened, Dina'le?" he asked softly. She collapsed in a chair and told him the whole story. Ephraim felt his heart close with dread as she related to him her conversation with Avrumie and the violent outburst it had ended with.

"Where do you think he could be?" he asked her.

"I don't know. It's possible that he's at Menachem's house. Menachem Geller." Ephraim probably hadn't even known about Menachem — he was hardly ever home, and Dina hadn't wanted to upset him by telling him.

"So let's call the Geller house," Ephraim suggested reasonably.

Dina looked down. "I'm — I'm too embarrassed," she said finally.

"But we have no choice," Ephraim pointed out. "It's better to suffer the shame and be able to sleep tonight knowing that Avrumie is at least safe in a warm house than to worry about him sleeping on some park bench or in the...." He broke off, the words too painful for him to finish.

"You're right," said Dina. "I'll call."

Her hands trembled as she flipped through the phone book. The Gellers were nice people, but not at all her type. Mr. Geller was a lawyer, and Mrs. Geller was The Lawyer's Wife to the T. Her style of dress, her hobbies and amusements all combined to make her a noncandidate for Dina's approval. She dialed their telephone number and waited anxiously. Ephraim stared at her with searching eyes.

The phone was finally picked up and she heard a female voice. "Hello?"

"Hello — Mrs. Geller?"

"Yes?"

"Hi — this is Dina Faber. My son Avrumie is friends with your Menachem." She paused, but the other woman said nothing.

"Um, I was just wondering. Avrumie didn't come home tonight and I thought that maybe he had met up with Menachem?"

"Yes, he did."

"Oh." Dina sighed with relief and nodded to her husband. "Do you know where they are now?"

"They went out a little while ago," said Mrs. Geller. "I think your son wanted to sleep over here."

Dina sucked in her breath. "Sleep over there? But why?" she laughed tightly. "He has his own bed to sleep in over here. Please ask him to call me when he gets back, or to come straight home. He did not ask for permission to sleep away tonight. I'm sure you know how it feels, as a mother...."

Mrs. Geller was silent. "I don't think we are as restrictive with

Menachem," she said after a pause. "I will give your message to Avrumie, though, if he comes home while I am still awake. Good night." She hung up the phone.

If she was still awake when they came home? Where could they possibly be?

"She said she'll tell Avrumie," she told her husband. "And if he doesn't listen, at least we'll know that he's sleeping at the Gellers. Of course, that's not acceptable, but at least it's — as you said, it could be...worse."

Ephraim nodded. "This Geller boy — I assume he's not the type we would pick to be friends with Avrumie."

Dina said nothing.

"I can't handle this right now, Dina," Ephraim said wearily. "I must get some sleep," he mumbled, and started up the stairs. Dina didn't move. She would wait by the phone in case Avrumie called. She reached for her *Tehillim* on the counter and opened the worn pages. It was fast becoming her best friend. "Please, Hashem, bring Avrumie back to us," she prayed. But Avrumie never called.

Seventeen

The pool hall was noisy and crowded when they arrived. Smoke hung heavily in the air and at first it was hard for Avrumie to make out anything in the dim light. He followed Mark closely, not wanting to get lost in the hubbub. They reached a table and Avrumie saw three guys and two girls standing together, laughing.

"Joe!" called Menachem, and a tall, dark boy turned around.

"Hey, Mark — haven't seen you in awhile." The two drew closer. "Who's your friend?"

"This is Abe. Abe — Joe, Stanley, Sherry, Monica, and Albert," Mark introduced his friends. They smiled at Avrumie. Avrumie looked at them and smiled back. He looked particularly hard at Albert — that guy looked so familiar. Suddenly Avrumie recognized him. He was Eliezer Spiegelman, a couple of years older than Avrumie, and he'd left yeshivah suddenly last year. Rumor had it he'd been kicked out for various misdemeanors. Now he was "Albert," and playing pool at ten o'clock at night. Avrumie felt a chill down his spine — was this where he was headed?

"You guys want to play with us?" asked the short, blond girl introduced as Sherry.

"Sure," Mark said. "Come on, Abe."

"I don't know how to play," Avrumie whispered frantically. Mark smiled condescendingly.

"Abe's gonna sit this one out and learn the ropes," he said, and Avrumie blushed.

Monica smiled at him kindly. "You'll learn it fast," she said. Avrumie smiled back at her. She looked a little like Chavie, he thought, then checked himself. He probably shouldn't even mention the two in the same thought! The game began, and Avrumie watched intently.

"Say, what's doing with Scott?" asked Mark, as he watched Joe set up his shot.

"You didn't hear?" asked Stanley in amazement.

"No — what happened?"

"He got canned three weeks ago," said Joe, not taking his eyes off the ball. "Drug dealing."

"I warned him," said Stanley.

"You're a big talker," snapped Joe.

"Hey, man — don't you go insinuating. I never did anything like that in my life, and I ain't going to do it either."

Avrumie stood, shocked. These boys were obviously Jewish, and he would bet a hundred dollars they had all come from *frum* backgrounds. But drugs? How could it be? He would talk to Menachem about this later.

Joe took a cigarette out of his pocket. "Got a match?" he asked Avrumie. The rest of the group tittered. They all knew he had never touched a cigarette. Avrumie felt embarrassed.

"Here's a stupid match, Ye*ho*nasan," Menachem said, disdain in his voice. He was a good friend, sticking up for Avrumie while risking his own acceptance. *I owe you one, buddy*, Avrumie thought.

Joe grabbed the match from Menachem angrily. Menachem had touched a raw nerve.

"Give me a puff," said Sherry, and Joe handed her the cigarette. Avrumie had never seen a girl smoke, and he was appalled. She passed the cigarette back to Joe, who inhaled deeply and blew out perfect smoke rings.

"Show off!" said Mark, waving the smoke from his eyes. "Whose turn is it to shoot?"

"It's mine," said Monica, taking up her stick.

"Enjoying yourself?" Mark asked Avrumie.

"Yeah, sure," said Avrumie. He was beginning to feel drawn to the atmosphere and the carefree gaiety that he had never before experienced.

Eliezer sidled up to Avrumie.

"How's yeshivah?" he asked quietly.

Avrumie rolled his eyes. "Let's just say you're smart for leaving," he said with a grimace.

"Yeah — I just couldn't take the rules. I felt like —" he made a strangling motion with his hands on his throat. "You gotta live life sometimes."

Avrumie nodded.

"You're still there, though — aren't you? I didn't hear anything about you getting bounced."

"No — I'm still there. In body more than spirit, though. I guess I'm just not creative enough to get kicked out!" Avrumie laughed ruefully. It was partly true.

"Have any idea of what you would do if you left?"

"No — that's one of the reasons that's pulling me back. What do you do?"

"Me?" asked Albert. "I work in a garage in the afternoons, hang out all night, and sleep all morning. What a life, eh? I moved out, got myself a little dig and a cute, beat-up car, and I'm hopping."

Avrumie was amazed. Although Eliezer was only two years his senior, he sounded very mature and capable. "Wow!" he said approvingly.

Albert regarded him cynically.

"It wasn't exactly my choice," he admitted. "I'll tell you something, kid," he said with a sardonic smile. "It ain't all it's cracked up to be."

"Hey, Al — your turn!" called Joe, and Eliezer turned away from Avrumie abruptly.

Avrumie was left in a state of confusion. What did Eliezer mean when he said it wasn't all it was cracked up to be? His life sounded ideal: free of parental supervision and pretty much all other authority, able to make his own hours, have his own money to spend as he pleased — what could be better? Eliezer was probably just being cynical. Either that, or he was being self-deprecating so as not to make Avrumie feel jealous and inferior.

"Wanna hear a joke?" Stanley asked, and he proceeded to tell an off-color, not-so-funny one-liner. The group laughed, and Avrumie laughed along with them, forcing the smile to his lips. He was beginning to really learn the ropes, and he was realizing that belonging took a lot of adaptation. Was he ready to make the necessary compromises?

"You know, I'm so mad," Sherry burst out. "My parents are just too much. They cut off my allowance and grounded me for two weeks 'cuz I slept over at Mandy without telling them. They're so....they're so medieval. They're like in the dark ages!"

"If you're grounded," Joe said, "then how come you're here playing pool?"

"You think I actually listened?!" laughed Sherry, and everyone laughed. Sherry put on a high-pitched, whining voice, " 'Rochel, we were so worried about you last night and sleeping out without permission is a very big thing in my book,' " she mimicked patronizingly. " 'Go to your room immediately, and take off that appalling nail polish!' "

"Wait — that sounds like my mom!" declared Monica. "Maybe they're twins. 'Miriam — you will wipe off that lipstick or you will not leave the house. And don't bother coming out of your room until you change that skirt!' " she imitated. They all laughed sympathetically.

"You girls think you have it bad — just come on over to my place," said Stan. "I bought myself a little color TV, right? And I was lying there in bed watching my favorite show, when my mom bursts in, without knocking, this 'now you're dead' look on her face. 'I just can't believe it,' she starts up, and you know the rest of the speech, right?" They all nodded. "Anyway, she confiscated the TV, told my dad who has his own particular way of disciplining —" Stanley's face went tight with anger as he put his fists up in a fighting stance; his father beat him for misbehavior — "and yours truly is not really here in this pool hall, he's in his room, grounded for life!"

Avrumie's blood went cold. He'd thought he had it bad, but his life was a picnic compared to his new friends'. One of them was beaten, one kicked out of his own house.... He scanned the group of faces. In the smoky darkness of the room, there was one uniting bond joining these strangers: bitterness and confusion.

"Say — you guys ever get the 'you're gonna go to Gehinnom' speech?" That was Eliezer.

"Oh — that's as old as my grandma," said Joe. "I'll bet the whole concept was made up by some rabbi who couldn't stand watching people having a good time." They laughed again, less heartily this time.

"How are your folks, Mark?" asked Sherry.

Menachem looked up from examining his fingernails. "Oh — actually, my parents are pretty cool. They don't try to make me into something I'm not, they don't try to put any restrictions on me that I can't keep. I don't feel like I have to go against everything they say just to live my life. My Dad's a lawyer, so I guess he's seen enough of what laws can do to a person," he joked.

"You're really lucky," said Avrumie. He hadn't intended to contribute to the conversation, but the words just slipped out. Everyone looked at him and he felt as if he had to quantify what he'd said.

"I mean — my parents, they just don't understand. They think that life is all about rules. They freak out if I even change the color of my shirt! I think restrictions make them happy — they feel that the *frummer* they are, the more fulfilling their life is." It was only after he said it that he realized what he had said and found that it was a feeling he'd had for awhile without being able to put his finger on it. It was true. His parents liked restricting themselves, even more than necessary. If it was okay to eat a certain *hechsher*, they would find problems with it and be more *machmir*. He had asked his father about that — honestly, rather than to bait him — and the answer had been unsatisfying.

"A person who truly loves Hashem, Avrumie, wants to do everything possible to serve Him whole-heartedly. If I have the choice of being *meikil* or being *machmir*, I try to choose being *machmir* because then I feel that I am truly being *oveid Hashem*. The harder it is, the more *sechar* you get, Avrumie. '*Lefum tza'ara agra.*' "

But weren't there so many other things to work on besides whether or not to eat a certain chocolate? Wasn't it better to try to control one's anger and learn to give selflessly than to make the decision to "graduate" to a larger yarmulke? Avrumie was lost in his own thoughts, and the conversation flowed around him, changing directions from parent-bashing to upcoming social events.

"I heard Avi's having an open house this weekend," Monica was saying when he surfaced from his thoughts. "You guys gonna go?"

"I already have plans," said Albert, "and besides — last time Avi did that, the neighbors called the cops."

"Serious?" asked Monica. "That's it — I'm not going."

"Scared?" laughed Joe.

Monica turned serious. "Listen — this is my life we're talking about. I don't want to do something stupid now that I'll regret ten years down the line, and spending a night in jail is definitely something I don't want coming to haunt me."

"You're totally right," agreed Sherry. Joe was quiet.

"You have a head on your shoulders," said Stanley. "I see so many kids living as though tomorrow was their last day on earth — and if they don't watch out, it will be!" He laughed ruefully.

There was a short period of silence which Mark broke.

"I'm gonna get going — I'm exhausted. Big test tomorrow. You coming, Abe?"

Avrumie nodded.

"Well, g'night, guys. Nice to see you all."

"Good night," said Avrumie. The group wished them a good night and Avrumie and Mark walked out of the pool hall and into the crisp night air.

Eighteen

"And so I told her, 'Ummmm, that's not exactly my type,' and burst out laughing right in her face!" concluded Chavie. Leah, Chanie, and Malky laughed appreciatively.

"It was really a tight purple dress without sleeves?!" Chanie demanded to know.

"I'm telling you — I never saw such an ugly, un-*tzenius* thing in my life!" asserted Chavie. "I can't imagine anyone buying it. Well, I told her I needed a party dress, and I guess this is what she would buy her daughter for a party!" The girls laughed again.

"So did you get anything in the end?" asked Leah.

"I got a pair of shoes, and a really nice headband to wear for Shabbos, but I don't know where I'm going to find the perfect dress."

"I know what you mean," commiserated Malky. "My sister's wedding is getting closer every day and every time I talk to my mother about what I'm going to wear, she tells me she's too busy to think about it. I'm telling you — I'm going to end up wearing my jean skirt!" More laughter, and some sympathetic clucking.

"Maybe we'll go shopping together, Malk," suggested Chavie. Shopping was Chavie's second-favorite occupation. Number one was talking. She could talk for hours on end without running out of things to say or feeling as though she was boring her audience.

"How was the *chumash* test?" asked Chanie. "We have it in another two periods, and I'm so nervous!"

"Well, we're not supposed to say anything about it, but all I'll tell you is, know that big *dikduk Rashi* very well," said Chavie.

Malky shushed her. "You're not supposed to say," she warned. "It's cheating."

"Did I say anything? I was just giving Chanie some advice. And anyway, Mrs. Friedman even said in class that we should study that *Rashi* well, so I'm not giving anything away," Chavie said self-righteously.

"Mrs. Friedman is such a hard teacher," complained Leah. "As much as I study for her tests, I just can't do well. Last year, with Mrs. Frisch, it was a breeze. I got straight *alefs*. This year I feel like a dunce!"

"Really? I like Mrs. Friedman," said Chavie.

Chanie was quick to agree with her. "So do I," she said. "She really knows her stuff, and she's so...she's such a *tzadeikes*."

"I know," said Malky. "My mother said that Mrs. Friedman is the one who started the *bikur cholim* committee that organizes girls to go visit the nursing homes and hospitals. She has a lot of kids, too."

Chavie turned philosophical. "Can you imagine, in twenty years from now, being married with our own huge housefuls of kids, and our husbands learning in *kollel*?" she asked wistfully.

"Oh, Chavie — you're too much!" laughed Malky. "I can't even think about graduating next year — how am I supposed to think about marriage?!"

"Being in the *shidduch parashah* is so much fun and so nerve-wracking," stated Chavie knowingly. "My friend Genendel tells me all about her dates." It wasn't an outright lie, but it wasn't completely true either. Genendel was her next-door neighbor, eighteen, and very mature. Chavie and Genendel had become friends quite recently, and Chavie was very proud of her coveted relationship with a postseminary girl.

"Really? What did Genendel say?" begged Chanie.

"You know I can't tell you," Chavie said scornfully, inwardly berating herself for getting caught in a little white lie. All Genendel had really said on the topic of *shidduchim* was that they drove her crazy and that she dreaded going out. "It's very private. But let's just say that it's a pretty complicated process. First the boy's family has to check you out and agree, and then the girl's family checks him out — right down to his great-grandparents and his first-grade report card!" That got a laugh. "Then the girl buys some nice suits — that's the best part!" laughed Chavie, and the four girls giggled together.

"It's not a joke, though," said Malky. "I heard stories of girls who boys wouldn't go out with because of their families. Ruchie told me that her neighbor has a sister with Down's syndrome and a very good *bachur* wouldn't go out with her because of it. Which is ridiculous, really."

"I just can't believe that! And Shoshie told me that she has a friend whose parents are divorced and she's having a very hard time with *shidduchim*," added Leah.

"It's true," confirmed Chanie. "I heard the same thing. Boy — you must feel like you're under a microscope!"

Something within Chavie's mind began buzzing with alarm. It was true — everything they had said. A girl was judged not only on her own merit, but on the way her family presented itself as well. What would people say about Avrumie when *she* was in *shidduchim*? Chavie had taken careful note of Avrumie's behavior over the past few months, but she had not discussed it with anyone. That was not something she wanted to share with her friends. She was planning on talking to Ima about it, but it was an uncomfortable topic. Ima had been looking very worn-out lately, and she was sure Avrumie was the cause of her stress. Avrumie hadn't even come home last night, and although all the children, by an unspoken agreement, had not mentioned his disappearance, she knew that trouble was afoot. She prayed that Avrumie would get over his stage and revert back to his regular old self — and fast.

Leah nudged her arm, and Chavie lost her train of thought.

"Wh-what?" she asked.

"I was asking you if you knew which seminary Rivka Hirsch applied to?"

"Oh — sorry. Yes, actually, I do...." The fears left Chavie's mind and she became absorbed in the conversation once more.

Nineteen

At precisely ten o'clock, Avrumie lifted his unwilling hand and forced himself to knock on the heavy, brown door. How many times had he swung open this very door — coming home from school, taking a snack break from a game of basketball, chasing one of the kids through the house — with so many different emotions: happiness after a victorious game, depression at being kicked out of class or getting back a bad grade, frustration and anger at getting into a fight at school. This was the first time he had ever approached the door with this curious mixture of terror, hope, and a strange detachment. The events of last night had made him feel completely foreign from his family. He took comfort in knowing that there was a place where he would be accepted by people his age struggling with the same problems he had. He felt as though he didn't need his family as much anymore, except for the mundane aspects of life: food, clothing, shelter — he stopped himself abruptly. When had he become so cold and calculating?

He rehearsed in his mind the speech he'd prepared to deliver to his mother. He had timed his return exactly: Abba would be in school and Ima would be in middle of feeding Bracha and thinking about making supper. She would be just distracted enough to be willing to forgive him, he hoped, and yet calm enough to be able to listen to him properly.

He took a deep breath and knocked on the door.

Dina had just finished washing the last breakfast bowl when she heard a knock at the door. She wiped her hands on a dishtowel and ran to open it. Could it be....

"Avrumie!" she practically shouted.

He looked at her curiously. "Hello."

She didn't know what to say. Feelings of rage, worry, love, and guilt surged through her simultaneously.

"Come in," she said dumbly, and he did.

Avrumie looked at his mother, at her pale, worn face, at her sad mouth and her worried eyes, and his whole self-confident, unyielding speech collapsed.

"I'm sorry, Ima ." The words came unbidden to his lips, but he meant them. Perhaps hearing what the other kids had had to say about their parents last night had made him realize that his own situation was pretty mild in comparison.

"I — I'm sorry too, Avrume'le," Dina said, choking back her tears. Impulsively she drew Avrumie towards her and he leaned his head on her shoulder. Dina let her tears fall silently on his shoulder, crying from joy that her son had come home and that he had apologized. It was a long moment before Avrumie pulled away, and was it Dina's imagination, or were his eyes damp?

"Do you want to talk, Avrumie?" she asked him searchingly.

Avrumie shook his head. "Not now, Ima. I'm not ready yet."

"Okay," said Dina. "When you're ready, I'm here."

Avrumie nodded. "Can I have some breakfast?"

Twenty

"And then the rabbit said, 'Thank you for those yummy carrots, Bill,' and he hopped away." Avrumie closed the book and put it on the shelf. "The end," he said to Bracha as she clapped her pudgy hands together. "Now it's time to go *shluffy*." He lifted her up onto his shoulder, then drew her away from him. "Iiiiima — Bracha has a dirty diaper!" he yelled downstairs.

"I'm coming!" called Ima from the living room. She was probably helping Sima with her homework. What was with Sima, Arumie wondered as he waited for his mother to relieve him. She was so...bumbling and awkward. She never could do anything right, and she was constantly criticized for it. Everything took her ages to do. But she did have a very sweet personality. Avrumie liked teasing her, and he would occasionally indulge in just a little exploitation, getting her to do his Friday jobs for him or take over his dishwashing responsibilities. Sima didn't have it easy, that was for sure.

He heard his mother run up the steps. Things had been much more relaxed between them, and he had agreed to her suggestion of making an appointment with the two of them and his rebbe for the next day. Ima had not mentioned Abba's name at all in the conversation, and Avrumie was glad of it. Maybe things could be worked out. He was beginning to hope.

"Thank you, Avrumie," said Dina as she hurried into the room. "What homework do you have for tonight?"

"Oh, Ma — I'm a big boy. I'll take care of everything — don't worry, 'kay?"

Dina looked at him.

"All right, my big boy, but something tells me that you're due for a math test some time soon, and we don't want a repeat of last math test...."

"Fine," he mumbled, leaving the room. He had failed his last calculus test — a combination of missing nearly every class and not catching up for the test. Math was his weak point, and Ima was right — they were having a test. On Monday. He turned to go to his room.

"Oh, and Avrumie?"

"Yeah."

"Shimshon called for you last night. Call him back."

Avrumie glanced at her, and a thread of guilt knotted inside him. He had been avoiding Shimshon lately, and Ima had probably noticed that. Shimshon was a good friend, a really nice guy, and yet lately Avrumie just didn't see eye-to-eye with him. Shimshon was already talking about where he wanted to go for *beis midrash*, while Avrumie was having a hard time getting through *yeshivah gedolah*. Avrumie also felt that Shimshon looked down on him. He couldn't quite pinpoint what it was that made him feel that way, but there was definitely something there. Another thing: Shimshon adored Abba. Abba had taught him in seventh grade while Avrumie had been in the parallel class, and Shimshon would often go off into raptures about how wonderful Rabbi Faber's class had been and how much he had gained from it. Did he do it to annoy Avrumie? To flatter him? To reproach him? Avrumie didn't know, but he had started distancing himself from Shimshon. Should he call him now? He'd have to see.

Avrumie went to his room and closed the door. The black walls added a nice ambience, he thought. He looked at his watch. Menachem was supposed to come at 7:30 to get some help on a paper for English class. Avrumie took out his math book and a notepad and got to work.

Images of the previous night intruded on his concentration. Although he had interacted pleasantly enough with Ima and it was nice to be home again, he felt curiously estranged. A layer of the "Other Side" clung to him, and he couldn't shake off the feeling. Was this the *tumah* his rebbe had alluded to on certain occasions in his *mussar shiur*?

"Iiiiiima!" He could hear Shira's screechy voice even through his closed door. That girl sure didn't need a microphone — she was a walking loudspeaker! He heard his mother rush downstairs to get the phone call. Then he got back to work.

Twenty-one

Dina picked up the telephone receiver which Shira had left dangling over a chair back.

"Hello?"

"Hello, Mrs. Faber?"

"Yes."

"This is Golda Katzman, Sima's *limudei kodesh* teacher. How are you?"

"Fine, *baruch Hashem*, and yourself?" Warning bells began clanging in Dina's head. What was she calling about?

"Oh, *baruch Hashem*, fine. I'm actually calling about your Sima."

My Sima, thought Dina. *Uh oh — this is trouble.*

"What about Sima?" she asked, trying to keep the annoyance and fear out of her voice.

"Well, I suppose you've noticed that her marks are not very good, and it seems that this is not the first year that she's having problems in school. She is a very sweet, polite girl, of course. Not one of the problematic ones in the class — you should be very proud of her." She paused for acknowledgment of such a generously dispensed compliment, and Dina obeyed.

"Yes, I know. Thank you. She seems to like you, too." Yeah, right — all Sima had to say about her *limudei kodesh* teacher was that she was mean, gave too much homework, and hated her.

"I have spoken to the principal about having Sima tested," Mrs. Katzman continued.

"Tested?! For what?"

"For learning disabilities. There is a great possibility that she has difficulty in different areas and that is what is holding her back. Some kids go through twelve years of school with no one knowing that they suffer from severe handicaps in their learning. It is a terrible ordeal for the children, and, when diagnosed later in life, learning disabilities are much harder to work on."

"Are you implying that my Sima is somehow...retarded?!" Dina spat out the words. Who was this woman who dared cast aspersions on her daughter? Granted, Sima wasn't bright, but she didn't have real problems. Dina sat down on one of the dining room chairs — she had taken the phone out of the kitchen, away from eagerly listening ears.

"Please don't misunderstand me," said Mrs. Katzman kindly. "I am not labeling Sima or saying anything bad about her. I just want to help her. I can't stand seeing the child sit in my class all morning, not understanding a single thing I say. When I ask her a question, she never knows the right answer. She tells me that she does her homework with you, and I believe her, but she doesn't know the material at all by the time she gets to class. That's a problem, Mrs. Faber, and I think you'll agree with me. We both have Sima's best interests in mind, don't we?"

Dina softened. The teacher was right. School was difficult for Sima. Dina would spend hours with her going over her homework, only to have Sima come home dejected after forgetting everything they had learned together.

"What is involved in the testing?"

"Oh, nothing much. We have someone very capable and professional who will administer the tests. It should take, at most, a few hours, and he is very pleasant to deal with. I am sure that Sima will cooperate if you speak to her about it and explain what it is all about."

"How much will this cost?"

"I am not sure of the exact amount, but if the money is an issue, the school will help you out. I mentioned to the principal that the expense might be a concern, and she implied that it could be taken care of. You must do this for your daughter, Mrs. Faber. She is not very happy."

"I know." Dina sighed. Lately Sima had been even more withdrawn and mopey than usual. She hardly spoke at home, and spent a lot of time in her room reading and writing. She didn't even show Dina her poems anymore like she once had.

"How do we schedule this test?" she asked.

"I have taken the liberty of making an appointment for you already. For tomorrow at ten o'clock, if that's good."

"That will work out fine," said Dina, making a mental note to get a babysitter for Bracha. Mrs. Katzman gave her the address to go to, wished her a good night, and hung up.

Dina walked to the kitchen slowly and put the phone on the hook. She had misjudged Mrs. Katzman — she was obviously very caring and concerned and had Sima's best interests in mind. But learning disabilities? What next? *Ribbono shel Olam — I have so much on my plate already,* Dina cried silently. *Isn't it enough?*

Her eyes caught sight of the picture on the wall — a smiling Dina and Ephraim, surrounded by five beautiful, grinning children.

For shame, Dina! a voice within her whispered. *Hashem is so good to you. There are bumps in your life, but look where they're getting you. You've never davened so well before, for one thing. You've been giving tzedakah consistently. You are forging a stronger bond with Hashem than you ever did before. The circumstances are difficult, but couldn't it just possibly be a hidden chesed? Life is not about riding smoothly — it's about hard work. So you've got some heavy duty weight lifting to do now — don't forget: Hashem only tests the ones strong enough to handle it. The potter only hits the jars that are truly strong, to demonstrate their strength. You always knew you were strong, Dina, but here's your opportunity to take your strength and use it for the best.*

Dina wiped her eyes hurriedly as she heard the sound of footsteps.

It was Sima.

Dina managed a smile.

"Ima," Sima said, "are you okay?"

"Yes, sweetheart," Dina replied. "I'm even better than okay." And for once, she meant it. She turned resolutely and secluded herself in her bedroom to say some tearful but grateful *Tehillim*.

Twenty-two

"Bye — have a great day!" Dina called after Chanan and Yosef as they ran out the front door. Now only Shira had to be pushed out, and then she would start her busy day.

"Why doesn't Sima have to go to school today?" demanded Shira.

"Sima has an appointment with me today, Shira, and besides, it's not your business. Do you have your lunch?"

"What kind of appointment? She's not sick — I'm the one with the stomachache."

"I asked you if you have your lunch," Dina said pointedly.

"Yes," Shira pouted.

"Good. The door is that way, Shira — hurry, or you'll be late." She kissed her cheek and patted her hair into place. "Have a great day!"

"I'm not going to have even a good day," were Shira's final, optimistic words as she stalked out of the house.

You win some, you lose some, thought Dina, as she closed the door. "Sima — are you almost ready?!" she called upstairs. No answer. Sima had not been pleased about the testing. In fact, she had outright refused — something she rarely did. Dina had pulled every trick in the book to make her agree to cooperate: candy, money, pizza, and an extended bedtime, but it was worth it, wasn't it?

"Sima?" she called again.

No answer. Dina dragged herself up the stairs and made her way to Sima's room. Sima was lying under her blanket, still in her nightgown. She looked up at her mother, standing in the doorway.

"I'm not going."

Dina's good mood dissipated. Sima could be very obstinate when she made up her mind.

"Oh, yes, you are, young lady. This is not a democracy. Get yourself out of bed this minute, and get your clothes on." She paused, and a sudden thought hit her. "Why don't you want to go, Sima?" she asked, in a more gentle tone.

"I don't want to have a stupid test, and then all the kids will know for sure that I'm stupid. It's bad enough that they just think so, but now they're gonna know it," she burst out angrily, her cheeks reddening.

Dina's heart went out to her daughter — she had so much on her young, frail shoulders. Dina sat down on her bed, put her arm on those shoulders, and held Sima close to her.

"Nobody thinks you're stupid, Simi, and this test is going to help us to help you. Don't worry about it — nobody's going to know that you took the test, except for us. It will be our secret, and we don't have to tell anyone else. In fact, we really shouldn't tell anyone else. It's nobody's business. Okay?"

Sima looked up at her mother. Maybe it would be okay. "You won't tell anyone?"

"No one," assured Dina. "And how about we go for donuts afterwards." Sima brightened. The way to her heart was definitely through her stomach! Dina smiled. "Okay, then, Simi — let's go!"

She wasn't feeling so excited, though, as she went downstairs to clean up the breakfast dishes. Panicky feelings were turning her stomach in knots, even as she told herself they were childish: What if someone saw them enter the psychologist's office and guessed what their purpose there was? Or worse, jumped to even more incriminating conclusions? "Keep away from that Faber family," she could hear them saying.

"One kid's got psychiatric problems, and the other one's going off the *derech*." She took herself tightly in hand. *That's enough, Dina,* she told herself sharply, and she forced her mind to think of something else.

Her thoughts turned automatically to Avrumie. She had set up a meeting with his rebbe later that evening while Ephraim would be with his *chavrusa*. She was dreading that appointment as well. What would the outcome be? How would Avrumie behave? What if Ephraim found out and was upset at her for hiding it from him?

"I'm ready, Ima." Sima was standing in the doorway, dressed. Wonder of wonders!

"I'm so proud of you, darling — that was very quick," Dina said approvingly. Fortunately, the babysitter had arrived already. "Let's go." She grabbed the keys and the two went out to the car, but Dina's thoughts were still distracted. Was she heaping even more taboo upon her family than they already had associated with them?

"Ima, you just missed a stop sign," piped up Sima from the passenger seat.

Dina was jarred back to reality. "Oh my goodness — did I really?! That's terrible. I'll be more careful now." She forced herself to concentrate on the road, and in no time, they had arrived. She parked the car, took Sima's hand, and the two walked into the pleasant office. The secretary looked at her watch, smiled, and told them to be seated. Dr. Simmons would be with them shortly.

Dina picked up a magazine from the coffee table and began flipping through the pages. She knew she should be talking to Sima, who was sitting huddled in her chair, terrified, but she felt too weak and scared herself. What would the tests show? What would be with Sima? What would be with them all?

The door opened, and a tall, graying man motioned them to come inside. "It's all right, Simi," Dina whispered as they entered the room.

"Well, you must be Sima," said Dr. Simmons, and he winked at her. Sima blushed, and Dina's eyebrows drew together involuntarily.

"And you must be Sima's older sister," said the doctor heartily. Dina was not amused.

"Well, you certainly look young enough!" he said, grinning.

Dina was too uptight to be drawn in by his attempt at humor.

"I believe we have some business to attend to," she said stiffly. He looked at Dina quizzically, and then at Sima.

"Indeed we do. You, young lady, tell me — how do you like school?"

Sima looked down at her hands and didn't say a word. Dina knew already that she wouldn't answer any of his questions — she was too shy and intimidated.

"Sima has a lot of problems in school, don't you, Sima?" she offered. Sima didn't look up.

"I was asking Sima," Dr. Simmons corrected her. "I'd really like to know how things are going for you this year, Sima."

Sima did not speak. Dina remained silent as well.

"Would you mind waiting outside for a bit, Mrs. Faber?" the psychologist asked kindly. "Sima and I need a little time to get to know each other."

Dina hesitated. Sima looked at her pleadingly.

"Would you mind if I stayed with my daughter?"

He smiled, and Dina found herself relaxing.

"That's perfectly fine — it's understandable. This is the first time we've met, so there's bound to be a bit of strangeness to it. Now let's see, when's your birthday, Sima?"

Dr. Simmons had turned out to be very kind and understanding, Dina acknowledged as she and Sima walked back to the car. Sima had done her best and displayed enormous patience, and now they would have to wait for the results. Dina didn't want to think about that part.

"Now donuts, Ima?" Sima asked plaintively.

"Yes, darling. You did very well, Simi. I'm so proud of you. Let's go have a *nosh*." Sima gave her the first real smile in a long time.

Twenty-three

Ephraim smiled to himself as he parked the car in the driveway. He had come home early; his night *seder* *chavrusa* was ill, and he had jumped at the opportunity to spend some extra time with the children. The day had gone well, *baruch Hashem* — he had worked out a complicated *inyan* in class and then had had a good afternoon *seder* with his brilliant *chavrusa*, Moshe Stein. As he walked to the door he smiled, thinking of the children, wondering who would be first to notice him and announce it to the rest of the family. He was surprising Dina as well, and she would be pleased.

It was Avrumie who first spotted him.

"Hi, Dad," he said. "You're home early."

"Hello, Avrume'le," Ephraim greeted him. Avrumie looked as if he was on his way out. "How's my *ben Torah* today?"

Avrumie said nothing, and Ephraim felt the irritation begin. Was the boy ignoring him? He would not let his pleasant day be ruined, Ephraim decided, and, controlling his annoyance, he forced himself to say something encouraging.

"Avrumie, tell me, what *sugya* are you learning these days? Maybe we can learn *b'chavrusa* a little after supper — if you're not already booked."

Avrumie looked at him, stared at him as though he were an alien from outer space. Avrumie, with his hair gelled in some new style, with his shirt rolled up to his forearms, hiking boots on his feet, glared at him with his eyes blazing fire.

And then came the storm.

"You don't understand me — you never have. When were you here for me? When did you take the time from your precious students to talk to me? You don't even know me. All you do is pin your stupid hopes on me and pretend that one day I'll be exactly the way you want me to be. Get real, Dad, because it's not happening. I'm sick of this! I hate this family, I hate this way of life. It's not for me! Your *'ben Torah'*?!! Go talk to Dovid about Torah 'cuz I'm not interested. Don't 'Avrume'le' me 'cuz ‑ it won't get you anywhere. Face it, Dad, I'm never going to be your *ben Torah*. Look at me — do I look like a *ben Torah*? Well, I ain't acting like one either. A *chavrusa shaff*? I'm through with yeshivah! Now what do you have to say? Huh? Now that you finally wake up and smell the coffee, what do you have to say?"

The words seared Ephraim, attacked him until he felt the wind knocked out of his chest and the blood rush from his face. Avrumie's voice had risen and the shouting had brought other family members. Shira stood there, listening to each scalding, hateful word. Yosef was coming downstairs. Sima was coming out of the kitchen. Ephraim knew he had to act.

"Enough!" he bellowed. "I will not have my son talking this way. No matter how old you are, you are my son, and I am your father, and this is my home. You will not talk this way, or you will leave. If you have something to tell me, you can speak to me in my study. This way of behaving and speaking will not be tolerated in this home! Get out!"

He turned away in anger and stalked into the kitchen. Avrumie ran outside, slamming the door behind him. Dina heard the noise and came running in from the laundry room, unaware of what had happened.

"Ephraim!" she exclaimed. "You're home so...." Then she saw his face. "What happened?" He looked at her, his eyes full of pain, of sadness, of a hopelessness that she had never seen before. She knew it was

Avrumie. "What happened?" she repeated. He could not even speak. She noticed Shira, standing stockstill in the hallway, and Yosef and Sima, quietly staring at their father.

"Yosef, Sima, please fold the laundry together — it's in the den. Shira, why don't you go and help them?" They looked at her somewhat knowingly and left the room. She poured her husband a glass of water and he sat down heavily in one of the sagging kitchen chairs. Finally he spoke.

"Where have I been, Dina? Am I blind? When did this happen? Could I not have seen my son changing so drastically? Sure, I saw his clothing change, but I thought — you know what I thought. When you asked me about it, I said it was a stage. Boys go through this all the time. Some earlier, some later. But he's still in yeshivah, he's learning fine — isn't he?" He looked at her desperately. She shook her head.

"I didn't want to tell you, Ephraim, but he...he hasn't been so consistent about yeshivah. He seems to have lost his *cheishek* to learn; he spends time daydreaming and kidding around. In fact, we had an appointment tonight with his rebbe to discuss...to discuss what to do next."

Ephraim looked at her dumbly. "Where have I been?" he repeated. "Can a father not know what is happening to his son? To discuss what to do next? You didn't even tell me there was a meeting."

Dina swallowed guiltily. "I'm sorry, Ephraim," she said quietly. "Avrumie wouldn't have it any other way. He refused to go if you were told about it."

Ephraim stared at her. "He wants nothing to do with me? My own son? How did this happen? The Friday night incident was one thing, but he's never done anything like this before. Those words, Dina — they were like razor blades, each one of them. But you can't go along with his conspiracy against me. You can't support him in his blatant chutzpah — how could you not have told me about this appointment? I — I feel so hurt, Dina."

Dina lowered her eyes. "I didn't know what to do, Ephraim," she said honestly.

"Not knowing what to do is one thing. Hiding things from your husband is another. We cannot let Avrumie get in the way of our *shalom bayis*, no matter what is happening with him. I must be involved in his *chinuch*, even though I appreciate all that you are doing. Dina, I feel as though you two were ganging up against me."

Dina was upset. "Me? Ganging up? Against you? Ephraim, don't be ridiculous. I had absolutely no choice. It was either lose my bond with Avrumie for the second time, or try to help him out of the problems he has now. I tried sticking up for you once, and he ran away and didn't even sleep at home that night. Should I risk it again? Who knows how far we can push him?"

"Sticking up for me, you say. What do you have to defend me for? What did I do? Am I not a good father? Is that what you're saying?" Ephraim burst out.

Dina halted, aghast. She knew that Ephraim was deeply hurt and that the conversation had gotten out of hand.

"*Chas veshalom*, Ephraim," she said softly. "You are an excellent father — a father any child would love to have. I used the wrong expression, and I'm sorry. I meant it from Avrumie's perspective. He seems to have some...some resentment towards you. But that will change soon, *b'ezras Hashem*. We have to help him together."

Ephraim's anger abated. "You're right, Dina. And I'm sorry I got so upset at you — I'm really upset at myself. I still can't get over what just happened. But is it only with me? Besides for when he ran away, has he had any outbursts with you?"

Dina sighed. "I feel like I'm constantly treading on thin ice — with any word I can fall. Every day he pushes me, tests me, wants me to break. I don't know what to do, Ephraim. The other day I found him without a yarmulke. And don't you notice the words he's using? The friends he's hanging out with?" She laughed bitterly. "I think I'm picking up his language — 'hanging out with' indeed. You've been so busy lately that I hardly had your time enough to discuss this with you. Even that night that he slept over at Menachem you were too tired to talk. I guess it's a blessing that you came home early tonight."

Ephraim sighed ruefully. "A blessing indeed," he said. "What are we going to do, Dina?"

"Maybe you could speak to Reb Nosson," she suggested quietly. She knew that he would resist speaking to his *rosh yeshivah*. If there was one thing Ephraim hated, it was discussing his problems with others. But did they have a choice?

"I'm not sure he's the one..." Ephraim began. Dina looked at him, and he shifted uncomfortably. "We can't make more of this than there really is," he finished. "After all, it really could be a passing thing, even though it is very shocking. And I would hate to involve the *rosh yeshivah* unless it were really a big problem. The way I see it, Avrumie needs some more structure. He's right that I haven't spent enough time with him. His chutzpah is appalling, but he is right about that. I think what we should do is concentrate extra hard on spending time with him, but at the same time, set guidelines for what he can and can't do. Not wearing a yarmulke is inexcusable, Dina. We can't have that in our home. A Jew wears a yarmulke, and finished."

Dina nodded her head and looked at the table. She was almost convinced that what Ephraim had said was reasonable. It would just be embarrassing to involve the *rosh yeshivah* at this point. Teenagers were so unpredictable that in another month Avrumie could be back in the *beis midrash*, in his black suit, as if nothing had happened, and what would they say then? And yet, was this normal? Were they missing the early signs of something serious?

Ephraim read her thoughts. "Don't you think that if this was something very serious, his rebbe would have made a bigger deal out of it? I know Sholom Ehrlang — he's very on top of his students. If he thought something drastic was going on, he would definitely have contacted me — no?"

"You're right," said Dina slowly.

"I really think so, Dina. I really think so. *Oy*, I got so angry at him tonight. I just couldn't control myself. And the kids were standing around listening. I haven't yelled like that since Chanan set fire to the living room curtains. Those kids were shaken up a little."

"This is your first real confrontation with Avrumie — besides for that Shabbos incident, which wasn't a direct attack on you — and it didn't go so well, Ephraim. You have to forgive yourself for the anger — it's very difficult to see him like this and to have him speaking like this."

"Do you think we should be worried that he left the house?"

"He'll come back, Ephraim. Where else would he go? He got angry, and he left, but soon he'll cool off and he'll be back, and he'll probably apologize for what he said. Just like he did last time, when he got upset at me. He has such a good heart, Ephraim. We can't forget. He's still our Avrumie, even if he dresses differently and has a new vocabulary."

"You're right, Dina. You're very right. *'Chochmas nashim bansah beisah.'* "

Dina blushed and lowered her eyes. Ephraim smiled wanly at her. "Now, how was your day?"

Twenty-four

Avrumie ran out into the cool, crisp air. The sky was a dark red as the sun made its descent behind the trees, but he hardly noticed. Anger, fear, and sadness boiled inside him, giving him extra energy, and he ran as he'd never run before. This was it — he had finally said what he had wanted to say for so long. He had hurt his father, and he knew it. He had seen Abba's look and the way he had reacted. And the kids had seen it, too. He really was a little ashamed that they had had to witness the run-in, but he pushed the discomfort away with a swift shake of his head. Good — let them see their father exposed as he really was. Not caring about anything except his own anger and disappointment, Avrumie ran and ran as the night thickened around him. This time he had somewhere to go. A place where he was accepted.

As he headed towards the pool hall, Avrumie hoped his friends were there tonight. Although he had only met them once, there had been such warmth between them that he felt sure they would welcome him again. Maybe they could help him to decide how next to proceed with his life. He took a deep breath and was amazed to see how his anger had abated so quickly — perhaps it was the fresh air, or maybe the thought of meeting his friends, but his mind felt clear, and he actually felt good.

He had to have a game plan, though. What was he going to do? Going home was surely out of the question. He had heard Abba clearly enough — if he continued to act the way he was acting, he would not be allowed at home. With Ima it was a different story — she was quick to forgive, and she really did love him, deep down. He felt a shock run up and down his spine. Was this it? Had he left home for good? The words sounded too final, too ominous. He was only seventeen, and although it felt good to have the heady sensation of independence and revenge bursting within him, he really felt a little scared. Abba would be sorry he had tormented his son so. As for the fear and finality of severing himself from his home, Avrumie felt a burst of sadness and loneliness and allowed himself to indulge in a measure of self-pity. He would miss Ima — her chocolate chip cookies and her warmth. They were so close to having done something together to make his situation better, and then his father came and ruined everything! And what about the kids? What would he do without having Bracha to cuddle? Would he ever get to see them again?

Don't be silly, he told himself. *You can always go home to visit when Abba's not home. Which is almost always*, he reminded himself bitterly. He wondered if anyone would miss him. Chavie probably wouldn't even notice that he was gone. She was much too preoccupied with her popularity and looks. Dovid would probably miss him in a strange way. Avrumie had always had a good relationship with Dovid. Yosef and Chanan would miss the games of baseball and tag that he used to play with them, but they'd get over it eventually. Sima, forget about — she probably wouldn't even register the fact that he had left. And Shira, the big mouth, would probably make nasty comments in her sing-song voice about Avrumie running away from home, and tell all her friends about it.

All her friends. Avrumie shuddered. Soon word would be out that he had run away from home. What would be the consequences of that? He certainly couldn't go to yeshivah anymore. His rebbeim would just give him speeches about his change in behavior, and *kibbud av va'eim*, and Abba would interfere. Anyway, hadn't he told his father that he was through with *yeshivah gedolah?* Perhaps he'd been speaking through anger at the time, but there was an element of truth to the statement. Yeshivah hadn't sat well with him for a long time now. Why not make it a clean break now, when the time seemed right? Yes, yeshivah was definitely a thing of the past, he decided, and it half-relieved him, half-terrified him. What would he do with all his time? How would he support himself? Was he capable of being independent at such a young age? And if he was in trouble, whom could he turn to for help? The community would have already labeled him a "runaway." Not that there hadn't been some mutterings already, when his style of dress had altered and he had given up the *"ben Torah"* scene.

"Ben Torah." The words rang hauntingly in his ears. "How's my *ben Torah?"* He could still hear his father's greeting, and his rage welled up inside him anew. Would Abba never understand?

"Hey — weren't you here last week?" A deep voice broke into his thoughts and Avrumie turned, stunned, to find a short, stout boy addressing him. He also noticed, with some surprise, that he was standing in the entrance of the Hall. Absorbed in his own thoughts, he had been completely oblivious to anything else.

"Yeah," he said guardedly. He had never met this guy before. "Who are you?"

"Just call me Mikey," said the other boy, and he smiled thinly.

"I'm Abe," said Avrumie, and the name came almost naturally to his lips.

"Hmmmm...." Mikey deliberated for one quick second. "Avrumie Faber, seventeen, from Yeshivah Zichron Yosef. Father, Rabbi Ephraim Faber, rebbe at Ohr Yechiel, seven siblings.... Shall I continue?"

Avrumie stood stock-still, shocked. Who was this boy? How did he know about him? Avrumie's guard clicked on again. Hadn't Ima always told him not to talk to strangers? Granted, he had been three years old and the strangers she had been referring to were grown-ups wearing dark glasses, offering him candy, but...one never knew. He turned abruptly away from Mikey — or whoever he was — and walked stiffly into the pool hall, not looking back.

"Hey!" Mikey called. "I'm really sorry — I didn't mean to offend you!" Avrumie kept walking, but Mikey ran after him and caught his arm.

"Listen, man, I didn't mean to make you all upset, okay? It's just my hobby — I always wanted to be a supersleuth, and so I hang out here and watch all the new guys and try to find out who they really are — or were. That's all. I didn't mean any harm, okay?"

Avrumie stopped and turned to look at him, but said nothing.

"I mean, I'm really Moishy," Mikey continued, almost babbling, in his eagerness to dispel Avrumie's coldness. "I was learning at Toras Tzion before they kicked me out a year ago. You might know my parents — Zelingoff?"

Avrumie started. Could this be Moishy Zelingoff? The Moishy Zelingoff he had heard of learned eighteen hours a day and did not wear cutoff jeans and a baseball cap. Hershel Zelingoff was a well-respected philanthropist who supported half the city with his generosity, and his sons were given everything they needed in order to sit and learn Torah in peace.

Mikey read his thoughts. "Oh, yes," he said bitterly. "Didn't you hear about the sudden disappearance of Moishy Zelingoff? Which version did you hear? The one about him going to learn in a *chashuv* yeshivah in Bnei Brak? The one about him having to recover from too much stress, in a convalescence center? The one about him going to Moscow to teach there?"

Avrumie felt his heart go out to this boy. He was probably in the same predicament as Avrumie was himself — if not worse.

"It must be tough," he finally offered.

Mikey looked up at Avrumie. "You have no idea," he said simply.

Was he right? Avrumie wondered. Could his situation really be child's play compared to what others were going through? Well, each person's problems were, to them, the end of the world, he decided self-righteously. His situation was certainly no picnic.

"Where do you live? What do you do?" he asked Mikey. He may as well find out for himself what the usual "route" was, and Mikey seemed ready to talk.

"Well, actually, I live with my aunt and uncle," said Mikey. "They're really cool. They don't say anything to anyone, and they watch what they say to me. They gave me their basement, and they kind of close their eyes, so we get along."

Mikey lived with his relatives! Why hadn't he thought of that? Uncle Yechiel and Aunt Minna were decent people, and their house was empty since Shuie had gone to a yeshivah in Eretz Yisrael and Chana had gotten married. And they were Ima's relatives, so he didn't have to worry about Abba poking his nose around. Maybe if he put it to them the right way, they would agree to have him live there for awhile. At least until he could make other arrangements.

"What was that you said?" he asked Mikey — he'd been too wrapped up in his new idea to hear what the other had said.

"I'm in public school," said Mikey. "It's not one of the standard schools, though, it's sort of a vocational school, where they teach you a trade. It's very hands-on and it's perfect for me. I take shop and woodworking, and plus you have to take regular subjects. It gives me kind of an outlet — y'know what I mean?"

Avrumie nodded. An outlet was a good thing. It let off steam. He had always been at a loss to find a permissible outlet. With his father demanding his absolute devotion to Torah, anything else was considered shameful. Even his baseketball games were discouraged. As Mikey rambled on about his new school, Avrumie thought back to a scene a year ago, when on the outside he had still been a "*ben Torah*," but his insides had begun to be infected by the niggling little worm of doubt and defiance. It came back to him, as clear as day.

He had had a good day of learning, and, as he'd left the *beis midrash* to get a good night's sleep, Shimshon had snagged him into playing a quick game of basketball. It had felt good to get the old juices flowing as he snapped the ball from the court to the net, to the accolades of his teammates and onlookers. He had left, sweaty but satisfied, his *gemara* tucked under his arm. He'd come home and was sitting in the kitchen, winding down with some cookies, when Abba had walked in.

"Avrumie!" He had seemed genuinely happy to see him. There was a time when his father had been very proud of him. The approval was a reward for conforming to the standards his father set.

"Hi, Abba," he had said, swallowing a bite.

"How was your day, *boychik?*"

"Great, Abba. Good day of learning, and fantastic game of basketball."

There had been a slight pause, and then a furrowing of eyebrows, and Avrumie had felt a pit in his stomach.

"Avrume'le, listen to your adjectives, and think carefully about where your true interests lie. Your basketball game was 'fantastic,' but your day of learning was only 'good'? Avrumie, surely you meant the reverse. And how can you ruin a day of *heilige* Torah by wasting precious minutes on a children's game of basketball. I am honestly surprised at you — I would have expected more from my *bechor.*"

The effect had been the same as if he were a full balloon and someone had just pricked him — all his euphoria and joy dissipated. As he had stared at his father's turned back, he had felt utterly and completely deflated and dishonored.

A sharp pain in the side, and he snapped out of his unpleasant reverie.

"You spacin' out on me, man?" Mikey looked hurt, and suddenly Avrumie realized that the boy had been baring his soul to him while he had been off in his own world.

"Gosh, I'm sorry," he apologized sincerely. "I'm so tired, you wouldn't believe it."

Mikey glared at him.

Avrumie fished around for something to say that would exonerate his lack of sympathy. "You have it tough, man," he said, and Mikey softened. "I mean, real tough. Not just anyone could do what you've done." Avrumie saw something light up in Mikey's countenance. *He's never been paid a compliment*, Avrumie thought wonderingly. *Never been encouraged.*

"You're a good one, Abe," Mikey said warmly, slapping him on the shoulder. And their friendship was cemented.

Twenty-five

Dina closed the car trunk, picked up the bags of groceries, and started the short walk up the path to the front door. Shira was playing ball in front of the garage, and Dina vaguely heard her cheerful sing-song:

"Avrumie over the water, Avrumie over the sea, Avrumie broke a bottle and blamed it on me. I told Ma, I told Pa, and Avrumie got a beating...."

She didn't have a chance to finish before Dina accosted her, nearly shaking her in her fury. Leave it to Shira to take the uppermost worry on her mind and turn it into a bouncing game. Avrumie had been gone for three days already. Without a trace. They had called everyone they knew. Menachem hadn't seen him, Shimshon definitely had no idea where he was. He hadn't been to yeshivah; he hadn't even been spotted at the basketball courts where he usually liked to play.

"What are you singing?!" Dina burst out angrily.

Shira looked at her, taken aback. "Whaaaaat?!!" she said in her high-pitched, "hurt" voice. "I needed a name for A so I said Avrumie." She paused and then delivered the final blow. "We're not allowed to say his name anymore just because he ran away from home?" she asked viciously.

Dina's eyes flew open, stunned. She hadn't heard the words spoken so bluntly, and they were like sharp, tiny knives in her heart. It was true:

Avrumie had run away from home. Suddenly, the anger rushed out of her like a tidal wave. Her rage had been completely unfounded. If Shira wanted to use her brother's name as an A, what was wrong with that? An innocent seven-year-old could not possibly know the pain and anguish ripping at her mother as she sang so carelessly and happily the cherished name of a wayward son.

"I — I'm sorry, Shira'le," apologized Dina, and she kissed her daughter on the forehead. "I don't know why I lost my temper." Shira just stared. "You can continue your game now," Dina said, picking up her bags and going into the house.

Twenty-six

"**T**his is a difficult *sugya*, boys, and we'll have to work on it more. You can leave to recess early." Rabbi Kaplan closed his *gemara* and nodded to his class. He watched as the confused faces broke into wide smiles and the boys ran out of the classroom, grabbing snacks and various balls, bats, and gloves in midstride.

Dovid took his bag of chocolate chip cookies from his knapsack and closed his knapsack carefully. He was one of the very few who didn't rejoice when an extended recess was declared. Why should he be happy? He was never picked for any team and was occasionally ridiculed and picked on by the bigger, more popular boys; he would much rather have stayed and plugged away at his *gemara*. But that would have attracted even more derogatory attention. He slowly shuffled out of the classroom and into the bright sunshine of the playground. The boys were already forming teams for their various sports. He heard Menashe organizing an elite basketball game under the nets, and the group cheering with excitement. He sat down on a tree stump and opened his snack.

His mind quickly turned to the long *Tosafos* they had been working on that morning, with the sweet, satisfying crunch of fresh cookies fueling his thoughts. Suddenly he noticed something awry. A group of his classmates was heading toward his quiet, deserted spot in the far corner of the playground.

Dovid felt a chill of alarm race up his spine. They never sought him out for anything commendable; he must be in trouble. What did he do this time? Shimmie was whispering animatedly to Gavriel as they walked towards him. Dovid's blood ran cold. Shimmie and Gavriel meant Trouble capital T. They had it in for him all the time, and he never understood why.

"Hey, Dovid," Shimmie drawled casually. "How's everything doing with you?" He paused. "How's your family?"

Dovid felt an electric bolt run through his entire body. He knew what game they were playing. He swallowed hard; there would be no escaping.

"What — you didn't hear? I just asked you a plain and simple question — how's your family? You know, like, your parents," Shimmie paused knowingly, "and your older brother, Avrumie — or did he change his name?!"

The group broke out into laughter, with Gavriel particularly amused. Dovid was ashamed to feel the sting of tears in the back of his throat. How could they be so cruel? Didn't they know how much he had been hurting for so long, ever since Avrumie, his model older brother, had started acting strangely? Couldn't they know that he was torn inside by the desire to imitate his brother in his new ways as he had always done, and yet pulled back by the feeling that they were wrong?

"Get away from me!" he cried, knowing that it sounded babyish and weak, yet unable to repress the feeling of revulsion towards the group.

"That's not such a nice thing to say," said Shimmie menacingly, and he took a step towards Dovid.

"What do you want from me?! How can you be such *resha'im*? Get away — all of you — now!" Dovid yelled hatefully.

Shimmie turned to Gavriel, looking uncertain. The rest of the boys shifted uncomfortably. Shimmie sent a look of disgust in Dovid's direction and turned to go.

"Let's not waste a good recess on such a baby," he said to the group.

There were murmurs of derision, and the boys filed away one by one. Only Gavriel looked back at Dovid.

"Who are you calling a *rasha?*" he said bitingly. "If anything, the *rasha* is your brother — and you're also a *rasha* if you stick up for him."

"Yeah," said Chananya. "He's right!"

And then the boys were gone. Dovid sat very still, Gavriel's final words echoing in his aching head. Could he be right?

Twenty-seven

I t took Avrumie Faber exactly two hours and fifteen minutes to get expelled from yeshivah.

Dina got the call at 10:30, and when it was over she felt like she would faint. Avrumie had done what?! Had said what?! When had her son learned such language? Where had he ever developed such an attitude? Certainly not from their home. She felt an overwhelming wave of depression, shame, and guilt. The uppermost fear in her mind was: what will Ephraim say?

As she waited for Avrumie to walk through the door, Dina wondered how she should greet him. Should she yell? Threaten? Punish? Ignore? She braced herself for his entrance, but he never even came home. As the hours ticked by she realized how foolish it had been to expect him back. He had left their home after the blow-up with Ephraim and who knew when he would come back. The classic expectation of a trounced-on child running home to his mother's skirt was almost a wistful dream in her mind. Avrumie had chosen to reject his father's home and thus the soothing comfort in his mother's skirt. At about three o'clock in the afternoon, Dina finally broke down and cried.

Avrumie, for his part, felt a certain relief at finally breaking away from the yeshivah. It had been too long that he'd been "out of things," not really feeling a part of it anyway. He'd felt like he'd been living a double life — half-heartedly going through the motions of *shiur* and *chazarah* in the morning, and hanging out with "the crowd" in the evening to well into the night. The gap between him and his rebbeim was ever-widening, and his friends had begun to shun him, realizing the direction he was taking: Avrumie Faber was "going off the *derech*."

As soon as he had endured the *rosh yeshivah*'s utterly dismayed harangue, Avrumie had packed up the few *sefarim* he hadn't already taken home, wrote a nasty comment on the washroom wall, and sauntered out of yeshivah, never looking behind him. At about three o'clock in the afternoon, he stretched out on a park bench with his backpack under his head and took a short nap. He wanted to be rested for the evening's excitement.

At about three o'clock in the afternoon, Ephraim was in the thick of a complicated *Tosafos*, arguing back and forth with his *chavrusa*, when Zev Sloty tapped him on the shoulder. Ephraim knew from his expression that something was wrong. Two minutes later, Ephraim's worst, hidden-away fear was realized: his son had been kicked out of yeshivah. And it was already public knowledge. He excused himself abruptly and sped home, his whole being a volcano of rage, shame, resentment, and bitter self-reproach. He felt like an utter failure.

Twenty-eight

"I get a *mazal tov!*"

"What for?"

Avrumie looked over at Mark across the table. "No more handcuffs." He held up his wrists dramatically and anounced, "No more yeshivah."

Mark grinned enthusiastically and Joe slapped him on the back. "What did you do?"

Avrumie's smile faded. It was one thing to have done it; it was another to speak about it boastfully. "Let's not get into the details," he said shortly. "But it worked."

"So what are you gonna do now, man?"

Avrumie looked at Joe and suddenly he felt afraid. What was he going to do?

"There's lots of jobs out there," Monica put in helpfully.

"Like what?"

"Well, depends on what you can do."

"Not much."

"If you can't get a job, you could always go to public school and at least get yourself a proper diploma. That's what I'm doing, and it's really not that bad." That was Alan, a more recent member of the group.

Avrumie made a face. "I dunno. I don't think I ever was really cut out for school. I'd just like to get out there and become rich and famous." He was surprised at the words coming out of his mouth. He sounded so confident and daring — not like the Avrumie of the past who'd been more reserved and indecisive.

Sherry banged on the table. "Well, anyone want to drink to Abe's new start?"

That brought a round of good wishes and someone produced a bottle of cheap whiskey which they all passed around. Avrumie held his breath and took a swig, not daring to abstain. He noticed that Monica politely delined and no one made any wisecracks about it.

The conversation flowed between them easily. They were all gathered together, in the late hours of the night, seeking a camaraderie that they desperately needed. Each young person sitting around the table was desperately searching for meaning and fulfillment. Avrumie felt a bond between himself and the rest of the group — they were there for each other, brought together by circumstances largely beyond their control.

"Where are you sleeping tonight?"

Avrumie looked at Mark. Up until now he'd been sleeping at Mark's house, and the latter hadn't said anything. Maybe it was time to move on.

"Why?" he asked cautiously.

Mark paused and looked uncomfortable. "Listen, Abe — I really like you and respect you and we've been through a lot together. But I think it's time to move on. My parents keep nagging me about you staying with us and I just think it would be better for you to get out on your own." He studied his fingers carefully. Avrumie felt deeply wounded, but he kept his expression neutral.

"It's okay. I know I should find my own place. Thanks a lot for letting me stay with you till now." He paused. "And thank your parents for me, too. I'll just swing by and get my stuff."

Mark nodded, and the conversation was over. Avrumie sat, lost in thought, feeling distinctly ashamed and abandoned. It was humiliating to have to rely on people for basic necessities. Along with his shame, he was overcome by the immensity of his dilemma: where would he sleep that night? Where did people sleep when they didn't have homes to go to and their friends couldn't take them in? He certainly wasn't going to approach one of the guys and broach the question, but what would he do? A sudden nostalgia pictured his own bed in his own room, with his own possessions neatly arranged right where he wanted them. He quickly shoved the tantalizing scene out of his mind. That bed belonged to a stranger named Avrumie who learned full-time in yeshivah and was an aspiring *ben Torah*. He was Abe, a yeshivah dropout, kicked out of his own home and aspiring to...who knew what!

After the group broke up, Avrumie hung back in a corner, his hands deep in his pockets, his mind working feverishly. What was he going to do?

"Why so glum, Abe?"

Avrumie looked at Monica. She was so sensitive to other people's feelings. He managed a half-smile.

"Just thinking."

"Depressing thoughts?"

"Yeah." He decided he could trust her. He glanced quickly to see where Mark was, but the latter was absorbed in a conversation with Joe. "You know any youth hostels around here?"

She didn't even bat an eyelash. "No place to sleep?"

"Kind of."

"Mmmmm, that's rough. My folks hate me and persecute me, but at least I can sleep in my own bed. Haven't heard of any hostels in this area — anyway, they're all downtown, and not a place for someone like you, from what I understand."

Avrumie felt a strange pride. It was good to be reminded that he was still a cut above the rest, with vestiges of self-respect — not a downtown street bum.

"Thanks for the concern, Mom," he joked lightly.

"There's plenty worse off than you." She shook her head sadly. "There was a kid who came in a couple of weeks ago. Acted really strange. We kind of laughed at him." She paused. "He's in the hospital now. He had a nervous breakdown. Can you believe it?"

Avrumie was taken aback. "What happened?"

"What do you mean what happened — it's obvious! Neal's problem wasn't 'frumminess,' it was obssesive parents. Nothing the guy did was good enough. He has two brothers ahead of him who got law degrees at Yale, and this poor kid just couldn't make the grade. Finally his parents kicked him out of the house, told him to shape up or he couldn't come back. He tried at first — he really did. But he's learning disabled, and he just couldn't handle the workload. They wouldn't give him a penny and he ended up in a pretty bad state. Finally he just collapsed. It happened last week — I heard it from his sister who's kind of shaken up."

"His parents must be kicking themselves now."

"Are you kidding? They're working around the clock to hush everyone up so that no one will ever find out what really happened. Bad for the family name, you know. Neal will just recover somewhat, quietly, without any noise, and one day he'll get a nice job being...a garbageman, or something. He'll never be allowed back home. And the craziest thing is that Nina, his sister, doesn't even think it's absurd! She's concerned for him and all, and she's not as close-minded as her folks, but she's not really freaking out about it. It's just a natural part of her life — you don't succeed, you don't belong in the family!"

Avrumie felt like his brain would burst. What was this world that he had entered? Here were kids his age, undergoing nightmares that he had never known could exist. He looked wordlessly at Monica, and she took pity on him.

"I'm sorry, Abe, but it's a cruel world out there. That's the reality. It's all about how you deal with it, you know? The fact is, this pool hall would be ten times fuller if most kids didn't chicken out of leaving their families and their situations. They kind of play the part because there's a certain comfort in routine. Sometimes I don't blame them. For me, dropping out of school was a really big, scary step." She paused. "Abe, you have to realize that however bad you think you have it, someone's got it worse."

"I hear you," said Avrumie listlessly. "Is there anyone helping out these kids, though?"

"Oh, so all of a sudden it's 'these kids,' huh?" she teased him. "See how I put things in perspective — you don't even consider yourself as having any problems anymore!"

He smiled. "But seriously, is anyone there helping them?"

"I guess so," Monica said vaguely. "There's this rabbi who comes around, and there are some helplines which people call. But it's not like a whole network, if that's what you're asking. That's why we have each other."

"Yeah, I guess so. Gosh, Monica, you really shook me up. I just realized how sheltered I am."

"You'll get used to it. It's a shame, though. There was a time when kids stayed innocent till they were at least twenty!" Her attempt at sounding flippant failed. "We do manage, though, don't we?" She shrugged. "Looks like your best bet is a park bench."

"Yeah." Avrumie glanced at his watch. It was five o'clock in the morning. Sleep was less of an issue than he had thought.

Twenty-nine

"It's seven o'clock, Binyomin," Tamara Woolf urged softly.

Her husband looked up from the *Rashi* he was learning with their twelve-year-old son.

"You're right — thank you. Bentzy, maybe you can ask Ima to finish this with you. I have to answer the phones now."

"You're on call, Abba?" the red-haired boy joked, grinning. Binyomin smiled back and tousled his hair. What a joy it was to learn with his eldest son. If it weren't for answering the crisis hotline, he would have spent three more hours on the *Rashi*.

The crisis hotline. His thoughts immediately switched tracks, even as he walked the short hall to his study and closed the door. In the two years since its inception, the hotline had become well-known in many troubled households, and he was gratified at the success it was experiencing. Unfortunately it had been his own pain which had spurred the idea: after a personal family tragedy they'd experienced, the grief had been overwhelming. In trying to deal with it, he and Tamara had become more involved with others who had gone through similar trials and seen how beneficial it was to talk about their feelings. The next step was opening the hotline, dedicated to the memory of their beloved child who had been taken from them.

Thank God there were few who called with such tragic problems, although each caller, on his own level, was experiencing untold trauma from seemingly smaller challenges. There were cases of spousal and child abuse, eating disorders, runaway children, and an ugly new trend: concerned parents calling about their children straying from the *derech haTorah*. This most insidious, most frightening of parental challenges was attacking more and more, amassing victims even amongst the strongest families in the community who took every measure to fortify themselves against the pervading influences of secular society. There was a pull that was sometimes too great to be overcome, and with the difficulties of the teenage years and sometimes behavioral or learning problems, the street was becoming horrifically overpopulated with deserting youth.

In fact, Binyomin had realized early on that he had been blessed with a knack for working with these searching, rebelling teenagers. His unassuming appearance, his sensitivity, respect, and willingness to listen, made him an unthreatening person to talk to. At night, he would often frequent the local hang-outs, offering a caring heart and a listening ear. *Baruch Hashem*, he was highly successful in establishing rapport, not only with the teenagers themselves, but with their estranged parents as well. Many a tense, explosive conversation had taken place in the small office, as Binyomin served as mediator between parents and children, and the magic of restored communication sometimes made all the difference.

Binyomin scanned his ample bookshelves and selected a *Mesillas Yesharim*. With the kinds of situations he faced as a result of the hotline, he needed to fortify himself daily to stay happy, inspired, and inspiring. The small jewellery store he owned brought in an adequate *parnassah*, and for that he was eternally grateful — it allowed him to devote himself entirely to his family and *klal Yisrael* in the evening hours. He opened the well-thumbed *sefer* and began to sway gently, becoming absorbed in the pages.

The telephone rang at 7:15. It was one of the regulars — an elderly man, abandoned by his children, calling to shmooze. They had a nice, ten-minute conversation about the weather, the neighbors, and the evils of crooked steps, and then Binyomin politely wished him well until next week, making a mental note to organize some girls from the Bais Yaakov to visit poor Mr. Friedman.

Tamara popped her head into the study at 7:45.

"Anything doing?"

"Not yet. How's everything in your end of the world?"

Tamara laughed, and the smile brightened her entire face. She was very tired, and the ghost of sadness and pain had never quite vanished.

"Oh — we're doing just great —"

She was interrupted by the ringing of the phone.

"*Hatzlachah!*" She closed the door. Binyomin watched her go with a mixture of admiration and respect. She was so careful to preserve the privacy of the callers. She never interrogated him afterwards — what he told her she listened to, but she didn't probe. He reached for the phone.

"Hello?"

A woman's voice, very hesitant, answered him. "Hello."

"How are you?" Binyomin kept his tone even and friendly. He knew how difficult it was for most people to make the call. Often they called from pay phones to hide the fact from their spouses, children, or even parents. But the hardest part for some was facing their own selves; acknowledging that there was, indeed, a problem. He was patient and kind, and he let each one take his time. He heard the woman clear her throat.

"I'm, I'm not really sure how to start. I think we have a terrible problem."

"Yes?"

"Is this call totally anonymous?"

Binyomin assured her it was. The woman paused again. She was ashamed to call, and she was probably not calling from home — Binyomin could hear traffic-like noise in the background.

"Please help me," she said. "Our son has left home!"

Binyomin sighed inwardly. The woman's pain tore at his heart.

"It must be very difficult for you," he said with feeling.

"Oh, I can't even tell you," cried the woman, and with that the dam burst. Dina Faber poured out her heart to the kind man on the other end of the phone line. She didn't know how she had worked up the courage to actually make the call, but she felt it was the only hope they had. Avrumie hadn't called in a week, and all their efforts to track him down had been in vain.

"And then he stormed out of the house...." Her voice trailed off and she dabbed at her eyes.

Binyomin had listened silently, occasionally murmuring sympathetically, and nodding in understanding. Now he spoke up.

"I think it's very important that you called tonight," he began. "This is the first step to helping your son. I hope I can offer some insight, but I want you to look inside yourself and problem solve together with me. It seems like there are a few problems here. One of the most obvious is your son's relationship with your husband."

"I know," Dina said miserably. "But all my husband wants is for our son to turn out to be the best he can be. He has such pure *kavanos* when he gives him *mussar* — how could it backfire like that?"

"It's so hard to understand," said Binyomin. "But think of it from your son's — let's call him Moishy — perspective. Things are difficult for him — he's more of a thinker, a bit different — not a dyed-in-the-wool *yeshivah bachur*. It sounds like he's the type who asks some difficult questions, not the most typical ones, and it also sounds like he's not getting answers. This is very frustrating for him. He's trying to work things out in his head — and that's pretty difficult to do. When his questions are shrugged off, or, even worse, when he's yelled at or shamed for asking them, the thought starts eating at him: maybe there really are no answers. Maybe these restrictions are all for nothing."

"But what about everything he's seen in our home? All the beauty?

Shabbos? Kashrus? Being together as a family? His father learning Torah? Where did that go?"

Binyomin softened his voice, "But was it really beautiful for 'Moishy'? For him maybe it was just rituals, mostly rote. To him, maybe Shabbos and kashrus are just 'don'ts' — two of many other 'don'ts.' "

His gentle words struck Dina full-force as she pondered their truth. Avrumie had always been asking questions, and his questions had never been answered. She remembered when he was nine years old and had asked her how she knew that Hashem really did exist. She remembered her shock, her dismay, her bafflement, but she did not remember giving him a satisfactory answer. Her reaction alone had probably unsettled him.

"He sounds like a very bright boy, this 'Moishy' of yours," Binyomin began again. "Very insightful, very *emesdik*."

"He is," Dina murmured, feeling the old rush of maternal pride, realizing suddenly it had been a while since she had felt it.

"He seems to be rejecting the whole idea of '*yeshivish*' entirely."

"Yes, it does seem that way."

"Do you know why he's trying to break away from the *yeshivish* way of life?"

Dina bit her lip and forced herself to speak, the words barely a whisper. "Because he hates his father and everything he stands for."

In the long pause that followed, Dina's thoughts raced back and forth, from Avrumie to Ephraim and back again. She loved them both, was fiercely dedicated to both of them, and yet they were like fire and water. But why? Binyomin, on his end of the phone, was weeping inside. How many cases had he seen of boys who had left the Torah way of life because of their antagonistic relationship with their fathers? In some cases it was outright physical abuse that turned them off, but in most, it was deep yet almost invisible emotional trauma that sawed apart the relationship. The son knew he could never please his father; the father was trying to live vicariously through his son or use the son as a trophy. He waited a few more seconds and then spoke.

"I think you have to speak to your husband," he said. "If you'd like, I will gladly speak to him myself, but the way he is now, the dreams he has for your son, the two of them can never live together under the same roof. You're probably very right. Your son is rejecting everything his father is, completely out of spite. It must tear your heart apart to see what is going on, but you have to understand that only you are able to stop it and actually bring them closer together."

"But I can't speak to my husband — he'll feel like I'm betraying him. I'll just hurt him and hurt our own relationship. I can't." She felt so helpless.

"If you feel that way, try to have him call me. Do you think he would? As I told you before, this, and every conversation, is strictly confidential. I don't know you, and you don't know me. Would you at least ask him to call the hotline?"

"I — I don't know," said Dina. She turned the idea over in her mind. Would Ephraim be upset? Insulted? Embarrassed? All three? She suddenly realized she had lost track of time, and her watch indicated that she had to be home fifteen minutes ago. "I — I have to think it over. I'll get back to you if he wants to call. Thank you very much."

"I'm very glad that you called. *Hatzlachah rabbah*, and may Hashem be with you," said Binyomin caringly. And then the phone clicked, and the woman was gone.

Thirty

phraim Faber rapped lightly on the brown door. He glanced at his watch. Rabbi Epstein had asked him to come to his office immediately, and Ephraim's heart was racing with nervousness.

"Come in!" someone called, and Ephraim entered.

The *menahel*'s face was very serious, and Ephraim felt beads of sweat break out on his forehead.

"Please be seated, Reb Ephraim. I have some unpleasant news to share with you."

The butterflies in Ephraim's stomach made him feel suffocated. Was his deepest, most secret fear coming true? Would he be fired?

He raised worried eyes to the *menahel*'s.

In response to Ephraim's questioning look, the *menahel* looked down at his hands. "It's about Elisha Tauber," he said.

Ephraim's relief at not being fired was replaced with dread over his *talmid*'s situation.

"What happened?" he asked anxiously.

"You know, I never told anyone this, but we never wanted to accept the boy in the first place. But his father has been a big supporter of the school, and he begged us. He wanted his son to get a good education, and I decided to give it a try, but there are limits, Ephraim, and it seems that we have been pushed past our limits."

"What did he do now?" Ephraim asked.

Rabbi Epstein hesitated.

"It's bad enough what he did. It's worse, though, how we found out." The *menahel* paused. "He went to a movie. We heard it from the neighbor of the girl he took with him."

Ephraim was shocked. Although he saw a wild streak in Elisha, he didn't think he would stoop so low.

"You see, Ephraim, that this can't go on. If the community already sees a *bachur* in our yeshivah doing these" — he paused — "things, then he destroys the reputation of the entire yeshivah. I had another call from a different source, reporting the same story. People are talking about it, Ephraim. It hurts me very much, but I'm afraid that Elisha must leave the yeshivah."

Ephraim did not know what to say. He could find no fault with the *menahel*'s reasoning.

"Where will he go?" he asked.

"I really don't know. With a track record like his, there aren't very many places that will accept him. He is definitely a problem child."

"But what will be with him? His parents will probably beat him for getting kicked out of yeshivah, then they'll bribe his way into a different school, with what will probably be very similar results.... He'll end up a broken kid, never given a fair chance. Couldn't we let him stay another year and a half? At least if he finishes *yeshivah ketanah* honorably, he'll have a better chance of getting into a *yeshivah gedolah*, and he'll have some chance at a future. Have you spoken to him about his behavior?"

Rabbi Epstein passed a hand across his eyes.

"I have spoken with the Va'ad HaChinuch extensively about this case. You can't imagine how concerned I am about Elisha Tauber's future, but I have a much larger future to be worried about which includes all the *talmidim* in this yeshivah, and the yeshivah itself. Aside from the bad reputation the yeshivah will develop, there is a dangerous risk of other students being influenced by the Tauber boy. What would you say if Yankel or Shmerel were taken in by Elisha and they also went to a movie with.... I'm sure you understand what I'm saying. You know the expression: 'One rotten apple spoils the bunch.' I think it applies very succinctly here. The Va'ad was very adamant that Elisha must leave. This was not a spur-of-the-moment decision, I assure you."

"I hear what you're saying," Ephraim conceded sadly. "But I can't help thinking what will happen to Elisha if he is expelled. Did you speak to him personally about his behavior?"

"No. Actually, I wanted you to be here when I spoke to him. I know that he has a lot of respect for you — perhaps more so than for the rest of the *hanhalah*."

Ephraim was not sure that that was the best idea, but he did not protest. Rabbi Epstein gave some short instructions to his secretary, and the two waited in silence. There was a light knock on the door, and Elisha Tauber walked in. He was dressed in the required black pants and jacket, and white shirt, with big Nike sneakers on his feet. He was slightly out of breath — he had probably been called away in middle of a basketball game. He was a short, slight boy, with ruddy cheeks and dark hair, a little too long for the yeshivah's liking. His smile could light up his face and everyone else's. He was not smiling as he entered the office.

"Hello, Elisha," said Rabbi Epstein. "Please have a seat."

Elisha glanced at his rebbe, then at the principal, and sat down.

Rabbi Epstein cleared his throat.

"Elisha, I'll be frank with you and put everything on the table. I got a call from a concerned parent yesterday. It seems that she thinks you went last night to...to a movie, with...with a girl...." He let the sentence trail off and scrutinized Elisha's face intently. Elisha stared and said nothing.

"Well, tell me, Elisha. Did you, or did you not go to a movie with a girl?" Rabbi Epstein demanded, losing patience.

"Elisha," began Rabbi Faber, "these two accusations are very serious, but we are trying to exonerate you. It's possible that this woman mixed you up with someone else, or that there was a misunderstanding.

Please tell us the truth, Elisha."

Elisha stared straight ahead. "No, it's true all right. I went to a movie, and I took a friend along." His tone was unsteady but defiant.

Rabbi Epstein's eyebrows drew together, and Ephraim was shocked.

"But how could you, Elisha? Never mind the yeshivah rules, how could you have been so *poreitz geder* to do such a thing? Where is your self-control? The *yetzer hara* tries to win us over every second, but our job is to fight it, not to submit to it. I am shocked and saddened, Elisha, and I am sure Rabbi Epstein shares in my disappointment."

The *menahel* nodded gravely. "I am indeed disappointed, Elisha. What came over you?"

Elisha's eyes narrowed and something came over his expression.

"Okay, I know already that by the time this meeting is over I'm gonna be kicked out of yeshivah, so I may as well say my piece. What came over me? You wanna know what came over me? I came to this yeshivah, not by my own choice, but because my parents had to keep their reputation. They couldn't let their only son get a bad name and have people talk about them. I never wanted to be here in the first place. Everyone looks at me like a *nebach* here. 'Let's play with Elisha,' the guys say, 'maybe we'll be *mekarev* him.' *Mekarev* me, my foot. If you only knew what I had to go home to every day —" he broke off, on the verge of tears.

The two men sat, stunned, but he was not finished. "Why should I listen to you if you don't even care about me?! All you're worried about is your reputation. Do you realize that this is the first time I've ever been called to the office? You didn't call me when I did well on my first *bechinah*, you didn't even speak to me when you accepted me into the school — now that I go against every rule in the book, you suddenly notice that I'm here?! Go ahead — kick me out of your yeshivah. I wouldn't stay here another minute if you paid me!" With that last word, he stood up and bolted out of the room, leaving a shocked, uneasy silence behind him.

Thirty-one

Ephraim rubbed his eyes groggily and tucked his tefillin bag under his arm. He had spent most of the night tossing and turning. Elisha Tauber had haunted him endlessly, the dark eyes flashing fire, the soul-searing words tossing in his mind like a tempest. What was there to say? What was there to do? Who was right, and who was wrong? An enormous burden of guilt lay upon Ephraim's shoulders. *I did not do enough for him. I should have given him more love and attention. Instead he had to seek it elsewhere....* It was too much to bear.

And now what would be? He had heard of what happened to boys who were expelled from yeshivah. They had tremendous difficulty getting into other yeshivos — once they'd been labeled "problematic," who wanted to deal with them? The yeshivos were so competitive that they could afford to turn away rejects, and they could ill-afford to accept them. What would become of Elisha?

Ephraim's feet felt leaden, but they traveled of their own accord to the nondescript brown door marked with a shabby plaque.

"Come in!" came a voice from within the office. Ephraim hesitantly turned the knob.

His eyes met the *menahel*'s. Rabbi Epstein looked away.

"Come in, Reb Ephraim," he said woodenly.

Ephraim sat down heavily.

"I know," the principal began.

Ephraim's eyebrows shot up. What did Rabbi Epstein mean? Was his conscience also bothering him?

"*Chinuch* is a precarious profession, Reb Ephraim. It's like walking a tightrope every single moment. One false move and there's a fatal, tragic consequence. Except that there's more at stake than just your own life on the line — there's a young *neshamah* affected by your mistakes. And that young *neshamah* is just the beginning of dozens of future generations of *neshamos*."

He was looking down at his desk as he spoke, but suddenly the *menahel* looked straight into Ephraim's eyes.

"Do you know how much I daven, Ephraim? Do you know that every morning, as I finish *Shemoneh Esrei*, I cry to Hashem. 'Ribbono shel Olam, I am trying to do Your holy work, but my shoulders are not big enough. I am only human — it's not an "only," but it's a "human." Humans are notorious for making mistakes. Please, Ribbono shel Olam, enable me to make the right decisions today. Put the right words in my mouth. Keep me from my own personal *negiyos* and poor judgments.' That is my *tefillah* every morning, and then again at *minchah* and *ma'ariv*. But I'm still human. I still make mistakes. On the other hand, sometimes I need to act against my humanity — against what feels right as a sympathetic human. '*Eis la'asos laHashem*,' Reb Ephraim — you yourself are very aware of that. When it comes to *chillul Hashem*, when it comes to a *bizayon* of Torah and a *shem ra* on a whole institution...then what do I do? Do I throw up my hands? Do I look the other way? What do I do?" His voice cracked.

Ephraim swallowed hard.

"After our meeting I felt like my head was on fire. You think I don't know what it means to expel a student — especially a student like Elisha Tauber, what with his family situation and all? You think I don't know? Of course I know! But I had consulted with the *rabbanim* on the Va'ad HaChinuch. We had spoken about it for over an hour, and this was the decision we all came to. It had to be done. It had to be done," he repeated lamely, his voice trailing off sadly.

"Money, it wasn't. *Kavod*, it wasn't. Discrimination, it wasn't. That I know for sure. What bothers me, though, is that he didn't feel the love. He never felt the love from his rebbeim or from me. That is a hefty *tainah*, Ephraim, a hefty *tainah*. What can I say? In a school of, *b'li ayin hara*, four hundred students, I never singled him out for praise or for a friendly shmooze, he said. And he's right to have a *tainah*. No child can grow without love and attention. And when they don't get the love and attention, they search for it elsewhere — in movie theaters, in pool halls, in who knows what."

He leaned forward and reached across the desk to touch Ephraim briefly on his arm.

"Ephraim, I am speaking to you like a father now. Please do not be offended by my ramblings, but I have heard that your precious son is faltering. Please, Reb Ephraim, all the remorse and guilt you felt for Elisha Tauber, your burning desire to make things right for him — which you no doubt came to talk to me about now — channel it all towards your Avrumie. He is your son, Reb Ephraim. No one else can be his father. He needs love and attention or he will seek it elsewhere. There is talk, Reb Ephraim — people love to talk. But I know you, and to know you is to respect you. You are *moser nefesh* for Torah, and you have no doubt tried to raise your children *b'derech haTorah*. You know that the Ribbono shel Olam tells us to do the best job we can, and He will take care of the rest. But every child is different. Every child is made in a different mold, with a different personality and substance. What works for one child is harmful for the next one."

Ephraim sat, open-mouthed, unsure of whether to cry or to rage. How did the *menahel* know about Avrumie? How had Rabbi Epstein gauged the seriousness of his son's situation, when he, the father, had been desperately trying to pretend that things would be back to normal in a short time? His mind raced.

"You must forgive me, Ephraim, for being so forthright with you. But I know — I truly know — the importance of acting quickly. The *yetzer hara* is a fast-moving snowball. Once it sinks its teeth into a young *neshamah*, it doesn't stop at anything. You are running out of time, Ephraim. Believe me when I say it, and don't fool yourself. '*Eis la'asos laHashem*,' Reb Ephraim. Now is the time to do something — for Hashem's sake. But it is about loving and caring, and getting into the mind of a child who is desperately trying to make sense of his life. It is not your mind, Reb Ephraim, and it is not my mind. It is Avrumie's mind, and he has shut you out of it but desperately wants you to gently push your way in."

Uri Epstein stroked his beard.

"We need to daven for *siyatta diShmaya* every step of the way, because ultimately the success of our children is in Hashem's hands. But don't forget about the *hishtadlus* part of the equation — you've got to give it all you've got."

He rose swiftly from his chair and walked out of the office, closing the door quietly behind. Ephraim sat stockstill, and finally let the tears fall freely from his eyes.

Thirty-two

Binyomin Woolf parked his car a block away from his intended destination, laid his jacket and hat on the passenger's seat, and slung his tie across the clutch. He checked his wallet, locked the doors, and set out determinedly, his footsteps echoing in the quiet of late evening. The pool hall, of course, was alive and brimming. Binyomin bought himself a Coke and sat unobtrusively, watching the goings-on. He could pick out a former yeshivah boy or ex-Bais Yaakov girl from the crowd a mile away. There was something distinct about those kids, he mused, as he sipped the ice-cold soda; they were always so unhappy. It was a few more minutes before he spotted his prey. In five seconds flat he had abandoned his drink and was making a beeline toward his target.

The boy was tall, handsome, and new on the scene. A baseball cap, no visible tzitzis, wearing jeans and a T-shirt. He seemed to have been accepted by "the *chevrah*," as Binyomin liked to call the regulars. He knew most of them by name; occasionally they came over to his house for drinks Friday night. They knew he was there because he liked them and wanted to see them happy and successful. When people asked him what his secret was he had only one thing to tell them: Love. Unconditional love.

The boy had been shmoozing with his newfound friends, but now he had wandered a little away from the group and was standing, hands in pockets, staring into space. Perfect.

"Hi, there — having a good time?"

The boy turned around and stared at him suspiciously. Binyomin saw the boy scrutinize him from head to foot. Nothing threatening. Nothing *yeshivish*.

"Yeah — it's fun."

"Good. You in middle of a game?"

The boy shifted uncomfortably. "I'm new at this. I don't really play."

"No?" Binyomin feigned surprise. He winked. "Tell you the truth — I'm not so hot at pool either. I'm more of a —" he paused. The boy was tall, and he certainly looked athletic. Maybe? "I'm more of a basketball kind of guy," he finished off conspiratorily.

He saw the boy's eyes light up. *Baruch Hashem*!

"No kidding! Basketball's my thing, too. Honestly, I don't know how anyone can stay awake in this boring game where you get a turn every five hours. Give me the net any day."

"Where do you play?"

The boy looked at him curiously, and Binyomin could read his thoughts: *I used to play in yeshivah*. He decided to help the boy out. "Probably around here somewhere, huh?"

"Yeah."

"Oh, sorry — I'm Binyomin. Binyomin Woolf. Who are you?"

"Av — Abe."

"Hi, Abe — nice to meet you. Maybe we can shoot baskets some day, or just plain talk. The guys around here know me — I hang out a little bit every now and then. And if you ever want to come around to my place, my wife makes a mean *cholent*."

Avrumie had been watching him carefully, but at the last remark his face softened into a smile.

"Thanks."

"Don't mention it. Here's my card. Where you living?"

Binyomin saw Avrumie tense again, but then he relaxed.

"I'm kind of in between places right now — you know what I mean?"

"Sure. Well, like I said, if you ever get stuck, come on over to my place. Any time of day, night, or real early morning. We're open twenty-four hours a day, seven days a week — got it? Like they say — 'We'll keep the light on for you!' "

"Yeah — thanks a lot."

"Sure. You looking for a job?"

"Yeah, actually."

"Any idea of what you want to do?"

Avrumie thought for a minute and realized that he didn't even know. "Ummmmmm — " he broke off, feeling foolish.

"Can't say I blame you — I didn't know what I wanted to do till I was twenty-five, and even then I wasn't so sure. Whatcha good at? Good with your hands? Your head?"

Avrumie smiled shyly. "Well, I guess I can think. I mean — that's pretty much all I have training in." He laughed ruefully and Binyomin smiled.

"Gotcha. Hmmmmm. It would be a shame, then, not to think at least part of the day, huh?" he offered carefully.

Avrumie took the bait. "You mean — you mean go to school part time?"

Binyomin shrugged his shoulders off-handedly. "Sure — school, there are even a couple of easy yeshivah options if you were so inclined.... You said it yourself, man, but maybe you're right — it's not a bad idea. If you could find the right place, you could learn part-time and support yourself the rest of the time. If you have a good head it would be a shame to waste it, no?"

"Yeah." Avrumie looked almost hopeful, but then a cloud descended over his features. "But there's no way I can go to a yeshivah. Especially after all this —" he paused. "It's a long story, but let's just say that I don't have the best rep in the yeshivah world, okay?"

137

"Sure — I hear what you're saying, but let me tell you something: I know plenty of guys in similar situations who found great yeshivahs and really felt happy and accepted there. I know a couple of the '*rosh*'es myself, and I could put in a good word for you, you know." He dropped his voice to a confidential whisper. "It's the guys who have the brains and the guts that make it back to yeshivah and get themselves a decent life. The other ones just get caught in the pool hall, wasting their lives until they hit rock bottom and have to pull themselves up by their *gatchkes*."

Avrumie smiled appreciatively. Whoever this guy was, he talked sense. And there was something very magnetic and very amiable about him. He really cared.

"I'd...I'd really appreciate if you could look into the, um, yeshivah thing for me," he said hesitantly. "I hope it's not too much trouble...."

Binyomin smiled. "It's not a problem at all. For you — anything! No, just kidding — really, it's my pleasure. You don't look all that happy around here, and I think it's more than just boredom."

"You're right," said Avrumie, and he felt as though a great load had been lifted off his shoulders. "I mean, if you had talked to me last week I would have laughed in your face. But to tell you the truth, I'm getting a little sick of this scene and my brain feels like it's turning to jello." He sighed ruefully.

"Give me a call tomorrow, say, six o'clock, and I'll let you know if I found something, okay?"

"Sure. Thanks a lot."

"Pleasure. Stay good, kid." And Binyomin left the smoky pool hall, humming.

It was only an instant later that Avrumie grasped the awesomeness of the entire encounter. This stranger was going to try to get his life back in shape. And he didn't even know Avrumie's real name.

Thirty-three

"**G**ood night, kids — be good!" Dina checked her makeup in the mirror one last time and put on her jacket.

"Remember — everyone in bed by the time we come home," warned Ephraim sternly.

"Oh, they will be, don't worry," Dina reassured him. "Where's your tie?"

"I'm getting it."

"Let's go — we already missed the *chuppah*."

Ephraim ran upstairs and came down, holding his tie.

"Thanks for babysitting, Chave'le," Dina said gratefully. It would be nice to get out a little bit.

"No problem, Ma — as long as I have the phone, I'm fine." Chavie grinned and Dina laughed. It was true.

"Have a great time!" Dina called out, and they walked out of the house.

Ephraim unlocked the car door for her.

"You look nice."

Dina smiled and blushed.

"So do you."

Ephraim smiled back. "Well, I am your Prince Charming, aren't I, so I must look nice!" he joked.

Dina laughed and felt herself relax. It had been a long time since Ephraim was in such a good mood.

"How was your day?" she asked as they pulled out of the driveway.

"The usual. Big class fight, Yossi broke his nose, I assigned a *bechinah* — business as usual." He smiled. Right now it wouldn't do to talk about his discussion with Rabbi Epstein. "And how was your day?"

"Okay."

"Just okay?"

Dina snuck a look at Ephraim. Maybe this was the time to talk to him, while he was in such a calm, cheerful mood. Then again, would bringing up the topic plunge his spirits down the drain? She decided to take a gamble.

"I'm, I'm a little nervous," she began. Ephraim waited.

"I'm so scared about Avrumie. What is he up to now? Who is he living with? What's going to be with him?"

Ephraim's voice was low. "I'm also worried, Dina. What do you think we should do?"

Dina pursed her lips. "Ummmm, well, you see, I kind of did a little research." *Research* sounded like a good word — very nonthreatening and scientific. "I spoke to somebody who deals with many situations like ours." She saw Ephraim's head jerk up, but she plowed ahead. There was no turning back. "Of course, my call was completely anonymous," she reassured him, but he did not relax. "He was very helpful and very sympathetic, and I think he had a lot of good suggestions...." She trailed off lamely. Ephraim was not pleased — she could tell by the set of his mouth. The whole evening's lightness had dissipated at the drop of a hat.

"Who is this person?" Ephraim's voice was hard. His precious privacy had been invaded.

"Ummmm, I'm not sure what his name is even, but he has a...a hotline." It wouldn't do to bring in the word *crisis* right now. "It's a toll-free number, I don't even know where he lives. I actually saw it in the *Jewish*

Vort this week. I called from a pay phone, and he didn't ask any questions, just listened and gave some advice."

"What did he say?"

Now was the hardest part. She couldn't tell Ephraim what the counsellor had said — it would be too hurtful, and it couldn't possibly come from her. But how could she get him to speak to the man himself?

"That's the problem," she started. "While he was talking, he made so much sense, but you know how hard it is for me to process things and take them *lemaiseh*. I really was hoping that you would speak to him yourself. That way you could tell me what you think of his *eitzah* and we could come to a plan together." The words had come out a little rushed, but surprisingly natural, and she was shocked at how easily she had improvised. It was slightly not true, but weren't there times when one had to fudge a bit? Wasn't this a woman's *binah* at work?

She felt, rather than saw, Ephraim uncurl his shoulders. "You think — you think he's the right person?" His voice was surprisingly meek, uncertain. Rabbi Epstein's words hammered in his head. He had to act quickly — or it might be too late. Was this Hashem sending him the appropriate messenger to save them from a serious situation?

"I really felt that he understood our situation. And in the ad I saw he had a lot of *haskamos* from *rabbanim*. He's our type also — he sounds like a real *ben Torah*. He's so patient also, and he doesn't interrupt you or berate you or anything."

Ephraim pulled the car over to the side of the road, and Dina looked at him uncertainly. His face was pale. Was everything okay?

"Dina," he said in a shaking voice, "I think you're right — I'd better speak to this person. I'm very worried about Avrumie. I feel as though I'm losing my son."

Thirty-four

"Got a place to sleep tonight?"

Avrumie turned around at the familiar voice and sighed. He'd been relatively well taken care of by the gang, who had let him spend the night on basement floors and remote sofas, but without a place to call home, sleeping was always an issue. He'd shown up early at the pool hall that night, simply because he needed to move out of Joe's place before he wore out his welcome.

"You know me too well, Mikey," he said dismally.

"I'm gonna need a bribe, though, if you wanna come on over to my place," Mikey taunted.

Avrumie was not amused. "Like what?" he asked cautiously.

"Well, let's just say that I got a very interesting offer to get involved in some very interesting business tonight, in a really wealthy part of town, and I need a partner to come along with me." He looked at Avrumie significantly.

"What's that supposed to mean?"

Mikey grabbed Avrumie by his jacket and pushed him roughly into a secluded corner of the Hall.

"What do you mean, what do I mean?" His voice was passionate, but his eyes were tinged with fear. "You and I are gonna make some money tonight. Can't live on nothing, y'know. It'll be quick and easy, and no one will even know the difference."

Avrumie gasped. "You mean —"

"You're catchin' on, Abe. That's real quick. So, are you in or not?"

Something in Avrumie's deepest inner self broke open and coursed through his entire body.

"Count me out," he spat at Mikey in a voice that he never knew he possessed. "How dare you even suggest such a thing! I've never stolen in my life, and I don't intend to start. How low can a person get? In fact, the Gemara says —" He stopped, shocked at his first reference to Torah in weeks. Avrumie blushed, but he did not stop.

"One day, you and I are gonna be living other lives, real lives, hopefully. And what are you gonna tell yourself when you think back to the night when you broke into someone's house and took something that didn't belong to you? How will you forgive yourself? How will you ever teach your kids not to steal when you yourself are a thief? There are plenty of things you and I can do to make a couple of bucks without selling our souls in the process. Like work, for instance," he concluded facetiously, staring daggers at an open-mouthed Mikey.

There was a long silence between the two. Mikey was the first to recover.

"You're such a goody two-shoes, Abe," he said acidly. "Giving me *mussar* like it comes naturally to you. Look at you, kid — take a good, long look at who you are right this minute. Y'think a guy like you is in a position to be giving *mussar seder*? You're a yeshivah dropout just like me. You also crumpled your tzitzis into a little ball in your knapsack. You're hanging out here just like the rest of us. So get off your high horse a little, will ya? It's getting to be a little irritating. Or maybe you oughtta start looking for a job in a *beis midrash* somewhere." His eyes blazing with hurt and anger, he spun around and stalked away.

Avrumie stood, rooted to the spot for an eternity. Mikey's words rang in his ears like a crowd of raucuous, accusing hecklers.

Y'think a guy like you is in a position to be giving mussar seder?

And to think he had been so close to contacting Binyomin Woolf about the possibility of learning part-time! Mikey was right, in a painful sort of way. There was no way that Avrumie could switch into Torah when a part of him had abandoned it so despicably. A feeling of rage and utter hopelessness washed over him. He reached into his pocket and pulled out the small card Binyomin had handed to him just the other night. Then, Avrumie had felt a glimmer of hope and encouragement. But Mikey's words would give him no rest. Viciously, he ripped the card in half, then in quarters and eighths, and he tossed the shreds to the wind outside the pool hall. There would be no *beis midrash*, no *mussar seder*, only the forlorn tzitzis in his backpack.

And to top it all off, he still had nowhere to sleep that night.

"He was?"

"You didn't see? He was wearing all kinds of clothes. Like Mario wears."

"Who's Mario?"

"The janitor."

"Oh." Deliberation. "You mean those kind of pants?"

"Yeah."

"But Mario doesn't wear a yarmulke."

"Oh, forget it, Yosef — you never know what I'm talking about."

"Oh, yeah?! Well, you can forget it! And I'm only asking Ima for permission to go on a ship for myself. And I know a secret and I'm not telling."

"Oh, don't be a baby."

"So take it back."

"What?"

"That I never know what you're talking about."

"Fine — you always know what I'm talking about — 'kay? Now what's the secret?"

"Promise you won't tell?"

"Promise."

"I saw Abba crying."

Thirty-six

Minna Feuer glanced in the mirror and smoothed her blond *sheitel* back. She smiled stiffly at her reflection, secretly pleased. She still looked young, she decided, even though her oldest daughter was already expecting a child of her own and her son was away in yeshivah. She grabbed her purse off the coffee table and was about to unlock the door when the phone rang.

"Hello?"

"Aunt Minna? It's Avrumie."

Minna swallowed hard. "Avrumie," she said, forcing her voice to be natural. It had been nearly two weeks since he'd run away and Dina was frantic. "Where are you, *zeeskeit*? Your mother is going crazy!"

Avrumie paused. "Yeah. I'm sorry," he said, and he sounded sincere. "I've been...I've been with friends."

"Well, I'm very glad you called, Avrume'le. What can I do for you?"

Avrumie cleared his throat. "Ummmmm, I was just wondering. You see, the situation is a little...difficult at home and I can't really stay with friends for that long, so I was wondering if, maybe...." He trailed off.

The idea had occurred to Avrumie on one of his first visits to the pool hall but had been abandoned when his friends had invited him in. Now, though, he had completely run out of invitations. Last night's altercation with Mikey had pretty much killed his chances of going there.

"You'd like to move in with me and Uncle Yechiel?" Minna could not keep the surprise from her voice. Although the families got together on several occasions throughout the year, she had never been very close to Avrumie. Maybe it would be a good thing.

"Well, that's kind of what I was thinking," said Avrumie. "I won't cause trouble," he continued. "And I'll even do dishes."

Minna smiled. "You know what, let me talk to Uncle Yechiel and see what he says. Give me a call back tomorrow, okay? And in the meantime, go call your poor mother — she's ready to go to the police!"

It was Avrumie's turn to smile. "I will, Aunt Minna. Thanks a lot."

"Good-bye, *zeeskeit* — talk to you later!" Minna hung up the phone and sighed. Could they really handle having Avrumie live with them? She looked at the clock. Yechiel would be home in an hour, and supper still wasn't ready. She picked up her purse for the second time and walked out the door, her eyebrows knitted together thoughtfully.

Thirty-seven

can't be doing this, Ephraim Faber told himself for the tenth time in five minutes. His hand moved of its own accord, picked up the phone, and dialed the number scribbled on the small white card. There was a pause, and then the purr as somewhere, in a different part of town, a phone rang and someone went to answer it.

You can hang up right now, Ephraim's reasonable side told him. Or was it the unreasonable side? His hand remained on the receiver, however unsteadily. Two rings, three rings, four....

"Hello?"

"Hello, is this...the hotline?" He realized he did not even know the organization's name, least of all the man who answered it. It was just as well.

"It is. How are you?"

Ephraim was caught off guard. "*Baruch Hashem*, well. I guess not so well, though, if I'm calling tonight." He chuckled ruefully.

"Would you like to talk about it?"

"Yes." Ephraim sighed wearily. "I believe my wife spoke with you last week. About our son...who's left home because of certain...difficulties we've had in our relationship."

"Yes, yes — I do remember. We spoke at length. I'm very glad you called. I'm sure it wasn't easy for you, but it's very important." He paused, but Ephraim did not answer.

"It sounds like this may be the first time you're acknowledging the fact that your relationship with your son may be a big part of why he left home."

Ephraim was astounded to realize that it was. He nodded dumbly, then remembered that the man on the other phone could not see him.

"Yes. You're right. It's...it's very hard, though. I try to be such a good father. I work very hard, but when I come home I really make an effort to give the kids attention. To ask them what they've learned in school. My wife and I work on our own relationship. I love my son so much. I don't know what happened." The words came out in a rush, but Ephraim was glad they had finally come out.

"Reb Yid, all I can say is that *tza'ar gidul banim* is a very real *tza'ar*. All we can do to alleviate it is to do our best. And it sounds like you do try very hard. Do you have a good relationship with the rest of your children?"

"I — I think so." He had never really thought about it much. The children were, well, they were children. Of course, each was a precious *neshamah*, needing careful direction and education, but....

"Your children feel that you are approachable? If they had problems they would come to you to confide in?"

Something nagged at Ephraim in a very irritating way.

"I'm not my children's social worker, if that's what you're asking. No, they don't come over to me and tell me all their deep, dark secrets. But they do shmooze with me and enjoy the time they spend with me." Did other children tell their fathers all their secrets? Was he an oddity among fathers? Perhaps he really didn't have a good relationship with his children!

It was almost as if the man read his thoughts. "Well, every parent-child relationship is different according to the parent and the child. You don't have to feel that you are not a good father. You definitely provide adequately for your children, do your best to be *mechanech* them properly —"

Ephraim broke in defensively. "I definitely do. That is something I take very seriously. My children know that my ideals and values are not to be compromised on. I am very dedicated to their *ruchniyus*, that is for sure."

Perhaps he had been too adamant in his assertion. Maybe he came across as a harsh, even abusive father, but he was still reeling from the realization that perhaps his relationship with his children was not quite up to par.

"That's very admirable. Children need firm guidance, especially in today's world." The man on the other end paused. "It's a very delicate balance, though. Do you agree?"

"Yes, of course. Don't misunderstand me — I'm not a monster, and I don't stuff my *hashkafah* down their throats, but a parent has a job to do, you know?"

"I do know. The question is, do the children know?"

Ephraim was taken aback. "Know? Know what? That I give them *tochachah* because it is my *heilige* responsibility? I, I hope so. I never told them straight out, even though my wife and I discuss it quite a bit."

"Then is it possible that some of your children just don't understand? That they don't see that you're doing this out of love and out of spiritual reasons, and they just see the — excuse the word — criticism?"

"Of course it's possible. Children never understand. Until they're older. When my father gave me *mussar*, I can't say I always took it like an angel. Sometimes I resented him. But now that I'm older, I see the wisdom and kindness in his rebuke. We cannot educate our children according to what our children want. Children want to eat candies and ice cream all day also, and we don't allow them to." Ephraim realized he had unconsciously shifted into the role of teacher, and stopped himself short. "Do you think that's the problem with our son?"

"Well, even though your wife gave me many details, I did not get the full story. Can you tell me how you and your son don't get along? What brings on the tension?"

Ephraim thought for a moment. "Well, sometimes he's just plain and simple *chutzpahdik*. Other times, it's as though he's baiting me. He asks me a question that he knows will anger me, and I fall for it every time."

"What sort of questions does he ask?"

Ephraim related the explosive Shabbos incident, feeling again the pain, the rage, the deep disappointment.

The man on the other end was silent. Finally he spoke.

"Has your son always been asking questions like this?"

"Yes, as a matter of fact. When he was a very young child he would ask questions about Hashem and the world. We thought he was just going through a stage and that he'd grow out of it. Then when he went to yeshivah, he gradually stopped asking questions and got down to business. The questions only surfaced recently, in the past six months or so."

"Do you think that perhaps the questions never went away? That they were buried inside your son, bothering him always, but forever being suppressed, until finally he couldn't stand it anymore and broke free?"

Ephraim sighed. "Truthfully, in the back of my mind, I know you're right. I feared all along that my son would always have these questions; that his *emunah* would always be shaky. I tried very hard to strengthen him, but it just didn't seem to work."

"But how were you strengthening him? When a patient comes to his doctor with a very serious infection on his arm, if the doctor simply puts a bandage over it, without treating the wound with antibiotics, the patient will be in big trouble. Is it possible that your approach was like putting a Band-aid, so to speak, on your son's questions, without getting to the real core of them? For a thinking child who gets no answers, the world is a very frustrating place, and he can begin to believe that there are no answers, when you and I both know that *Yiddishkeit* has all the answers."

"You're right," Ephraim said simply, the truth of the man's words hitting him squarely in his heart. "You're absolutely right." He paused, and when he finally found his voice, it was plaintive. "So what can I do now?"

Thirty-eight

"Ima, can I invite Gila over to play?"

"I guess so, Shira. Did you do your homework already?"

"Yup."

"Good girl. Sima, what about you?"

No response.

"Sim-Sim, do you have homework to do?"

"Yeah."

"Please get started on it, then. And I'd like some help with supper." Dina went back to peeling the potatoes, quelling the frustration that was bubbling inside her. Why was Sima always so hard to deal with? She thought back to their appointment together at the psychologist. When would the results of the test come back? What would they show? She certainly hoped that someone could help them deal with Sima — she was so unhappy. She had started to adopt a certain belligerent attitude, too, and her stubborn rudeness grated on Dina's nerves. It reminded her somehow of...Avrumie.

Dina tucked a stray hair back into her snood and her thoughts turned quickly to Avrumie. He had left a message on the answering machine for her; had called when she was out, of all things. He had said that he was fine, that she shouldn't worry, and that he hoped he'd be able to call back soon, but that was it. No telephone number, no address, no

"I love you" at the end.

"Ima, it's for youuuuuuuu," cried Shira.

Dina dropped the potato and ran for the phone. You never knew.... "Hello?"

"Dina, how are you?"

"Oh — Minna, it's you." She tried to keep the disappointment from her voice.

"You sound real excited to hear me. Sorry. Should I hang up?"

"No, no — it's okay. I'm sorry, it's just that every time the phone rings I think.... Well, I can't help but think that maybe it's Avrumie calling...." Her voice trailed off wistfully.

"Well, I might not be Avrumie himself, but you could say I'm sort of his secretary."

"What?!"

"Well, this is the thing: Avrumie called and asked if he could live by us."

Dina was shocked. Although she had nothing against Minna and Yechiel, the two families had never been particularly close. Strong emotions clashed in her mind, unbidden: jealousy — he would go live at her sister instead of living with his own family; sadness — he had no plans of coming home; hope — well, at least he'd be living in a *frum* home. Finally she found her voice.

"What did you tell him?"

"Well, of course we wanted to speak to you and Ephraim about it before we made a final decision."

"Would you be willing to have him stay by you?"

"Well, I talked to Yechiel, and we couldn't find any objections. The house is pretty empty, and he's old enough to take care of himself. And I figured that it's better for him to live with us than with his friends, if you know what I mean...."

Dina knew exactly what she meant, and she felt at once the motherly defensiveness for her son and the stinging pain of jealousy shoot through her.

"I'll have to speak to Ephraim," she said tightly. "I'll get back to you."

"I didn't mean to hurt you, Dina," said Minna gently.

But Dina had already hung up the phone.

Thirty-nine

"What a loooooong day!" Chavie sighed as she slung her schoolbag across her shoulder and settled down in the bus seat, smoothing down her skirt.

"Oh, yeah," Malky agreed.

They had had two tests, and another two projects assigned for the coming month. The end of the term could not come soon enough.

"What are you doing tonight?"

"My mother wants me to help bake for Shabbos. We're having a lot of guests." Malky's family was famous for their *hachnasas orchim*, despite their strained financial situation. Her father was a rebbe, her mother a secretary in a local yeshivah, and with eight children to provide for, each bill deadline they were able to meet was an outright miracle.

"My mother never lets me bake." It was true. Dina liked to do the baking and cooking herself, although the girls helped her with preparatory jobs. Chavie didn't mind that much, though it always seemed like fun when she heard other girls talk about baking and cooking.

"Really? How are you ever going to learn, then? *B'ezras Hashem*, when you get married, chances are your husband probably isn't going to be able to teach you!"

"Oh — I can just see that one, all right," Chavie joked. "He'll have the chocolate chip cookie recipe written on the first page of his *gemara*!"

They laughed together, but inwardly, Chavie was perturbed. Malky was right. What would be when she had to have a house of her own? She chided herself slightly for the ridiculousness of it all: she was all of sixteen, and she was already thinking seriously about marriage?

"Where are you, Chavie?" Malky asked. "Are you spacing out again?"

"Oh — sorry. I was just thinking. I do think sometimes!" They chuckled together. "Here's my stop — I'll see you tomorrow, *b'ezras Hashem*. Have fun with the *navi* assignment!" Chavie picked up her schoolbag and stepped agilely from the bus.

It was a full five-minute walk from the bus stop to the house, and Chavie utilized the time to think again about her conversation with Malky. Despite her relative youthfulness, she felt ready to get married tomorrow. Everyone else said so, too. Mrs. Hiller, the neighborhood *yenta*, would tell her mother, "Your Chavie is going to be our senior *kallah* — no doubt about it." Ima would smile vaguely and change the subject. On the few occasions that Chavie had brought up marriage herself, Ima had reacted similarly. She didn't seem to understand Chavie's desire to settle down and build her own family.

"You have plenty of time," she had told Chavie.

"But not really," Chavie had corrected. "I mean, I'm already sixteen, and there have been girls — girls who, you know — who get engaged at seventeen."

"Let's leave it up to Hashem," Ima had answered. "Now please give Bracha a bath." Discussion over.

Of course, there was another cloud on the marriage horizon, aside from her complete inability to create anything in the kitchen. Avrumie. Her friends had become aware of his disappearance, and, although they tried hard to be tactful and not prying, their curiosity was beginning to overwhelm them.

"How's everything?" Shulamis had asked her significantly, with slightly sympathetic, inviting eyes.

Chavie hadn't taken the hint. "Great, *baruch Hashem*. How's everything with you? I heard your sister had a girl — *mazal tov!*"

Shulamis had answered her half-heartedly, and Chavie knew what she was really asking: *How's everything with your brother?*

She walked up the driveway and knocked quickly on the door. It was unlocked, as usual, and she put her schoolbag away in the hall closet before making her way into the kitchen. Ima wasn't in the kitchen, which was unusual. The house seemed quiet — Shira was probably at a friend's, and Sima was most likely buried in a book. Bracha was probably resting. Ima must be at the supermarket.

Chavie poured a glass of orange juice for herself and took some freshly baked cookies from the pan where they were cooling on the counter. She smiled to herself — hadn't these very cookies just been the focus of her thoughts! She glanced at her watch. An hour until *minchah*, and then that *navi* worksheet. She could afford to relax a bit. She selected a book from the shelf in the dining room and headed upstairs to her room to read comfortably.

Halfway up the stairs, she heard the sound. It was muffled crying and it was coming from her parents' room. Through the partially open door, Chavie saw her mother standing in the corner of the room, her back to her unseen daughter. Ima was whispering and sobbing simultaneously. Chavie, hidden in the shadows of the hall, could just barely hear her.

"Ribbono shel Olam, help us. We don't know what to do. This is so bitter and so difficult — you must help us. We tried so hard, but now it's time for You to do Your part. Give us back our son. He has strayed so far, but in Your *chesed*, have mercy on him and on us, and return him to us and to Your mitzvos. Ribbono shel Olam, the gates of tears are never locked. Give us back the son that you entrusted to us — he is such a blessing!"

Chavie felt the tears spring to her own eyes. She tiptoed to her room, silently closed the door, and offered her own prayer to Hashem that He help Avrumie and take away her parents' anguish and suffering.

Forty

olda Katzman turned wearily to the pile of papers awaiting her on the kitchen table. Teaching was a twenty-four-hours-a-day, seven-days-a-week job, as she always said to the young seminary students who came regularly to observe her in the classroom. It was hard but holy work. She lifted the top paper off the pile, glanced at the name, and smiled. Liba Shafer — just the test she wanted to mark first. Liba scored nothing less than 99 percent and she could use her paper to mark the others. She scanned the neatly written answers, frowned once at a minor slip-up, and took out her "*metzuyan*" stamp. Liba had done it again.

Next paper. She looked at the name — it was blank. Golda felt her blood pressure rise. Name omission was her pet peeve, and she emphasized this in class numerous times. How could a student forget to identify her paper? The idea was, to her, as foreign as forgetting one's own shoes in school. She looked carefully at the handwriting on the test. There was no mistaking it. She shook her head sadly. It was Sima Faber's test. What was going to be with that girl? Another thought struck her: what had been the results of her testing? She reached across the table for the phone.

"Hello, Dr. Simmons — it's Golda Katzman. I'm sorry for bothering you at home, but...."

"Oh, Golda — it's never a bother. Like you always say, a teacher is a teacher twenty-four hours a day, seven days a week."

Golda smiled. "Yes, absolutely. Actually, I wanted to know whatever happened with the Faber girl who you tested. It seems to me that she went to you awhile ago, maybe three weeks, was it?"

"Faber? Faber? Oh, yes — Faber. Very sweet girl."

"Uh huh."

"Hmmmm. I definitely did write up the report. Now, what happened to it in the end?"

"Well, what were your conclusions?"

"I'm sorry, Golda — as much as I respect you as a person and as a remarkable teacher, the results are completely confidential and you'll need the parents' permission before I can inform you. You know that."

"Yes, I suppose I do. Well, what happened with the results?"

"I'm trying to think. I wouldn't have just held them on my desk. I probably sent them to the parents. Oh, yes — I do remember mailing them out. A while ago, though — about a week ago."

"I'll speak to the mother and get back to you if we need to resend it. Thank you very much, Doctor."

"Anytime. All the best."

Golda hung up the phone and retrieved her list of parent phone numbers. She quickly dialed the Faber residence.

"Hello?"

"Hello, Mrs. Faber please."

"Speaking."

"Oh, Mrs. Faber? This is Golda Katzman, Sima's teacher. How are you?"

"Fine, thank you."

Pause.

"Well, I was just wondering whether you ever received the results of Dr. Simmons testing — he said he sent them in the mail awhile ago. About a week ago."

"A week ago? That's strange. No, we never received them." A slight tremor in Dina's voice. "Did — did he tell you what he found?"

"No, of course not. That information is completely confidential."

"Good. I don't know what could have happened to them, though."

"Perhaps your husband took the mail in?"

"No, no — I always get to the mail first. Unless...." Hesitation. "You know what, let me call you back in a little while, please."

Golda was confused. "Okay — I'll be up late tonight."

She hung up the phone.

Forty-one

Dina set her mouth in a firm line, wiped her hands on the dishtowel, and headed upstairs. Sima was lying on her bed reading a book when Dina opened her door.

"Sima, I'd like a word with you."

Sima looked at her and reddened. There was trouble brewing.

"Sima, I just got a call from Mrs. Katzman. She was wondering whether we had ever gotten the results of your test with Dr. Simmons." Dina paused significantly. "It's very odd that they never arrived at this house, considering that the doctor mailed them a week ago."

Sima stared down at her book and Dina felt the irritation begin.

"Sima, I am speaking to you and I expect you to look at me, please."

Sima reluctantly raised her eyes and stared at a tiny grease spot on her mother's white shirt.

"Sima, do you know what happened to that report?"

There, she had said it, just the slightest edge to her voice. Now what would be?

Sima looked down at her carpet and moved her toe in a circular motion. Dina, mustering every last shred of her patience, stared at her expectantly.

"Sima, Ima is talking to you. I would like an answer. Now. Do you know what happened to the doctor's report?"

When Sima spoke, it was in a voice that Dina had never heard.

"No," she spat out.

Dina stepped back abruptly. Where was her quiet, meek little Sima? Who was this defiant, confident child who had shouted so vehemently? Sima was no longer staring at the floor — her eyes flashed a strange fire and she gazed triumphantly at her mother.

Dina lost it.

"Don't you stare at me like that!" she shouted. "What do you mean by yelling at your mother like that? What happened to your *derech eretz*? Not in this home, young lady. Now answer me truthfully — did you take those test results or not? I want the truth, and I want it now."

Sima continued to glare at her, but she would not respond. Her eyes flitted involuntarily to her desk, where her books and precious objects were stored. Dina inadvertently followed her daughter's eyes and they rested on an envelope peeking out of the corner of a book. With a cry of anger, she ran over to the desk and pulled the protruding envelope from its hiding place. It was printed with Dr. A. Simmons's letterhead. And it had been opened.

"Liar!" The word escaped with venom from Dina's lips and she realized she was shaking with rage. How dare this child intercept personal mail, open a letter which was not addressed to her, hide it away from her parents, and then lie as to what she had done? It was simply unthinkable. Sima had turned white, but her fearless defiance had not broken. Indeed, she seemed a different person. Dina's hand reacted almost instinctively — she raised her palm and slapped Sima across her pale face. Sima jolted back in shock and nearly lost her balance. Then she turned to face her mother, her eyes brimming with tears.

"I hate you!" she screamed, and she ran out of the room.

Forty-two

Dina stood stockstill in the middle of Sima's empty bedroom, holding the opened envelope in her hand. Her palm hurt where she had hit Sima, and the throbbing ache ran down her entire arm, straight to her heart. What had she done? She tried to reconstruct the details of the past five minutes, but they were already blurry in her mind. What had she said? What had Sima said? What had led to the slapping? Dina couldn't remember slapping any of her children that way — except, except perhaps one of them. Dina shuddered. She remembered once having hit Avrumie. And she couldn't even remember what he had done to deserve it.

If he really deserved it at all, she berated herself fiercely. Had Sima really "deserved" to be slapped? And across the face, at that?

No, she decided resolutely, the punishment definitely did not fit the action.

But her conscience (or was it her pride?) nagged. The child had done something very underhanded and invasive, and had been deceitful. The memory of Sima's tone of voice and mocking air struck her anew. What had come over her daughter? What demon had entered her, transforming her from a docile, obedient child to a rebellious adolescent?

Dina stared blankly at the pale yellow walls — Sima had begged for the color and they had granted her wish on her last birthday. She moved her hand to instinctively smooth down a wrinkle in the bedspread, and felt the envelope in her hand. She hadn't even seen the test results. She opened the torn envelope, withdrew the paper inside, and scanned the blue handwriting. Outside, the hallway echoed with an eerie silence and the front door slammed shut.

Forty-three

Avrumie looked at himself good and hard in the mirror. He hadn't shaved in three days and he needed a haircut. Badly. And wasn't that a stain on the lapel of his designer shirt? His eyes were bloodshot from lack of sleep — thank God it wasn't from anything else. He had resisted the temptation at Jonathan's party the night before — endured scorn and condescension by refusing to drink. But it was worth it. All he needed at this point was a hangover!

He felt sick and depressed. With good reason, he told himself. It had been a month since he left home — three weeks and three days, to be exact — and since then he'd done, well, basically nothing, with his life. He had done a little shopping so that he could dress more like his friends and looked foward to talking with them at the pool hall every night. He and Mikey had avoided each other for a few days until they both realized the necessity of making up. Living on the fringe was a lonely existence, and a guy couldn't afford to bear grudges. In fact, after they had talked for about an hour, Mikey had invited Avrumie to live with him at his aunt and uncle's house until something else panned out, and Avrumie had eagerly agreed, since he was still waiting for a definite answer from Aunt Minna. The topic of Mikey stealing had never been mentioned again, by unspoken agreement.

Mikey had a television in his room, and that was Avrumie's bosom companion for most of the day. He would get up from the couch feeling heavy and stupid. *You're wasting your life*, his mind would tell him, and he knew it was true.

It's only temporary, he would tell himself. *I'll pick things up and get my act together.* But the whispers of his conscience continued to plague him: *Remember how good you felt after a long day at yeshivah? Remember how nice it was to come home to a loving family? Remember what Ima's suppers were like?* The thoughts tormented him and gave him no peace. He had thought moving out on his own would be the answer to all his problems, and instead he was feeling worse than ever.

Well, at least I don't have to deal with Abba, he would tell himself firmly, attempting to see the silver lining in an otherwise depressing cloud. It was true — there were no more conflicts and feelings of disappointment, guilt, and frustration. But was it worth it?

Avrumie would lie awake listening to Mikey's contented snores, trying to piece together what had been his life. Had it really been as bad as he had thought? Oddly, he couldn't remember everything. The passage of time lent a soft blur to events in his mind, softening them from the way he had seen them previously. Maybe it hadn't been so difficult to get along with Abba. He would think back to the times he and his father would talk together about what he was learning — the two getting caught up in the discourse, arguing animatedly until one of them admitted defeat. And he could remember Ima's fond look of pride as she watched the sparks fly, knowing that Torah was their joy and lifeblood.

Well, that had certainly changed, hadn't it? Avrumie winced at the metamorphosis his Torah commitment had undergone. Abe Faber wasn't exactly known in the streets for his *mishnayos ba'al peh*! The thought, while comical enough, brought a lump to his throat. Was this the life he really wanted?

He had his moments of contentment, when he was sure he'd made the right decision about leaving home, but they were few and far between. Once he'd seen past the glitz of the nightlife, the thrill of being independent, the experience was fast becoming stale. He continued going to the pool hall, enjoying the new friendships he had made, but now it all felt so empty. He had avoided Rabbi Wolf the one or two times he'd seen him, ashamed of himself and his own inability to do anything productive.

He realized that he was still eyeing himself in the mirror, hands in the pockets of his torn jeans — a gift from Mikey. He pulled a face at himself, then was reminded of all the faces he used to make to entertain Bracha, and he felt a pang of loneliness. Maybe he could stop in at home just for a while. Abba wouldn't be home now.... He'd written a letter to Ima a few days ago, thinking the time had come.

His homesickness was interrupted by the opening of the door and Mikey's heavy footsteps in the hallway.

"Hey, Fabe — whatcha doing?"

Avrumie turned around, vaguely annoyed. He didn't like the new nickname Mikey had made up for him, and although he repeatedly told him so, it was to no avail. He also wasn't in a very talkative mood, and from the way Mikey was looking at him, Avrumie knew he wanted to unload.

"Just looking in the mirror."

"What are you — a pretty boy? You don't look all that great, my friend."

Avrumie snorted. "Thanks — I needed that. You don't look like such a beauty queen yourself."

Mikey was offended. Avrumie was constantly amazed at how sensitive his friend was. Probably a result of his complete lack of self-esteem. The guy was a time bomb, waiting to be ticked off.

"Okay, okay," he said, "I'm sorry. I'm in a crummy mood."

Mikey sulked. Avrumie reconsidered.

"Hey, man — I'm sorry. I really didn't mean it. You know that — I just was all down on myself and I snapped at you. Hey — how 'bout going out for a bit. For ice cream. On me."

Mike practically lit up. "Sure, Fabe — you're a buddy."

Avrumie grabbed his wallet and checked to make sure he had money. Bless his meager salary, and the banking system — without ATMs he would have been lost long ago. Slowly, over the past three weeks, his bank account was nearing empty. All the bar mitzvah money, counselor wages, and prizes he'd received for *mishnayos* learning were dwindling in the face of his expenses. Mikey refused to take a cent from him — he was at least living rent free, but it was a mediocre situation at best.

"Y'ready?" Mike sprayed himself liberally with his cheap cologne.

"Yup," said Avrumie, putting his wallet into his back pocket. He headed towards the door.

"Hold on a sec — you're not going like that, are you?"

"Like what?"

"Like...that." Mike pointed emphatically.

"Oh." Avrumie paused for what seemed an eternity. Although he normally wore a baseball cap, his yarmulke had been a more comfortable option that morning. But now it felt like a leaden weight on his head as Mikey stared at him significantly.

With a shrug, he reached up to his head and pulled off his yarmulke. He wouldn't be needing it now.

Forty-four

Sima never knew she had the power to run as fast as she did that crisp afternoon. She literally flew. Out of the house, down the block, out of the neighborhood, until she felt her lungs would burst. She was surprised to see that her eyes were dry and that she actually felt good. What had just happened?

She went over the events of the last few hours. She had seen the envelope in the mailbox that afternoon. Ima usually checked the mail first, but apparently she had forgotten, and once she had seen it, it had been too much of a temptation. In the first place, she had been dreading the envelope since they had been to the doctor's. Nearly every night in the past two weeks she had woken up with recurring nightmares: Her parents putting her into an institution, her teacher announcing to the entire class that Sima was retarded and was being put back to first grade.... The dreams haunted her, becoming very real, and her only hope had seemed to be destroying the envelope.

Of course she knew that eventually they would probably realize what had happened and speak to the doctor themselves. But at least she could buy time. Maybe she could even improve in school and prove the tests wrong. Of course, nosy Mrs. Katzman had interfered and poked her long, ugly nose into her business. That's what had started all the trouble in the first place, and today she had caused the real fireworks. She knew that Ima would find the envelope, but she didn't know how she would react. This was the first time in her life that Sima could remember actually standing up to her mother. Not buckling down or being timid. Where had she gotten that strength from? She didn't even know.

Or maybe she did. Sima was just plain sick of being the *nebach*. Everyone thought she was a *nebach*. She could read all their faces — from the family to her classmates, they all looked at her with pity and a hint of disgust. What she had ever done to deserve the "honor" she didn't know, but enough was enough. Sima sat down on a low wall and hugged her legs. Her dress flew up a bit in the wind, and she could hear Ima's voice: "Sima, put down your dress — the whole world can see your underwear. It's very not *tznius'dik!*" She let the dress billow as it pleased. She was free! Her cheek burned where Ima had slapped her, but that didn't matter. She was never going back home. Never.

The voice of reason and practicality tapped lightly on Sima's thoughts, and she reluctantly admitted it in. *Where will you go?* it asked. *You can't stay here much longer — it's getting dark outside. And besides, you're hungry.* Sima grudgingly acknowledged that it was true. She couldn't very well spend the night on a little stoop in another part of town with a very empty stomach. The question was: where to go?

She walked aimlessly along the main road for what seemed like hours. Where was she, even? Her surroundings were unfamiliar, but then again, how often had she run away from the safety and confines of her home? Sima came to a fork in the street. It was time to make a major decision. Which way should she walk? Both directions were unfamiliar to her. She looked both ways, then resolutely turned right. With a newfound confidence, she strode toward...toward she didn't even know what.

The walking helped her think. It was really unbelievable that everything that had happened had really happened. It wasn't a dream. She wouldn't wake up to Shira pulling off her covers or Bracha demanding a bottle. She was free, and she, Sima Faber, felt very good. Like Avrumie.

The thought jumped into her head unbidden. It was true, though. This must have been what Avrumie had felt when he left home. Sima had often wondered what was happening with Avrumie, but she knew better than to ask. It was more than three weeks since he'd left, and there was an unspoken ban on his name in the house. Of course, her classmates missed no opportunity to ask her about her brother.

"Sima, how's your brother? Is he still keeping kosher?"

She had become numb to the comments, and yet she could not fathom the cruelty that produced them. How could they say such things to her? Didn't they know that Avrumie was a good person who had it just a little too hard? And besides, it wasn't their business.

She shuddered to think what they would have said had they found out about her learning disabilities. That would have been the breaking point. Didn't Ima understand that absolutely no one could know that she had a problem of any kind? Of course not. Ima didn't understand anything. Least of all her own twelve-year-old daughter.

Forty-five

Dear Ima,

I know you're probably going out of your mind worrying about me, but don't worry (yeah, right!). I'm okay, and I'm sleeping at friends' houses, and yeah, I've been eating all my vegetables and taking showers. I just feel like I need a little time away, on my own, so that I can think. I hope you got my message the other day. I don't want to speak on the phone — even to you — even though what happened wasn't really your fault, because I want to work things out before I talk. Meanwhile I wanted to write this letter so you'd know that I'm safe and sound and not getting into trouble. My friends aren't exactly the kind that you would approve of (as you might have guessed), but they are good, decent people, and they like me and respect me, which is a lot more than I can say about some other folks I know!

I'm sorry that I'm worrying you. I'm also sorry that I'm disappointing you and everyone else. This is something I have to do, though — please understand it and try not to nag me too much about stuff.

Aunt Minna might have called you and told you that I was thinking of maybe moving in with her. I thought maybe that would be a good solution 'cuz I can't live at home, and it's getting hard to keep having to ask friends to stay with them. I'm looking into getting my high school diploma at some place other than Zichron Yosef (I hope you've figured out by now that I'm not going back there. I mean, it's not exactly rocket science).

I would really rather you didn't show this letter to Abba, but I know you're going to, so there's no point in forbidding you to. I really don't want to have anything to do with him, though — it's just one long, painful story and we can never see eye-to-eye on anything. With you, I feel sort of that you're more lenient and less hung up on things, even though you sure do have your hang-ups (just smile, Ma, and admit it!).

Please tell all the kids that I miss them and give Bracha a big hug from me.

Gotta go.

Avrumie

P.S. I hope you don't mind that I came into the house when no one was home and took some of my stuff. I really needed my pajamas.

Forty-six

"Iiiima!" Shira's screechy voice carried across the house shrilly.

"What, Shira?" All Dina wanted to do right now was go to her room and cry. As if it wasn't enough that Sima had just run away, here was Avrumie's letter, attempting to allay her fears but in fact just adding to them. Her deepest, most secret worries surfaced, scampering across her mind like rodents: Maybe Avrumie had been kidnapped and was forced to write this letter. Maybe he had a Mohawk now and had joined a biker gang. Maybe he was writing from jail.

Don't be ridiculous, Dina, she told herself firmly. *He just needs a little time, and then he'll be fine. Meanwhile we'll prepare ourselves so we can deal with him properly when he comes back.* She was speaking to Rabbi Woolf from the crisis hotline nearly every night, expressing all her fears and asking him for his advice. He was a fount of knowledge, and his insight was inordinately valuable. She knew she needed to come to terms with the fact that Avrumie wanted to live with Minna and Yechiel instead of with his own parents, but that was a step she hadn't reached yet.

"Iiiima!" Shira was standing in front of her, hands on her hips. Dina cringed inwardly.

"I've been calling and calling, and you're just ignoring me," Shira whined demandingly.

Dina didn't have the strength to discipline the chutzpah. "What do you want, Shira?" she asked in her best pseudopatient voice.

"I wanted to know if I could have permission to ride Sima's bike. All my friends have bikes, and I don't have one, and they're all going out riding. Can I? I'll be very careful, and Sima isn't even home. You always let me ride her bike — right? Where is Sima?"

Dina cried inwardly as Shira's innocently intended words pierced her very heart.

"You may not use Sima's bike — it's hers, and she's not here so we can't ask permission from her. Either you'll run beside them, or you'll play something else."

Shira considered arguing and throwing a tantrum, but one look at her mother's face and she slunk away, defeated.

The entire tragedy of her encounter with Sima came crashing down on Dina with a force too heavy for her to bear. She sank into a kitchen chair. Where was Ephraim? She needed to talk to him. She realized her hands were shaking as she dialed the yeshivah's pay phone. The words of Rivkah Imeinu came to her mind, "*Lamah eshkal gam shneichem yom echad* — Why should I lose both of my sons in the same day?" Rivkah's pain was her own pain — today she had lost Sima, and it seemed to her, in her bleak despair, that Avrumie was lost from them, too.

The phone was answered abruptly.

"May I please speak to Ephraim Faber? It's very urgent."

"I'll try to get him."

She heard the receiver dangling and hit the wall. *Please find Ephraim*, she prayed, and then his voice came through the phone, weary but concerned.

"Hello?"

"Ephraim!"

"Dina — what's the matter?"

Suddenly she didn't even know how to begin. The emotions flooded inside her, the tears sprang to her eyes, and she couldn't say a word.

"Dina — what's wrong?" He was very alarmed. She never called him in middle of his learning. "Dina — talk to me."

"Come home, Ephraim. Please come home," she wept.

"Okay — I'm coming right now," Ephraim stammered. He slammed down the phone and raced out of the *beis midrash*, without even stopping to get his hat on the way out.

Forty-seven

Dear Diary,

Hi — my name is Shira, and you probably don't know me 'cuz I just started you today. I never wrote in a diary before, but now all my friends are, so I decided to. Well, I don't have that much to tell you, but I do have a little to tell you and it goes like this.

Ima always says I have big ears and big eyes and a big mouth and I guess it's true because I always hear things I'm not supposed to and see things that people would never want me seeing. So that's what happened today and a few weeks ago. I'll tell you first about today.

I saw Ima with her eyes all red (again!) and she had a piece of paper in her hand, and I happened to see that she put it in her telephone book (the one where she keeps all her friends' numbers). So when she left the kitchen — and I know it was a big aveirah, but I really couldn't help it — I looked at the paper. She didn't catch me, and I feel very bad that I did it, but I'm just so curious about everything.

Anyway, it was from Avrumie — he's my biggest brother, and I like him but I don't think he really likes me. It's kind of hard to explain, but he ran away from home because he hates Abba. Don't think Abba's so bad, it's just that they didn't get along together, so Avrumie is living with his friends who aren't really such great peo-

ple. He doesn't want to come home just yet and he's not even going to yeshivah. I think he's doing something really stupid (I'm allowed to write that word here, because Ima's never going to read it, otherwise she would punish me!). I mean, imagine not even living at your house and having to worry about where you're gonna sleep, and stuff! Okay, that's one thing. And then the second thing is about my sister Sima. See, Sima's very hard to explain. She's really pretty nice, I guess, but she's so quiet and she's always, kind of, well, nebach looking. And it's not just me who says it — it's all my friends, too. And I think Ima and Abba both think so also. She does really badly in school, and I always get higher marks than her, even when I don't try hard and she does. I think she probably hates me, because I sometimes make fun of her and tease her, but I don't do it meanly, just kind of to have fun. I know, I know — it's a big aveirah.

I think there's something going on with her, too, because Ima took her to a very private appointment a few weeks ago, and I overheard her talking to Sima's teacher about her having problems. It's so crazy around here. It seems like everyone in this family has problems. I just hope I don't start having problems, too!

Forty-eight

It was not a good part of town. Sima knew this even though she had never really encountered a "bad" part of town before. Perhaps it was the filth, the broken stoops and boarded-up buildings, but it had an air of mystery and danger that made her rethink her decision. It was a busy street, though, and the sun was just setting, and she took comfort in the remaining daylight and the people around her.

A woman, her head encased in a ragged turban, bumped into her accidentally.

" 'Scuse me, missy — 'scuse me."

Sima smiled, ashamed, and walked on. This was certainly a new experience for her.

She passed a convenience store, the sound of video games blaring from its doorway, its cramped insides crowded with rowdy teenagers. She passed a seedy-looking restaurant with a half burnt-out neon sign proclaiming "The Joint." She slowed her pace to take in the scene around her, even as she heard Ima's voice in her head. "Sima, no talking to strangers." "Sima, watch where you're going." "Sima, never accept a ride from a stranger." She looked into the faded display of a frame store, a dusty collection of various photographs ensconced in its yellowed window. She lingered outside a candy store, looking longingly at its wares, hardly noticing the chill in the air as her hunger became more acute.

And then she saw him. Across the street, holding an ice cream cone, laughing with a boy, clad in torn jeans and an oversized shirt. It was Avrumie. Unmistakably. Sima's heart beat faster. Of all the unexpected things in the world! What should she do now? Her first instinct was to hide. Surely he would be embarrassed to see her, especially if he was with a friend. "Four Eyes" Sima was definitely not his favorite relative. Then she rethought the situation. It was almost dark, and it wasn't safe for her to be alone. Maybe Avrumie would help her out. Maybe he'd even change his thoughts about her when he heard her triumphant story. Maybe now they finally had something in common. She quickly looked both ways, then ran across the street, thrilled at her own daring.

He wasn't looking at her — he was talking to his friend, and the two were gaping at a motorcycle parked on the street. She noticed he was not wearing a yarmulke, and that he looked more unkempt than she'd ever seen him. With faltering steps, Sima slowly approached her brother.

"It's a Harley!" Avrumie's friend was saying gleefully. "You know how much this thing must have cost!"

"Cool it, Mike — the owner's just inside the store. We don't need him getting mad." He turned instinctively towards the doorway where the motorcycle's proud rider had just entered, and in that moment, his eyes caught Sima's. For a split second, Avrumie thought he was dreaming. It couldn't be. But it was.

"Hi." She smiled shyly and half-waved.

"What are you doing here?!" His voice came out half-shocked, half-aghast, and completely bewildered.

"It's a long story," she said simply. Avrumie looked at her long and hard. Had she come to track him down? No — she wouldn't do that. If his parents would send someone out looking for him, they sure wouldn't send out Sima! But she looked different. Something about her seemed very much changed. She was standing straighter, more confidently. Her hair wasn't in her eyes, and her eyes were even sparkling a bit. He became aware that Mikey was eyeing her questioningly.

"Uh, Mike — this is, um, my sister, Sima. Sima, this is, uh, Mike."

"Nice to meet you," Mikey said pleasantly. Avrumie could hear the thoughts clicking in his mind. Mikey was not slow.

"Uh, you know what, Mike — I think Sima and I need a little time alone. Do you mind if I meet you a little later?"

"Sure." Mike looked at Avrumie a little knowingly and started off down the road, his ice cream melting in his hand.

"Come with me," Avrumie said to Sima, and she followed him.

"Can I have some of your ice cream?" she asked, and her courage astounded her. "I'm really starving."

"I'll bet," said Avrumie, looking at her as if he'd never seen her before. He handed her his dripping cone and led her to a bench outside a pizza shop.

"Now shoot," he said. "I want the whole story."

Forty-nine

"We're going out, Dina," Ephraim said firmly. "Chavie!" he called upstairs. Chavie appeared at the top of the staircase.

"Chavie, Ima and I have to go out for a bit. Please make sure that everything is under control."

"Is everything all right?" Chavie knew that everything was not all right. Shira, Miss Know-it-all, had reported two pieces of distressing news: Avrumie wasn't coming home, and Sima had run away. The first part wasn't so shocking to her, but the second tidbit she simply could not believe. Sima? Little, quiet, awkward Sima? She didn't have the guts to refuse her celery, let alone go anywhere without permission. What had happened? Swallowing her pride, she had pumped Shira for details, but Shira was unsure of what exactly had transpired. *What is happening to this family?* Chavie thought hysterically, but she quickly calmed herself down. Everything was going to be okay.

"I hope so." Abba was talking, but Chavie was still lost in thought. "Good-bye."

Dina and Ephraim walked outside together. "Do you want to take the car?"

"No, let's just walk," said Dina. "It's not so cold tonight, and we'll be able to talk better."

"Okay."

They continued on until the end of the block.

"Now tell me the whole, wretched story."

"It really is wretched," Dina agreed. She had gathered her thoughts together, and she told Ephraim what had happened, not missing out a single detail. He was very quiet, and she could see his eyebrows drawn together.

"I never would have imagined it in a million years, Dina," he said quietly. "I think we have made a grave mistake with Sima."

"We definitely have. We've ignored all the warning signals, until it's almost too late."

"It's never too late," Ephraim cut her off emphatically. "Sima is a little child. She can't manage on her own. She'll definitely come back. The thing is, though, we have to reevaluate where she stands. And where we stand with her."

Dina regarded Ephraim with a mixture of pride and surprise. The Ephraim of a month ago would have said something along the lines of "This is unacceptable. A child does not leave home under any circumstances. We will have to deal with her very firmly." Before her, though, was a transformed Ephraim. Much more attuned to the feelings and needs of his children. She silently thanked Hashem that He had sent them to Binyomin Woolf. Ephraim had met with him — in person — many times over the last week, and the two were even developing a sort of friendship, as the young rabbi helped guide Ephraim toward understanding his troubled son.

"One thing is sure: she has not been happy for a very long time." As soon as she said it, Dina felt a tremendous wave of guilt hit her. It was true. Sima had suffered for so long, and not just because of her acute learning disability. Friends, she had none. She was always excluded from birthday parties, always left out of games and sports events, and constantly picked on by teachers and classmates alike. It had been twelve long years of rejection and pain. Was there any way to make up for them?

Dina realized her own metamorphosis — from wavering, anxious-to-conform mother, to a stronger, more caring parent. She was adapting slowly but surely, and it hadn't taken very long.

"This is all my fault," she began, feeling tears spring to her eyes. "I don't know what came over me. I was worrying about Avrumie, and thinking about the results of the evaluation, and feeling like an inferior mother, and then, all of a sudden, I was confronted with this...this Sima that I'd never known before. And to think that she had intercepted the mail! It was just too much for me. It was the straw that broke the camel's back. But it's really inexcusable that I hit her — I can never forgive myself for that. It was just this blind anger that came over me — I can't explain it rationally. In the heat of the moment I called her a terrible name and I slapped her. Oh, Ephraim, what should I do?" Dina covered her face with her hands and wept.

"Calm down, Dina'le. We're not perfect, and we all make mistakes. This was a mistake, and I'm sure it can be corrected. What we need to focus on now is bringing Sima back and making her life better. I guess we need to do the same with Avrumie, but Sima might be a bit more malleable at this point." He grimaced.

"What do you say we take Sima out with us for a night. As soon as she gets back. I think she needs a lot of love and a lot of attention." There were Uri Epstein's words, ringing through his very being. That man was a *malach*!

Dina smiled through her tears. "I think you're a genius."

"We'll give her until nine o'clock and then we go out searching," Ephraim said resolutely. "Until then, I think it's definitely *Tehillim* time."

Fifty

A vrumie just stared at his little sister. Her eyes blazed fire, and her mouth was set in a taut line. Much like his own, he noticed, amazed. They both had something in them — some rebellious spirit, waiting to be unleashed from its prison. But she was only a twelve-year-old kid! Now she was silent, waiting for his comments. And he didn't know what to say.

"Sim — I can't even believe this is you talking! What happened to my shy little 'Four Eyes'?"

He was teasing her, but in good humor, and she smiled. She also felt proud.

"I guess I just got sick of it. I was so unhappy, and so scared of what the kids in my class would say, that I just said whatever was on my mind, instead of burying it, like I usually do."

"I know what you mean, kid."

"Can I move in with you?"

Avrumie laughed ruefully. "Dream on, Sima. I'm living at a friend's house, and even that is just temporary. This is a kind of 'on the go' life that I'm leading right now." He felt sorry for himself, suddenly, and sorry for her. "Listen, Sima — it's not all it's cracked up to be." Déjà vu took hold of him, and the cryptic words of Albert, formerly Eliezer, came back to him: "I'll tell you something, kid," he had said. "It ain't all it's cracked up to be."

"But what should I do? How am I supposed to go back home? I can't stand Ima. Abba, I really have nothing to do with, but Ima — she always has it in for me. And besides, they're just going to force me to go back to school, and the whole school will find out about my — my problem. And that's the end of me, I can tell you that much!"

Avrumie's heart went out to his sister. He knew how she felt. But there was no way she could make it on her own — not at this age, at least. He steeled himself and began.

"Sima, I know how you feel. Believe me, I know. But you have to be reasonable and weigh the different sides. There's no way you can move in with me, and truthfully, I'd hate to see you leave home now. Even though Ima and Abba have their problems, they're okay people, on the whole." He was surprised at how naturally the words came to his lips — he hadn't even forced the word "Abba" to come out, even in the context of "okay people."

Sima was regarding him with an almost worshiping gaze.

"It's not what you think — this kind of life is no life," he said gruffly, blinking away the sudden moisture in his eyes. "Imagine having nothing to do a whole day. Feeling so unaccomplished, like such a...such a bum!" He practically spat out the words. "Not coming home to anyone who really cares about you — I mean, my friends are great and all," he put in defensively, "but they're just not like...like family, I guess." He stared out into space. "If I could, I would go back this instant," he said softly, almost wistfully.

Sima felt like crying — for Avrumie, for his friends who were all probably equally as miserable, for her parents, and for herself.

Abruptly, Avrumie returned to his old self, ashamed at himself for revealing his rawest feelings.

"There's no two ways about it, Sima. You have to go home," he said gruffly. "But what you can do is, you can try to talk to them. Explain to them how you feel. Don't be all closed up inside yourself — they're not mind readers. I'm sure you can come to some kind of solution between the three of you. I had a really good talk with Ima once, and she really was very patient and wanted to sort things out. She's not a bad person, she just doesn't understand things sometimes."

"You really think they'll listen to me? I'm the stupid idiot that can't even remember things properly. I'm 'Sim-Sim' who sticks out all the time and who can't get over 60 on a test! They're not exactly going to sit up and listen to me."

"I'm not sure about that. They probably got quite a scare with you running away, and they realize that there's a massive problem. It's probably hard enough there with me gone." He paused. "Do...do they say anything about me?" His voice faltered.

"Yeah — they talk about you all the time, but in kind of a whisper. We're not allowed to say your name, otherwise Ima starts yelling. And they've been talking to all kinds of people about you."

"They have?!" Avrumie sat up straighter. "What kind of people?"

"Well, you know — everything I ever know I find out from Shira." Avrumie couldn't help but laugh.

"Shira says that they're talking to a rabbi who's helping them work out what to do with you, and how to relate to you properly."

Avrumie was astounded. "Both of them?"

Sima wasn't stupid. "Yeah — Abba, too."

"Have they been acting any differently to the rest of the kids?"

"Well, not to me they haven't — right?" Sima laughed bitterly. "I don't know — they seem a little calmer, maybe. And on Shabbos Chanan asked Ima a question about the parashah and she got a funny look on her face and she really went out of her way to give him an answer. And Abba actually asked Dovid if he wanted to play chess with him the other night."

Avrumie could not believe his ears. His parents? His one-track-minded, unquestioning, and unanswering parents? It just couldn't be.

"Are you for real, Sim?"

"It's true, Avrumie. You have to believe me." She paused and snuck a look at him out of the corner of her eye. "Maybe it's time for you to come home," she said quietly. Avrumie looked at her sharply, but she avoided his gaze.

"Not just yet," he said, a little uneasily. "There's a time for everything. I still need to sort some things out."

"Yeah — and you need a haircut!"

The words flew out and Sima couldn't believe she had actually said them, but Avrumie just laughed and tousled her hair. "You're right, kiddo."

The sun had long since set, and the ominous sounds of suspicious night life were filling the streets. The traffic had dwindled and the street lamps cast grotesque shadows across the roads and alleyways. Avrumie looked at his watch.

"Yikes! I think you've given them enough of a scare. Come on — I'll walk you back."

"Do you have any money?"

"Yeah, a little — why?"

" 'Cuz I'm so hungry I don't even know if I can get up!"

"Come on, Sim — I'll get you some chips."

In the comforting darkness, the two walked together: a tall, lanky boy, and a shorter, younger girl with a curiously confident stride, heading toward the place they both knew as home.

Fifty-one

"I'm calling the police."

Ephraim looked at his wife worriedly. Maybe she was right and they should involve the authorities. It was already well past nine o'clock and Sima had left the house at four. Ephraim had driven around the neighborhood extensively, but with no results. They didn't hear the quiet footsteps until Dovid was in the kitchen.

"I'm sorry to bother you, but...is everything okay with Sima?" He looked very scared.

Dina glanced at Ephraim. He cleared his throat.

"Sima left home and we're waiting for her to come back. *B'ezras Hashem*, she's all right and she'll be home very soon, but meanwhile, you can say *Tehillim* if you want to. Don't be so afraid, Dovid. It'll be okay." His voice was gentle, but Dovid was not calmed.

"What's happening to this family?!" His voice was barely a whisper, and yet it seemed like a scream in the hollow silence of the kitchen. "First Avrumie, then Sima — everyone's running away. What's happening? And is Sima also going to leave *Yiddishkeit*?" He saw the shock and torment on his parents' faces, and stopped. "I'm sorry — I didn't mean to hurt you, but it's so hard for me..." he broke off, and the tears ran freely down his cheeks.

Dina's heart felt like it would burst. The whole day had been one long epiphany of sorts: she was seeing into the minds of her children, getting to know them as they really were, not as she wanted them to be. She could tell that Ephraim's thoughts mirrored her own. She reached out and hugged Dovid close to her.

"It's so hard, Dovid — for all of us. But it's good that you told us what you were feeling. I'm sorry, *zeeskeit*, that it's been so hard on you. You look up to Avrumie so much. He'll come back, Dovid. We just have to daven very hard, and try to accept him and love him. You'll see — he'll come back. And Sima will be back very soon, we hope. With Sima we'll have to be extra careful — she's suffered a lot."

Dovid wept softly, and Dina let her own tears fall. Ephraim had wrapped his arm around Dovid, and his eyes, too, were moist. They stood that way for many long moments, the sound of the kitchen clock ticking the only real noise.

When the knock on the door was heard, they all jumped simultaneously and ran for the door. Ephraim reached it first, and he pulled it open with force.

Framed in the light of the porch lamp was Sima. Her face was tired, her hair unkempt, but her eyes were clear and content. Before she could even utter a word, Ephraim had seized her and hugged her tight in an uncharacteristic show of emotion. Dina followed, smothering Sima with kisses all over her pale face and moist hair. In their wonderful, ecstatic reunion, they failed to see a tall, lone figure watching silently from the edge of the lawn before he turned away and disappeared into the night.

Fifty-two

"Anyone seen Abe?"

The Hall was crowded that night — several newcomers had joined the scene. Albert repeated his question to the gang surrounding the pool table.

"Abe, anyone?"

"He hasn't shown up tonight," said Sherry. "Since when are you guys close?"

Albert shrugged. "Nah — there's a guy here who was looking for him and gave me a note to pass on to him."

"Who?"

"What's it your business — since when are *you* guys so close?!" he taunted.

Sherry pulled a face. "Sometimes you can be a real pain, Al."

"Okay, okay — let's knock it off. It's that rabbi dude — he asked me if I'd seen Abe, so I'm just making a few discreet inquiries."

"Wow — you're so discreet you should work for the FBI!"

"Very funny. Maybe I do. Oh — here he comes."

"That rabbi dude" was fast approaching. Binyomin Woolf sauntered over to the group, hands in the pockets of his suit pants.

"Hi, everyone!"

He recognized maybe four out of the ten kids, and they smiled at him warmly. The other six regarded him warily. He had a beard. He turned to his nearest compatriot. "These guys are all eyeballing me, Joe — why don't you introduce me?"

Joe smiled, slightly abashed. "Yeah, guys — this is Rabbi Ben. He kind of hangs around here. If you ever need someone to talk to, or a great *cholent*, he's the man. Go ahead — introduce yourselves!"

There was a round of handshaking during which Binyomin was impressed to see that the girls did not offer their hands. To each, Binyomin gave a friendly smile. Then he removed himself from the spotlight unobtrusively and retreated to the outskirts of the playing area, eyeing the crowd. He spotted his victim in under twenty seconds. The boy was slim and dark-eyed, but his shoulders were slumped, and he looked unkempt.

"Hey — what's your name again?"

The boy looked up at him, surprised. "Johnny."

"What's doing with you, everything good?"

"Yeah."

Yeah, right.

"Whatcha up to these days?"

Johnny nodded vaguely. "Oh, a bit of this and a bit of that. Keeping busy."

I'll say, thought Binyomin. He could smell the tell-tale odor on the boy's clothing. "You got your own place?"

"Nah — costs too much. I get by, though."

"Yeah, you look like the capable type."

Johnny stared at him for a moment, eyes wide. "Huh?"

"I know 'em when I see 'em. Seems like a real shame for you to be out here wasting your time when you could be going places, huh?"

Johnny's stare turned into a gape. Nobody had ever said anything remotely similar to him before. "You're darn right," he said angrily. "You think I have nothing better to do? You think I don't want to get some place? You think I like it out here with no life and nowhere to go? No way, Rabbi, but I ain't got much of a choice. Listen, I don't have to get into the whole messy story, but I didn't ditch home like 'cuz I wanted to, right?"

"Hey, I'm no rocket scientist, but I kind of understood that, Johnny boy. It must have been pretty tough for you there, but out here it's not that much better."

"Yeah, but anything's better than there." Johnny frowned and his face darkened.

"Well, this is just talking through my hat, you understand, but I've got a buddy who's really desperate. Looking for someone to work in his store. Needs someone good, though — none of them slimey characters with jello for brains, you know. He's willing to pay pretty nice too, and it's a full-time job. So here I am, talking to you, and all of a sudden the lightbulb's going off in my head and I'm thinking — maybe you're the one! Whaddaya say, Johnny?"

Yona Blum could not even open his mouth. Here was a complete stranger who didn't know him from Adam, offering him a decent job, and acknowledging that he actually had more than jello between his ears! He could only nod mutely, his eyes filled with gratitude and joy.

"Tell you what — meet me at my place in an hour, and we'll shmooze some more, okay? I gotta go now, but I want to talk to you about some details here and there. Let me give you my address." Binyomin pulled out a piece of paper and scribbled directions to his house. "Eleven o'clock you'll be there?"

"You betcha," said Johnny with conviction. And Binyomin knew he would keep his word.

"See ya then!" He clapped Johnny on the back and hurried out of the pool hall. He had one hour to find the kid an employer.

Fifty-three

ina felt a flutter of nervousness. She and Ephraim had sat together that afternoon, alone, and role-played what they thought would be a successful conversation. Now it was in Hashem's capable hands. Ephraim came down the stairs, and Dina noticed that he had straightened his tie and combed his hair. He must be nervous, too. Shira was slinking around the kitchen unhappily, munching on a cookie. She felt left out of all of this, unused as she was to Sima getting attention.

"Where're you going, Ima?"

Dina looked down at Yosef. "Abba and I are taking Sima out for a little bit tonight, darling. You be good and behave with Chavie, and I'll bring you a special treat."

"Okay." He paused. "Will you also take me and Chanan out some time?"

Dina looked at him, surprised. "Would you two like that?"

"Yeah. We're always getting left out of everything. Just because we're younger doesn't mean we can't do stuff, you know."

Dina ruffled his hair. "You're absolutely right, little guy. Let's make a date for — how about next week?"

"You'll take us to a restaurant?"

Dina smiled. "Well, I guess that's not a bad idea."

"You and Abba?"

"Yes."

"And I can order hot dogs?"

"Yes."

"Two of them?"

"Uh huh."

"Thanks." He ran upstairs, no doubt to tell Chanan about their upcoming adventure. Dina checked her lipstick again. It had been awhile since she'd gone out to eat, and she was slightly excited at the prospect. She heard soft footfalls on the staircase and caught a glimpse of Sima in the mirror.

It was the new, self-confident Sima, looking very pretty with her hair pulled back in a clip, and her favorite blue outfit.

"Hi, Sim-Sim — you ready?"

"Yeah. Could you just call me plain 'Sima'?"

Dina's breath caught in her throat.

"Sure," she said, in as neutral a manner as she could muster. The rules of the game had definitely changed.

"Thanks."

Sima's voice was so distant. Could they bridge the gap? "You look very nice," Dina said, as casually as she could.

"Thanks."

"Ephraim!" Dina called her husband from where he was helping Dovid with a piece of *gemara*.

"Are we ready?" he asked, looking up with a smile.

"Yes."

"Then let's go!" He cheerfully ushered Dina and Sima out the front door. Dina wondered if his good mood was forced or genuine, but either way it was very necessary.

"Have fun!" Chavie called over her shoulder, and Dina breathed a silent sigh of relief.

It was amazing what a difference Rabbi Woolf had made in their lives. He had encouraged Dina and Ephraim to be open with the children, to "lay the cards on the table," as he had phrased it. He had guided them in taking concrete steps toward improving their relationships with each of their children and lightening the atmosphere in their home. Now if only they could bridge the gap between them and Sima...and then, of course, there was Avrumie.... Dina had actually called her sister the day before and formally granted her permission to take Avrumie in. Perhaps he would be coming home one day, she thought wistfully.

The ride to the restaurant was quiet, except for some small talk, and Sima's only question was where they were going. They had chosen a nice, stylish place, with good food and relatively low prices. Even Sima was impressed as they were greeted by the maitre d' at the entrance.

"It's so fancy, Ima," she whispered, letting down her guard. Dina smiled and a surge of hope welled up inside her.

After they were seated and had placed their orders, silence fell thickly upon the trio.

"Water, anyone?" Ephraim asked.

"I'll take some," said Dina. "What about you, honey?"

Sima avoided her gaze. "No, thanks."

"We're so glad we got to do this, all together, tonight," Dina began, looking at Ephraim for support. "We think it's very important to...talk things out between us. Everything that happened over the past few days was very sudden and very...big."

"We really love you," Ephraim continued. "It hurts us to see one of our children in such pain. We want to work out the things that are bothering you so that we can all be happier."

Sima said nothing.

"Honey," Dina began, "the thing we want you to realize is that we really love you. We might have...made mistakes in certain things. We didn't know, for example, that you were having such a hard time in school...."

"How could you not know?!" Sima demanded harshly. "Didn't you see how sad I was? How I always hated going to school? Didn't you ever realize that I didn't have any friends? I'm never invited to any of the parties, I never get any phone calls. Everyone just makes fun of me. And even at home everyone hates me. How do I even know that you love me? Just because you say so doesn't really mean it."

"Sima," Ephraim started, remembering the advice Rabbi Woolf had given them, "there's no way we can absolutely prove to you that we love you — in fact, until you yourself are a parent you probably won't understand how deep our love is for you. We hope to show you this love through our actions. Can you try to reassure yourself that we do, indeed, love you, and then move on to talk about what's wrong and how we can fix it?"

Sima looked at her father strangely. It was unlike Abba to be so calm and rational — she had thought he would have become upset at her last comment. He was right, in a way. Her parents could never really prove beyond a shadow of a doubt that they loved her, but here they were, on a regular Wednesday evening, taking her out for a fancy dinner and seeming genuinely concerned about her.

"Okay," she said quietly, and Dina heaved a small sigh of relief.

"I brought a piece of paper," she said quickly, withdrawing a pad and some pens. "I think we should write down the problems and then problem-solve together. How's that?"

"That's a wonderful idea, Ima," enthused Ephraim. "Except for one thing — I'm really hungry!" He pulled a comical face and even Sima cracked a smile. Things were looking up already, and they were only on the first course.

Fifty-four

Avrumie picked up the old sock he'd been given and proceeded to wipe the dust off the dresser. He scanned the small room uncertainly, taking in the small window on its left-most wall, and the three stark shelves that stood out from the wallpaper like intruders. He sprayed the mirror with some Windex and swished the cloth across it. Dark smears stood out where the dust had mingled with the liquid. He stared into the streaked mirror momentarily. His face looked tired, and the lone bulb that hung from the center of the ceiling did nothing to enhance his appearance. He scratched the two days' worth of stubble on his chin and kicked at a box on the floor. So this was the place he was to call home for the next little while.

It had taken Aunt Minna an inordinately long amount of time to give him a definite response, and when she had finally called Mikey was on the verge of throwing him out. Two weeks of rooming together had just about done them in, and Avrumie had been ecstatic when his aunt and uncle had agreed to house him.

Of course, the move to their basement would change the rules of the game a little bit. Until now, he had been maintaining a good cover — his parents knew nothing about his whereabouts, and he was free to do as he wished. Now they would know exactly where he was living. Avrumie let that thought swish around his mind for a few moments, considering the possible ramifications of his parents knowing his location.

A polite knock on the door broke into his musings, and Avrumie whirled around.

Aunt Minna stood in the doorway, holding a plate of cookies and a glass of milk. "Here you go — moving is hard work. Enjoy!"

He smiled weakly, but he was touched. "Thanks a lot. I'm really hungry."

"Well, you're more than welcome to join us for supper upstairs whenever you'd like. You do have your own cooking facilities — sort of." She eyed the single burner and sink in the far corner of the room dubiously, and Avrumie shared her hesitation. "Just remember that even though you're our tenant, you're still our nephew." She smiled at him encouragingly, and Avrumie felt himself melt further.

"Thanks."

Minna's pleasant demeanor successfully hid the emotions that bubbled inside her. There had been several back-and-forth conversations between her and Dina, many of which were tinged with animosity. In fact, she had been very close to telling Avrumie she could not take him in. But Yechiel had assured her that it was only Dina's guilt and pain that prompted her to be so problematic about Avrumie staying with them.

"Uh, is there a phone jack?" Avrumie asked his aunt.

"I think it's on that wall, behind the bed." They both searched together and found it. "This is your own line — we installed it for Chana a few years back. You know — with *shidduchim* and everything, we felt it was the right time. You'll pay your own phone bill — I won't even open it, okay?"

"Okay." Avrumie felt his stomach tense. Where would he get the money from? And they hadn't even discussed the arrangement with rent — was he supposed to pay them a monthly fee? On the one hand, he had been thinking of offering and hoping beyond hope that they would refuse to be paid, but on the other hand, what if they accepted? That was all he needed!

Aunt Minna was eyeing him expectantly, and he felt uncomfortable. Just then he heard the plodding of feet coming down the steps, and Uncle Yechiel appeared in the room. "Well, looks like you're all ready to have guests, huh?" He grinned broadly and winked at Avrumie.

Avrumie had always liked Uncle Yechiel. His good sense of humor and infectious laugh marked him as an honest, unpretentious person.

"I really appreciate you guys having me stay here," he began.

"Nonsense!" Uncle Yechiel waved him away. "It's our absolute pleasure. The house is too quiet, isn't it, Minna? I always try pushing Shuie to move back home, but you know how it is — the grass is always greener on the other side! Come, Minna — we'd better let him unpack."

Minna glanced at her husband meaningfully and didn't move. "Ummm, Avrumie, there are just a few things we wanted to discuss with you," she began. Avrumie felt himself tightening up. He could smell trouble. He saw his uncle's face take on a frown of sorts, but his aunt plowed ahead.

"We're not your parents, obviously, but we do want to set down a few rules," Minna started out quickly. She looked at Avrumie for approval, but he remained impassive.

His uncle broke in. "It's like this, Avrumie. There are three things we do not want in this house. What you do out of the house is your own business, but we'd like to ask you to honor these three requests: No girls, drugs, or *chillul Shabbos.*"

Avrumie felt as if he'd been punched in the stomach. Was this what his aunt and uncle thought of him? That he was some low-life drug user who would bring girls home with him; that he had given up on Torah observance entirely? True, he was becoming increasingly lax in many areas, but for them to suspect him so blatantly was a shocking, hurtful thing. He felt the old rush of anger, hatred, and deep shame. Why had he ever thought to move here? They were all the same, these people. Always judging him, always suspecting him, always acting holier than thou.

They were no different from his parents! They probably had set down these rules to protect their own self-image, worried as they likely were about guests or neighbors thinking badly of them because of illicit activity on Avrumie's part.

Minna and Yechiel were looking a little anxiously in Avrumie's direction, awaiting a response of some sort. He could not even look them in the eye.

"We didn't mean..." Minna started, but Avrumie tuned out the rest of what she was saying. He had an urge to run out of the house, run out of their lives and be done with every vestige of hypocritical religion, but his practical side restrained him. After all, he had nowhere to run to, and the street, as he had seen, was not worth its price.

"Let's let Avrumie think about it, Minna." Uncle Yechiel, ever the diplomat, interrupted his wife, giving her a long look. "You let us know, Avrumie — we're right upstairs. I hope you're comfortable here. If there's anything you need, just call — you know our number!" He forced a laugh at his feeble joke, and they both left the room, closing the door gently behind them.

Avrumie sank down on the bed, his thoughts racing. After the initial rage had subsided, he was able to think somewhat rationally. His aunt and uncle had always been good people, he realized, and just a few minutes ago he had really liked them. Of course, it was extremely disturbing to him that they had such a low opinion of his current religious status, but then again, he wasn't exactly broadcasting the image of a Torah-true Jew. He eyed his cutoff jeans, high-top sneakers, and open-necked polo shirt which revealed no sign of tzitzis, and acknowledged the fact that he looked, well, like a bum. His new hairstyle and the noticeable absence of a *kippah* didn't do much to lead them to believe that he wasn't into girls and was still keeping Shabbos. As for drugs, they probably automatically associated all dropouts with drug use, because, unfortunately, many of them did resort to it. Could he blame them for their stereotyping and for their wanting to retain a modicum of self-restraint and propriety in their own home?

As he looked at the situation more openly, he felt his anger subside and embarrassment take its place. Did he want people looking at him and thinking that he was completely irreligious and possibly into drugs? As much as he tried to tell himself that no one's opinion mattered, and that everyone was prejudiced anyway, he was forced to acknowledge to himself that it did matter. And if his own aunt and uncle, whom he knew to be extremely caring, wonderful people, and who were, admittedly, less inclined to be hypocritically judgmental, had this impression of him, what was everyone else thinking?

He tried to shake the feeling of shame, self-consciousness, and uneasiness, but it wouldn't leave. And there, on a sagging bed in a bare, dusty room, Avrumie Faber was forced to come to terms with an unsettling fact: He was not comfortable with the new life he had tried to make for himself.

Fifty-five

Shira had a problem. And it wasn't even something she could discuss with her best friend Gila, because Ima had emphasized that it was complete and absolute *lashon hara* for her to tell anyone, and deep down, Shira's seven-year-old conscience was almost as big as her mouth. The problem was...Sima. Well, that was nothing new. Sima had always been a problem, as far as Shira was concerned. Sima's bumbling behavior and failure at school had become a thorn in Shira's side ever since her friends had started teasing her about it. "Your sister's such a dunce!" they would tell her, and to maintain her own popularity, she had felt it necessary to develop the automatic, flippant response, "I know — I think she's adopted!" This graduated to a directly antagonistic attitude towards Sima in general. It wasn't that she hated her, she just felt sorry for her, and upset at Sima for reflecting badly on her own image. And that was the problem.

Ima had just given her a ten-minute speech (Shira had surreptitiously watched the kitchen clock) about how hurt Sima was and how she had left home because of it and how the whole family had to make a tremendous effort to be extra-super nice to Sima and change their attitude towards her. And Ima hadn't stopped there. She had given detailed examples of behavior she expected "her Shira" to exhibit: Walking home from school with Sima, not teasing her at all ("But not even when she buttons up her shirt wrong?!" "No, not even then, Shira. You can just tell her gently, without embarrassing her, that her buttons are wrong and she should fix them"), inviting Sima to go to the toy store together with her (where the two would no doubt be seen by Shira's friends who would then realize that she was actually spending time with her "*neb*" of a sister!), and the list went on. And the worst, very worst part about it was that Ima had her around the neck — she had promised Shira an unthinkable, unimaginable, absolutely desired prize: she would be allowed to go along with Ima and Abba to cousin Aryeh Leib's *chasunah* in Los Angeles! By airplane! Only her!

Thus the excruciating dilemma. It was a toss-up between her own self-pride and the unpleasant, potentially devastating prospect of her classmates' ridicule, and the dream of going exclusively with her parents, for the first time in her life on an airplane, to the exotic lure of California! Surely, if she had fallen from grace in the eyes of her friends, their opinions would change when they heard about her rise to travel fame, she argued with herself. Then again, some of them, like Shoshana, for instance, wouldn't even be impressed. She probably flew to China three times a year!

And what else had Ima told her? That she knew how hard it would be for Shira, but that she knew what a beautiful, wonderful person Shira was, and that she would certainly be able to change her behavior overnight. Another of Ima's points reverberated in Shira's head, nagging at her uncomfortably. Ima had emphasized the fact that truly good people would never have their laughs at someone else's expense, and that true friends would never break a friendship because their friend was trying to work on her *middos*. Ima was right, too, and Shira admitted to herself that some of the friendships she had built in her class were quite dubious in nature and strength.

Take Shoshana, for instance. If Shira was completely honest with herself (which she was trying to be, at this very moment), she knew that the only reason she valued her friendship with Shoshana was because she wanted something out of her; whether it was being treated to a cookie at the bakery (because everyone knew that Shoshana's allowance was $10 a week, and more if she needed it!), or playing with her special, brand new dolls, or just for the pride of being friends with such a wealthy, popular girl. She wrinkled her nose unconsciously — the truth was slightly distasteful.

Then there was Raizy. Raizy was the smartest girl in the class, and even though she wasn't exactly popular, she was very well-respected. But Shira knew why she coveted Raizy's friendship: to get valuable help on her homework, studying, and sometimes — but extremely rarely — on a test itself (here Shira's conscience really gave it to her, but she had promised herself solemnly that she would never cheat again, *b'li neder*!). Hmmm, so that was Raizy.

Next came Chumie. Now, Chumie was a completely different story. In fact, Shira could openly admit to herself that she didn't like Chumie at all and couldn't understand how anyone else did. But the fact was that she had to be friends with Chumie because Chumie had the sharpest tongue and cattiest mind of anyone in the class, and not to be friends with her was to be constantly ridiculed, shamed, rejected, and completely ruined in the eyes of the entire class. Chumie hung out all the dirty laundry she could find, so to speak. She knew every girl's weak point and wasted no time in filling everyone else in — if that girl wasn't lucky enough to be her friend. So that was her coercive relationship with Chumie.

Of course, then there was Gila. The situation with Gila was more sensitive, because she and Gila were supposed to be best friends. How this best friendship had evolved was beyond Shira's comprehension, but the fact was that they had to do everything together, tell lots of secrets, exclude other girls from their games, and, most of all, spend a nice chunk of time making fun of "*nebs*." Therein, of course, was the rub. Gila's chief "*neb*" was...Sima! It wasn't clear exactly how this had developed, but Shira had the distinctly uncomfortable feeling that making fun of Sima was really the crux of their relationship. Becoming friendlier with Sima would mean distancing herself completely from Gila.

Shira perched herself glumly on a tree stump and frowned. It was so nice being popular and liked. It would be horrible to be shunned and rejected. *That's what Sima feels like right now*, said a soft voice in her head, and she knew it was true. *Then again*, she shot back, *my being nice to Sima won't make everyone nice to her, so it's not like it'll make things all better for her anyhow!* She shrugged, but she hadn't convinced herself. And of course, the image of the promised airplane trip floated in her head like a delicious fantasy — and it could be a reality! She sighed. Why did she have it so hard?

Fifty-six

"You boys are dismissed. Dovid Faber, can you come here for a minute, please?"

Amidst the ruckus of collecting sports gear and snacks, Dovid being singled out by the rebbe went blessedly unnoticed. His heart beating wildly with fear and apprehension, he approached Rabbi Kaplan's desk. What had he done wrong? Maybe it was the *bechinah* they had taken that week. He had studied, but perhaps not well enough. He relaxed a little when he saw the rebbe's eyes looking kindly at him.

"We'll just wait until the classroom is empty, Dovid," Rabbi Kaplan said with a small smile, and Dovid nodded uncertainly.

After the last boy had exited the room, the rebbe turned to his *talmid*.

"You're wondering why you had the special privilege of missing recess today, huh?" he said jokingly. Dovid permitted himself a small smile, but his stomach was still in knots.

"Well, Dovid, I just wanted to see how everything is going with you. It has come to my attention that there have been some…difficulties in your family, which must be very hard on you." He paused, and Dovid swallowed hard. A rush of shame filled him, and his face flushed. Even the rebbe knew what was going on with Avrumie? Then surely the whole city was talking about it! How humiliating!

Why did Avrumie always have to be this way? Always so angry and stubborn, always getting on everyone's bad side? True, Avrumie had always been his idol, but his reverence for his brother had cooled substantially since Avrumie had left home. Dovid studied the floor and willed his cheeks to return to their natural pallor. The rebbe seemed to be waiting for some kind of answer, but what should he say?

"I want you to know that if you ever want to talk about anything, I'm always available, Dovid," Rabbi Kaplan continued in a gentle tone. There was something about the way he said it, though, that made Dovid's heart sink. He knew the rebbe was trying to be helpful, but instead he felt like a *nebach*.

"There's something else I wanted to speak to you about, Dovid." Rabbi Kaplan paused and looked at Dovid rather sharply. He must have been put off by Dovid's lack of response. "Are you still with me, Dovid?"

Dovid started. "Y-yes, of course I'm listening to Rebbe. I'm sorry, I-I just don't know what to say."

Rabbi Kaplan nodded. "I assume that you've started thinking about *yeshivah gedolah*."

Dovid nodded in the affirmative. It was all the boys were talking about lately, and, although Dovid hardly joined their conversations, he too was thinking about it constantly. There were many options relatively close to home, and the yeshivah had even taken the boys to see two out-of-town yeshivos, one which Dovid had found very much to his liking. He hadn't spoken to Abba and Ima yet about the subject at all — they were much too busy with Avrumie, and now with Sima. He still had a bit of time.

"Have you narrowed it down to a few choices?"

"Not really."

"Dovid, I'm surprised. I thought all the boys are dreaming about *yeshivah gedolah* in their sleep already!"

Dovid smiled weakly. "Well, I haven't really had a chance to discuss it with my parents yet. They've been...kind of busy."

The rebbe nodded understandingly. "When you've done a little more research, you're welcome to speak to me about it also, Dovid. I know some of the *menahelim* at other yeshivos, and I would be glad to speak to them about you getting in."

Dovid looked at his rebbe appreciatively. He really was going out of his way to help him. "Thank you," he said simply.

"I do think, however, that...under the circumstances...." Rabbi Kaplan paused. "Because of other things that aren't really in your control, you should pay extra attention to your learning and your grades. It's very competitive in these yeshivos, as I'm sure you've heard."

Dovid was surprised. He had thought he was doing quite well in the rebbe's class. "But I thought I was getting good grades," he protested quietly.

"You are," Rabbi Kaplan was quick to assure him. "It's just that in your case, you have to really be at the top of the class. To show them that you're not following the same trend as.... It's hard for a yeshivah not to judge a boy based on his...family."

Dovid started. What the rebbe was saying was that the yeshivos could disqualify him based on Avrumie! But that was preposterous! How could he be held responsible for something his older brother had done?! His complete shock compelled him to speak up despite his natural shyness. "But Rebbe, I don't understand! How can a yeshivah judge a boy because of his older brother? If they see I'm doing well, what do they care about the rest of my family? It's just not fair!"

Rabbi Kaplan squirmed uncomfortably. "I'm not saying that it definitely happens, Dovid," he hurried to say. "I'm just saying that...in certain circumstances, the yeshivos might be nervous about accepting a *bachur* with family difficulties. After all, doesn't it say regarding *shidduchim* that one should inquire after the girl's brother? You just never know.

"Of course," he hastened to add, "you are a very serious *bachur*, very bright and capable, and a real *lamdan*. That is why I say that you should have no trouble, but being extra cautious can't hurt." Obviously the rebbe felt that the subject had been exhausted, and he turned to the sheaf of papers on his desk. Dovid shifted, his stomach in knots of anxiety, anger, and tension, but he realized the discussion was over.

"Thank you," he said half-heartedly, and he shuffled out of the classroom. The noisy hallways did nothing to alleviate his aggravation. He stumbled outside into the bright sunlight only to be pushed roughly by two sixth graders scrambling for a football. The world closed in on him like a bleak curtain, and he felt the tears stinging his eyes. That was all he needed now, for everyone to see him cry like a baby! He headed back inside to the relative safety of the school building and was about to head for the washrooms when he felt a strong hand on his shoulder. He swung around. It was Abba.

"Dovidel — I was hoping I would see you!" Ephraim had recently been going out of his way to find Dovid during recess and say hello. His cheerful smile vanished when he saw his son's red-rimmed eyes. "*Oy vey*, it looks like we'd better have a talk."

Dovid, too weepy to even speak, nodded gratefully and followed his father out the main entrance.

Ephraim steered Dovid out the front door and into the parking lot, where they got into the white station wagon. As he drove over to a small park beside the school, he wondered just what had happened to Dovid. He also wondered at his own abilities to talk to his son properly. Half a year ago he probably would have just ignored the teariness and tried to be *mechazek* him in some joking kind of way, but now he was a different person. A different father.

Dovid sat in the passenger's seat, staring out the window.

"*Nu*, Dovidel, you don't look so happy," Ephraim started out, forcing a light note into his voice. Dovid said nothing.

"Should I pull out my glass ball, or do you want to give me a clue?"

Dovid smiled feebly. Suddenly he felt very close to his father. Maybe Abba would understand. Maybe Abba would be able to explain to him

213

how such an unfair system could have developed, and how he could defeat it. The whole story spilled out in one long breath. Abba kept his eyes on the road, but his facial expressions conveyed his feelings to Dovid. His mouth was taut, his eyebrows knitted together. He was clearly very upset.

Ephraim pulled the car over to the shoulder of the road. They didn't need the park anymore.

"I feel your pain, Dovid, because it hurts me, too," he began. The words flowed to his lips straight from his heart, and he realized that this was his first time really talking with his son. "But I can tell you that, unfortunately, sometimes these things happen. And I'm also very ashamed to say that there was a time when I, too, looked down on people who came from backgrounds less than...perfect." He chuckled bitterly, recalling how he had condemned entire families because of one of their children. No more.

"What can I tell you, Dovid? It happens, and we just can't beat the system. What we can do is work on ourselves to fight the natural tendency within us to be that way. I think that all the *yissurim* we're going through — and I mean 'we,' the whole family — are really a gift in disguise. They are opening our eyes to things we would never have seen before. Making us better people. Now we know how it feels to be in 'Shmerel's' place. Now we can stop judging other people because we know how it feels to be judged. Isn't that worth something?"

Dovid gazed at his father admiringly. In a few sentences Abba had swept away all his anger and consternation. Abba was right! It was useless to try to change people, but it was imperative to change oneself. He thought back over the course of the year — at the tauntings he endured from his classmates, at the tension and pain at home, at the loss of his secret idol — and saw something other than blind suffering. He saw growth, victories, and the overwhelming sense of truth and virtue borne of challenge and nurtured through sadness.

"You're right," he said softly, and Ephraim felt a warm flush go through him at his son's praise.

"It's a good barometer, Dovid," he said softly, "for seeing the way people really are. If, when push comes to shove, they can't deal with the problems or difficulties that you have, they're probably not worth dealing with for the long term. In everything: yeshivos, social circles, even in *shidduchim*." He bit his lip, deep in thought. Was this really Ephraim Faber speaking? He surely wouldn't have thought this way a scant few months ago. But ever since Avrumie had left home he had been treated to a different picture of life. Suddenly, acquaintances avoided him at *simchah*s and certain people had stopped coming to him for advice. Even a *chaver* that he had approached about learning *b'chavrusa* had squirmed uncomfortably and awkwardly declined. And the man had expressed great interest in learning with him only half a year ago!

"You know, Dovid," he said very gently, "life is a never-ending learning experience. The important thing is to do *retzon Hashem* — real *retzon Hashem*. But we can't judge people. I'm sure that if we do the right thing and the proper *hishtadlus*, Hashem will make the best *yeshivah gedolah* arrangements for you. Better than you and I could possibly do on our own, even if we didn't have other issues to worry about." He glanced at his watch. "Speaking of learning experiences, maybe we should head back to class!"

Smiling, father and son drove back together to the tall, brick building, the conversation flowing easily between them. Dovid would continue to concentrate on his studies as he had always done. Ephraim would look into yeshivos and speak to Dina about the various options, and then the three would decide together where to apply. It was all in Hashem's hands anyhow.

Fifty-seven

"Hey, Abe, where've you been? Haven't seen you around these parts much."

It was Joe, a familiar face, and Avrumie was glad to see him.

"Oh, I've been pretty busy."

"Really?" Was that jealousy he could detect in the other boy's eyes? "Good to see you back." Joe walked away.

The truth was, he hadn't been that busy, but he'd been trying to avoid the pool hall. There was something so empty about the scene, and, especially after his introspection had turned up a lot of mixed feelings, he had wanted to take a break from the hollow nightlife. After a long hour of reflecting deeply on where he was now and where he was headed, he had finally come to the conclusion that something had to change. Like right away. He had told his aunt and uncle that he agreed to their rules, in as offhand a manner as he could muster. They had appreciated it and Avrumie felt good. They were okay, his relatives.

So why was he back in the pool hall? He told himself that he had come hoping to meet the rabbi he'd seen a few weeks ago so he could re-open the conversation about yeshivos. He now regretted his hastiness in throwing out the rabbi's card. But he felt the uncomfortable nag of a half-truth and knew, deep down, that he had come to the pool hall to give in to his sense of loneliness and boredom. He had spent the last few days setting up a job for himself in a local hardware store where they'd pay him a little over minimum wage for helping customers and arranging merchandise. It had felt good to finally have some kind of schedule — he'd be working all day, which left him the evening hours to work on home study courses so he could get his diploma. He had also written one more letter to his mother, telling her about the job development and reassuring her not to worry. He knew that Aunt Minna gave her a blow-by-blow update on his every move and it didn't really bother him. He'd been having terrible pangs of homesickness lately, and he'd even been entertaining the idea of dropping in on his mother for a visit. But now he was in the mood of a little easygoing fun.

"Well, look who's here!" It was Sherry. Avrumie waved and smiled — the whole *chevrah* was gathered around their usual place, the dusty pool table in a dim corner of the hall.

"What's up with you, Abe? We thought we'd never see you again!" It was Albert, with a wry smile on his face.

He probably thought I went back to yeshivah, Avrumie thought suddenly. His next thought surprised him: *I wish I had.*

"Nah, I'm still around. I got myself my own place, and a job, and I've been kind of busy. Any news around here? Anything going on?"

Sherry and Monica locked eyes, and then Monica said to Stanley, "You tell him." Avrumie felt a prickle of apprehension run up his spine.

"The cops busted this place last week. Lots of kids ended up in the slammer. Drugs and stuff. It was really wild."

"Scary," put in Sherry. "We tried to run out the back door, but they had surrounded the place. Losers!"

"Who — the cops, or the kids who were caught?" That was Joe.

"Both, I guess." Sherry shrugged and made a face.

Avrumie was shocked and afraid. Police meant trouble. Deep trouble. Was he getting himself involved in a potentially dangerous situation, just by being involved in this nightlife? He shuddered at the thought of being questioned by the cops. What if they had thrown him in jail just for being at the scene of the crime? Could there be a deeper shame than having his parents called to bail him out? He suddenly felt a burning desire to leave the place and never come back.

"Oh, Abe — I forgot. The rabbi said to give you this."

Avrumie, surprised, took the proferred note from Joe. "I'll be seeing you, guys," he mumbled, and he strode out the door into the cool evening air.

He opened the note under a lamppost and read the hasty scrawl.

"Give me a call — I may have something. 651-7640. Binyomin Woolf."

Avrumie felt his heart skip a beat. The rabbi hadn't forgotten about him, hadn't given up on him! Truthfully, he wasn't ready to go back to a yeshivah setting, even one with a looser atmosphere than Zichron Yosef's. But Rabbi Woolf could help him put together all the confusing elements of his life, all the pieces that contradicted one another, and give him some idea of what to do next, besides working at the hardware store. Oh, to be in a yeshivah again; to have some structure; some...self-esteem!

He practically ran home, tumbled down the stairs, and closed the door to his room. He caught his breath as he waited for the phone to be picked up. It rang three times, and finally a woman answered.

"Hello?" She had a pleasant voice, but Avrumie was momentarily flustered.

"H-hi, ummmm...."

"Hold on one second — let me get my husband," she said pleasantly, and Avrumie appreciated her intuitiveness. "Binyomin — phone call!"

Ten seconds later, he heard the rabbi's voice over the phone wires. "Hello?"

"Uh, hi, this is Avru — I met you at the pool place." He stopped — that last bit sounded so foolish; so amateur. But the rabbi helped him out.

"Oh yeah, I remember you. Boy, you sure took your time calling me, huh?"

"I'm sorry," Avrumie apologized. "I just got the message."

"Well, that's a good sign, I guess; you've been keeping away from there?"

"I've been trying." Avrumie grinned sheepishly and felt good.

"Listen, I hate talking over the phone. Why don't you come over?"

"Tonight?"

"Yeah, why not? The night's young. I'll stay home from the Hall tonight if you are."

Avrumie chuckled. He liked this guy. "Okay — I'll be right over. 'Bye."

"Hang on one second — maybe you want my address?"

They both laughed, and thirty seconds later Avrumie Faber was out the door, feeling happier than he'd felt in a long time.

Fifty-eight

Sima inspected herself in the mirror. She'd had her hair cut the day before, and she definitely liked the results. What would her friends say when she got to school? Just thinking the word *friends* brightened her smile. Her situation at school had changed so much in the past two months. After their dinner together, her parents had suggested that Sima meet with a counselor to talk about the issues she had in school and at home. At first, Sima had balked. After all, that was the last thing she needed — another person to make her feel like a *neb*. But Ima had pressed her to meet Mrs. Goldstein just once, and their meeting had gone so well that Sima eagerly agreed to continue. In Mrs. Goldstein's words, their sessions were helping her sort through her feelings and her self-image, one step at a time.

In fact, her classmates seemed to be treating her differently since she had begun counseling. She actually got a phone call — her first this year — from Sara Neuman, asking her what that day's homework was. Although the reason for the call was a little lame, Sima was ecstatic that someone had actually thought to call her, of all people.

"Well, why not, Sima? You're a sweet, intelligent, with-it girl," Mrs. Goldstein had said kindly. "I think your classmates are going to see that more and more, and this may be the start of many more phone calls. I wouldn't be surprised if your parents were to be forced to install a separate phone line when your popularity peaks!"

At home, things were enormously better, too. For some reason, Shira hadn't been cutting into her as much, which really made a big difference. And Chavie had somehow discovered that Sima was an excellent massage therapist, and she frequently begged for a back rub, a service that Sima was only too eager to dispense. The two had had some good conversations that way, and it seemed that there was a mutual desire between them to get to know each other better. Actually, Chavie had been the one to take her to the fancy salon with a name she couldn't pronounce for her haircut.

Sima had also been getting help with study skills and alternative learning methods, based on her evaluation by Dr. Simmons. At first, she'd thought that the girls would laugh at her and make cruel remarks about her getting called out of class to go to the Resource Room. Strangely enough, however, no one seemed to notice, and there was even another girl in her class who got tutored as well. So many anticipated tragedies had turned out to be, in reality, very minor obstacles.

It was almost time to leave for school. Sima had been trying to come on time now that she no longer dreaded the hours spent in the classroom. She took one last look at the mirror and fixed her necklace. The necklace always brought a secret smile to her face because Avrumie had given it to her. On their way home after their talk together, he had given her the necklace that he said he'd worn once himself, just to be cool. The thought of Avrumie wearing the gold-plated chain was enough to make her burst out laughing, but it thrilled her to no end when Avrumie conferred his gift upon her.

"This will be our little secret, Sim-Sim," he'd said before they parted at the edge of the front lawn. "And remember: you tell Ima and Abba where you found me, and I'll k— I'll be furious with you." He had tapped her arm gently then, and she'd gone home, the necklace carefully cradled in her hand.

"Siiiiiiiiima!"

Shira's voice carried across the house.

Sima rolled her eyes, then stopped herself. "What, Shira?"

Shira ran down the steps, clutching her backpack. "Oh, good — you're still here. Wanna walk to school with me?"

"Sure," Sima said, grabbing her coat and her own book bag.

They walked out the door together for the first time all year.

Dina had been ironing in the laundry room, but the last exchange had caught her attention. "Sima? Shira? Where did they go?"

The foyer was empty — no sign of either of the girls.

"Am I starting to imagine things?" she asked the mirror in the hallway. "I don't believe what just happened. I think I just saw Sima and Shira walking to school together!"

Fifty-nine

"**H**ey, look at this, Eemes!"

Dina looked up from her cookbook at Yosef's offering and gasped. It was a large, full-color picture of the common cockroach.

"Ughhhh, Yosef, get that away!"

"What's wrong, Ima — it's just a bug. And it doesn't even bite. Hey — what's that crawling up your leg...!!" He ran away laughing as Dina swatted at him good-naturedly. Yosef could bring a smile to anyone's face, no matter what their previous mood.

Chavie sauntered into the kitchen. "What's for supper?"

"I don't even know myself," Dina admitted. Here it was, already five o'clock, and she hadn't prepared a single thing. She was tired, and cooking held no appeal.

"Why don't you let me cook something?"

Dina looked at her in surprise. Chavie, cook? She had never even been near the stove, except to sample or scorn.

"I'm serious, Ima. I've been thinking about it a lot." Chavie stopped and looked anxiously at her mother. Was this a good time to broach the subject that had been occupying her mind for so long? Ima looked tired, but she seemed to be in a good mood, and there was no one else in the kitchen. She took a deep breath. "I've been talking to other girls about it, and all their mothers have them cooking and baking already. I know

223

you still think of me as a little girl, but I'm really not. I'm almost...I'm almost ready to start thinking about getting married."

She snuck a look at her mother. Dina regarded her daughter intently. It had been a very long time since she and Chavie had had a heart-to-heart, and she welcomed the opportunity to bond. Truthfully, she did realize how fast Chavie was growing up, but the thought scared her. *Shidduchim?* Let them first get Sima through high school! "Go on, Chav," she said reassuringly.

Chavie sat down across from her mother. "It really scares me, Ima. All the girls are talking about *shidduchim* and marriage, but I feel so unprepared for it. I don't even know how to boil an egg!"

"I know how you feel, Chavie," Dina empathized. "When I married Abba I didn't know the first thing about cooking. I learned pretty quickly, though, and it turned out to be very enjoyable. If you want to start practicing, I guess I wouldn't object to it too strongly. I always feel like it's my responsibility, though, and it's something I enjoy."

"I really would like to try it out. But — but there's more to this *shidduch* business than just the cooking." Chavie paused. How could she say it? "I was talking to my friends the other day about the whole *shidduch* process, and one of them said something very disturbing. She said that a girl isn't just judged by herself, but she's judged also by her family. I — I'm nervous what people will say about...."

"About Avrumie?" Dina could not believe her voice had come out so steadily, considering that she felt like the wind had been knocked out of her. Of course this conversation had been just waiting to happen, but once the words and thoughts had come out in the open they were terrifyingly real. She looked at Chavie, who was studiously examining the pattern of the tablecloth, realizing the bomb she had dropped, but feeling relieved she had said it. Dina sighed. What could she say?

"It's hard for all of us, Chavie. For Abba and I, but also for you kids. The one thing we have to keep in mind, though, is that we have to do what's best for us, not for the rest of the world. We have to love Avrumie and see him as part of the family even if we are looked down upon by everyone else. Sometimes people are very shallow, Chavie, and we ourselves can be shallow, too. It's certainly not your fault that Avrumie is holding where he's holding right now. If a boy doesn't want to go out with you based on our family circumstances, I really don't think he's the right boy for you. You don't want to marry someone who is only concerned about what other people will say, right?"

"You're right, Ima. It's just...I can't help feeling frustrated at the whole situation, and even angry at Avrumie. How can he do this to everyone? I know how hard it is on you and Abba. I've caught you crying, and I know that Abba has been so tense. It's just not fair! And all the kids are feeling it, too. Shira is miserable — she feels like it's her fault that Avrumie left, because she used to tease him so much. Dovid doesn't know what to think anymore, but he's scared that Avrumie joined a cult, and Chanan and Yosef have a special *tzedakah* box where they're collecting money for Avrumie because they think he's in jail!"

"Whaaaat?!!" Dina was shocked, horrified, and amused all at once. She hadn't known any of this inside information, and the last part really shook her. It was, she realized, her own fault that the children had such distorted views of Avrumie's circumstances. She had never actually told them where he was and what he was doing. She would have to lay the facts on the table — and soon, unless she wanted things to really get out of hand. "I'm really glad you're telling me this, Chav, because it's important for me to know it. Never underestimate the imagination of kids, I guess."

"Well, you haven't really told us anything, and we don't want to pry," Chavie said slightly accusingly.

"You're right, and I'm going to have to set things straight. I'll tell you first, because you're the oldest and you deserve to know. Avrumie is living in Aunt Minna's basement. He's working in a hardware store during the day, since he's not in school. He hangs out with certain people who do not exactly excite me and does certain things that make me very unhappy like smoking and playing pool, but he does avoid doing

225

anything very serious, like drugs or *chillul Shabbos*. I've been in touch with him a little bit, and he seems to be pulling himself together a bit and reevaluating things. For our part, Abba and I have been getting some guidance on how to relate to Avrumie, and it seems to be helping all of us."

"You know, I've really noticed the difference in the house. You seem much less tense, and Abba isn't as strict as he used to be."

Dina was again surprised by her daughter's astuteness. She had never known Chavie to be so incisive. "Thank you for saying that, darling. We've really been trying. Even though this is a really hard situation for all of us, we've seen a lot of good come out of it. Even the fact that we're sitting here having a good conversation is a big step, I think."

"It's true. What about Abba? Is he in touch with Avrumie?"

Dina shifted uncomfortably. "Ummm, no, they haven't spoken yet. It's very difficult for both of them, but eventually, *b'ezras Hashem*, they'll be able to have a good relationship."

Dina was quiet, lost in thought, envisioning Ephraim and Avrumie sitting together learning *b'chavrusa*. Chavie was also quiet.

"Ima?"

"Hmmm?"

"Why don't we invite Avrumie over for Shabbos this week?"

Dina was startled at the idea. "That's an interesting suggestion. I don't really know if he'd come, but...I'll talk it over with Abba."

"That way we'd show him that we really miss him and that we still love him, right?"

Dina smiled at Chavie's infectious enthusiasm and warmth. Why hadn't she thought of the idea herself?

"You're absolutely right, honey. You're one smart, sensitive young woman. Any boy who doesn't want to go out with you ought to have his head examined!" She glanced at the kitchen clock. "And I'd better make supper now — it's so late!" She paused. "You know what? You're in charge of the soup!"

Sixty

"You want to what?!"

"I want to invite Avrumie for Shabbos," Dina repeated as calmly as she could. But Ephraim looked no less panicky.

"It's about time, Ephraim. It's been, what — three months since he left home? That's ridiculous. For him not to see the family for such a long time is tragic. It wasn't even my suggestion; it was Chavie's."

Ephraim seemed not to hear her. His own mind was in overload, running through possible scenarios, his heart struggling with conflicting emotions. He had grown so much since Avrumie had left home. Together with Rabbi Woolf and a lot of introspection on his part, he had become a new person. But could his whole new personality crumble if put to the test of his oldest son? He was frightened and unnerved, and yet he yearned for Avrumie to return. Every night since the fateful argument he begged Hashem to forgive his deficiencies as a parent and to return Avrumie to them and to *Yiddishkeit*. He had started a private Avrumie Fund, giving large amounts of *tzedakah* as a *zechus* for his son. And yet, when it came down to the wire, what would happen when he and Avrumie were reunited?

Dina watched Ephraim's face anxiously, aware that he was struggling, and yet not able to read his thoughts. Finally he turned away from her and sighed.

"I'm scared, Dina. What will I say when I see him the first time? Will I accept him back as my son? Will I hug him? Does he still hate me? What if he shows up without a yarmulke? How will I react? What if he baits me at the table again, in front of the children? What if he's *mechallel Shabbos* in our very own home?"

Dina cut him off sharply. "Listen to what you're saying, Ephraim! Don't you have any faith in Avrumie? Do you think he would really be so disrespectful and uncaring? You're being *choshed* him without even seeing him and where he's holding! And what happened to the new Ephraim who was able to deal so well with Sima and Dovid and all the others? Has everything you've resolved with Rabbi Woolf gone out the window all of a sudden? Have all our talks about acceptance and love and reasonable expectations gone out the window? What's wrong with you, Ephraim?!"

Ephraim hung his head meekly and couldn't meet his wife's eyes. She was right, and he was wrong. It was unlike Dina to be so aggressive, but she was justified in her anger and disappointment. Dina, realizing that her point had been made, fell silent, examining her sleeve. It was just so frustrating!

The alarm clock ticked loudly in the uncomfortable silence. Ephraim finally lifted his head.

"You're right, Dina," he said softly. "I was speaking from fear and I didn't mean to say what I said. We daven to Hashem each morning not to put us into challenging situations, and there's a reason for that. I feel like meeting Avrumie will be a tremendous challenge for me, and I want to prepare myself properly for it. I really want to see him — please believe me. I really...I really love him."

Dina looked warmly at her husband. He was so strong and so true to himself and to her. "I'm also scared, Ephraim," she said gently. "But I'm very hopeful. This could be a real turning point for us. If he decides to come, that is."

"I think I'll speak to Rabbi Woolf about it right away. Maybe we'll role-play some possible scenarios so that I feel more prepared."

"Can I come with you also? I think it would help me, too."

"Of course, my wonderful wife." He smiled as she blushed. "Go ahead and invite Avrumie. It will be a golden opportunity for him to see how we've grown and for us to gauge where he's holding. How do you think the children will react?"

"Well, I mentioned it to Dovid tonight. He seemed very excited, but also nervous. I think he feels some anger towards Avrumie, and he doesn't know how to deal with it."

"I can imagine. Maybe we should speak to all the kids tomorrow night. I'll come home for supper and we can have a little conference."

Dina smiled. "That's a great idea! I hope it doesn't backfire on us, though. Can you imagine this: Avrumie sits down at the Shabbos table and Shira pipes up, 'Avrumie, we're all being nice to you, just like Abba and Ima said to be.' "

They both laughed. "Maybe we should ship that one out for Shabbos!"

"Or muzzle her!"

"*Kinaina harah* — each of them have such unique personalities."

"Unique is a good word."

They eyed each other happily. Ephraim felt that a huge weight had been lifted from his heart. Avrumie would be coming back home, albeit just for one Shabbos, but that was a good start. Dina felt elated — Ephraim was excited to see Avrumie, and this time they would really try hard to give him what he had needed all along: genuine, unconditional love.

Sixty-one

Avrumie opened the door as quietly as possible and eased himself into the house. He knew it was later than his aunt and uncle would appreciate, and he did not want them seeing the way he looked at the moment. He stank of cigarette smoke and his eyes were bloodshot. It had been a long day and an even longer night, and he was absolutely exhausted.

Although he no longer frequented the pool hall, he still met his friends in the pizza shop downtown and in various other hangouts. Tonight he'd made an exception and had gone to the Hall — after learning with his *chavrusa* for an hour — in honor of Mikey's birthday. He smiled despite his exhaustion at the thought of his learning session with Akiva Jacobs, the *chavrusa* Binyomin Woolf had set up for him. His once-a-week sessions with Akiva were helping him to slowly renew his connection to *Yiddishkeit*.

He crept to the staircase and saw the note attached to the wall. Probably Aunt Minna reminding him to put his wet laundry in the dryer. He staggered downstairs and groped his way to the door handle of his room.

The room was a disaster area. Clothes strewn everywhere, papers crumpled up around the wastebasket, and an unhealthy stench in the air. One of these days he would have to clean up. Either that or hire a cleaning woman. Boy, he sure was funny at four in the morning — cleaning woman indeed! He lay down on the bed and kicked off his boots. They were a hand-me-down gift from Mark, who was always tiring of his old clothes and buying new stuff. Avrumie withdrew Aunt Minna's note from his pocket and smoothed it out. As he glanced at the handwriting, he started. It wasn't Aunt Minna's; it was his mother's.

Dear Avrumie,

Abba and I and all the children would like to invite you to spend Shabbos with us this week. We all miss you very much and would love your company. If it doesn't work out with your schedule, you can come over for only one of the meals. We'd really love to see you. No need to r.s.v.p.!

Kisses,

Ima

Avrumie reread the letter and fingered it for a long time. What should he do? He was overcome with an urge to see the family again. It had been much too long since he'd been with them — Bracha must have grown up already! It would be very awkward, of course, but that would soon smooth over. The real question in his head was Abba. Ima had deliberately written "Abba and I" to give him the message that his father missed him, too, but was that the real truth? Were these Shabbos plans just an accident waiting to happen; another big blowup between him and his father? Then again, they'd both had lots of time to cool off since he'd left home. Avrumie had even found himself, at times, hoping that his father missed him; wishing that perhaps Abba might call, then chiding himself for imagining the impossible.

The alternative to accepting the family's Shabbos invitation was not very tantalizing. Shabbos had become a problem for Avrumie. His new lifestyle had necessitated some alterations in his Shabbos observance, and that meant that he couldn't stay with any fully *shomer Shabbos* family, so as not to offend them. He'd tried staying at friends' for Shabbos, but their total carelessness in Shabbos observance shocked and appalled him, and so he'd often wind up eating by himself, in the dark basement, and sleeping most of the day. Of course, Aunt Minna constantly invited him to join them, but the multitudes of guests they had over each week were definitely not his type, and he felt he would only embarrass his aunt and uncle by showing up.

Avrumie drummed his fingers on the wall to break the silence. A wave of homesickness washed over him, and he knew he would accept Ima's invitation. For the first in a long time, he offered a silent prayer to God: *Please — no disasters!*

Sixty-two

Avrumie stood outside in the darkness, staring at the familiar door, and hesitated. It had been so long. There was a chill in the night air, and in the overwhelming silence he could hear faint sounds from inside the house, beckoning to him. Finally he got up the courage to knock. He steadied himself and found that his hands were shaking. It seemed an eternity until he heard the key turn in the lock. And then the door was flung open and light washed over the whole scene.

"Avrummmiiiiiiieee!!" Chanan was the first to tackle him, engulfing him in a bear hug. Yosef followed, trying to jump onto Avrumie's shoulders. Avrumie let himself be swept along in the rush of love and affection.

"Hey, leggo!" he yelled good-naturedly as someone banged him on the head. Dovid came up to him shyly, and Avrumie embraced him. Dovid looked grateful that Avrumie had made the first move, and he held his brother tightly, smiling.

"Vrum-vrum!" It was Shira, and even she looked like she was glad he was home. He picked her up and swooped her in the air, enjoying her delighted shrieks.

"You gained fifteen pounds, Shira!" he said as he dropped her on the floor.

There was Chavie, smiling, standing in the doorway. Avrumie

bowed to her and they both laughed. "Hi, big bro!" she said, swatting at him as he ducked.

Sima approached him hesitantly, and he instantly gave her a high-five. "Hey, Sim-Sim!" Her eyes lit up.

In the whole, wonderful ruckus, there were two important people missing, and Avrumie noticed it just as Ima and Abba walked into the room. Ima came first, practically running at him, smothering him in a huge hug.

"We wanted to give the kids their fair share of you," she explained into his shirt as he held her tightly.

Ephraim watched Avrumie hug his mother, and he felt the tears prick the back of his eyes. Then she was released from his embrace, and it was his turn. He walked over to Avrumie and impulsively grabbed him tightly. Avrumie did not struggle, and his smile did not falter. Dina watched from the corner of her eye and left the hallway quickly as she felt her tears spring forth. The children had already occupied themselves with other things and Avrumie and Ephraim were left in the hallway alone.

"We're so glad that you came," Ephraim said in a slightly choked voice.

"It's good to be back," Avrumie said, trying to sound off-handed but failing utterly. He also seemed emotionally charged.

Was this the moment for a heart-to-heart exchange? Ephraim wondered. He quickly checked himself. The talks could wait until after the meal. He grabbed Avrumie by the hand.

"What are we standing here for — let's start!"

Minutes later, everyone had seated himself at the table, after waging battles over who got to sit next to Avrumie. Avrumie bounced Bracha on his lap during *Shalom Aleichem* and she gurgled happily. Dina looked at her oldest son and at the other smiling faces at the table, and she felt her heart would burst with joy. It was a miracle of sorts that they were all together again, and she prayed that nothing would burst the wonderful bubble. Avrumie was dressed nicely in black slacks and a starched white shirt. He was wearing a *kippah*, of course, and his hair was combed stylishly, if not to her taste. He seemed relaxed and happy.

Serving the soup, Dina went over Rabbi Woolf's instructions in her mind: Don't bring up the past, just focus on the present; show him unconditional acceptance and love; make his favorite dishes; keep away from offensive *divrei Torah* and just let things flow lightly and naturally. So far they were doing okay. Chanan had recited his version of his rebbe's *d'var Torah* — an incomprehensible mash of words that were supposed to highlight the gravity of the *chait ha'eigel*. Yosef had already spilled his soup — onto Chavie's lap, and the two had handled it surprisingly well.

"Well, I see nothing around here has changed," Avrumie remarked jokingly after the soup calamity, and Dina and Ephraim exchanged secret smiles. Things *had* changed. Big time.

Dina cleared the bowls and got the main course ready.

"So, what are you doing lately, O Big Brother?" asked Chavie, smiling.

Avrumie stiffened slightly, but relaxed again. There was something about the atmosphere that felt very safe and nonthreatening. "Oh, I do a bit of this and a bit of that. I have a job in a store which keeps me pretty busy. And I'm just so popular that my social life takes up every spare second," he said wryly.

"You've always been a people person," said Ephraim, surprised at how naturally the words came out. "You must make a lot of sales."

Avrumie looked at him in shock. *Did Abba just compliment me?* was the first thought that ran through his mind. He could only nod feebly and say, "Yeah, I guess so."

Ephraim offered silent thanks to Hashem.

"What kind of store?" Trust Shira to ask.

"Hardware — no Barbies there, Shira — sorry!"

Shira stuck her tongue out at him. "I never played with Barbies."

"You mean they have all kinds of tools there?" Chanan's eyes were alight with the thought.

"Yeah — they have a whole section of them, and every single nail and screw you could imagine."

"Really?" Yosef was drooling. "Can we get some for free because you work there?"

Avrumie laughed. "I'll see what I can do," he promised. Just then Dina appeared with the main course. "Speaking of presents and stuff, here's something for everyone to share, for dessert." He took two chocolate bars from his pocket and handed them to his mother.

"Oh — how thoughtful of you, Avrumie!" Genuinely touched, she leaned over and kissed him on the head.

"You could have just brought us a screwdriver," Chanan said sourly.

"You're welcome," replied Avrumie sarcastically, but he was hiding a smile.

"Can I read my parashah sheets?" Shira spoke up, screeching, as usual, in her excitement.

"Stop whining, Shira."

"Stop whining, Sima."

"Who wants potato kugel?" Instant chaos reigned at the prospect of Ima's delectable kugel.

"Very smooth, Ima," complimented Ephraim on Dina's swift change of tracks.

Avrumie observed the whole exchange in a kind of wonder. Things were different than he remembered. The table was much more peaceful and relaxed. Abba hadn't called anyone his "little *tzaddikel*," and Ima and Abba were actually giving each other small fond looks. Sima and Shira weren't at each other's throats, like they used to be, and everyone looked, well, happier. Even Ima looked less tense than she used to.

A vicious thought ran through his mind: *They're much better off without me here*. Was it just self-pity, or could it be true? Avrumie knew he had created a lot of tension in the house — that was certain. But, he argued with himself, perhaps he had just reacted from existing tension that had been there all along. Who could say for certain? The other explanation would be that his leaving had brought them all to the realization that something, somewhere, needed fixing. He hoped it was the latter, but the thought that perhaps he had been the cause of all the tension in the household filled him with guilt. He attacked his chicken unhappily.

"Does it need salt, Avrumie?"

He started. "It's fine," he answered shortly, and took another forkful. Bracha began to whine, and he ran to pick her up.

"That child has hardly touched the floor tonight," Dina chided good-naturedly.

Bracha's happy gurgles dissipated Avrumie's surliness, and he found himself singing along with the rest of the family when they broke into a hearty "*Kah Ribbon.*"

When Dina brought out the dessert, she was rewarded for all her efforts by Avrumie's facial expression and the lavish praise that followed.

"You made all my favourite stuff, Ima," he accused her, grinning with delight. "You want me to get fat."

"You're already fat." Shira stuck her tongue out at him and he threw his napkin on her head.

"Ima, you're the best. I haven't eaten like this in...a long time."

There was a sudden silence as the family acknowledged Avrumie's long absence. Ephraim came to the rescue with a cheerful, "Is this stuff for show, or can we make quick work of it?!"

The meal was over almost too quickly, and then, before they knew it, the table was cleared, *bensch*ing was over, and everyone had retreated to his or her own favorite Friday night spot. Avrumie, however, stood in the corner of the room awkwardly. Should he leave now? He felt unsure of where he stood in the eyes of the family: on the one hand, they had treated him like a son and brother; on the other hand, he had just come back into their lives after a very long, painful separation. He almost wished that Yosef and Chanan would ask him to help them spy on Sima, or that Dovid would come over to him and shmooze, but they seemed oblivious to him. Ima was lying on the sofa for a much-needed rest, and Abba had retreated to his library. Abba. He had been especially caring and sensitive tonight; hadn't rubbed Avrumie the wrong way at all. Was it just a show, or had he really changed? Should Avrumie swallow his pride and go to speak to him?

As he deliberated, the subject of his thoughts entered the living room.

Ephraim found Avrumie standing uncertainly in the corner of the room. Was this the time he had been waiting for? He forced himself to smile through his nervousness.

"Are you in a rush to leave?"

Avrumie shook his head uncomfortably. He hadn't really exchanged very many words with his father in the course of the evening. His thoughts had been too jumbled. Should he forgive Abba for all the pain he had caused him and just focus on how much he had changed? Should they discuss all the hurt so he could get it out of his system at last?

"Do you feel like talking now, Avrumie?"

Avrumie shrugged. "I guess."

"You're not too tired?" Ephraim was giving him a way out.

"Nah — I'm fine; I'm used to late nights by now." Avrumie decided to lay all his cards out on the table. He didn't want Abba living any delusions: this was who he was, and Abba could either accept him or reject him.

Ephraim winced slightly, but he quickly turned toward his study and Avrumie followed. Ephraim closed the door behind them.

Ephraim sat down behind his desk and motioned Avrumie to sit. Avrumie sat down casually, a tornado of thoughts as he eyed his father and the bookshelves that lined the walls. The life that had once been flew back before his eyes, along with the warm memories of learning *b'chavrusa* with Abba in this very office, and the praise he'd received within these walls. How times had changed. Sometimes Avrumie felt as if this whole period of upheaval was one long nightmare and that suddenly he would wake up and find himself back where he had once been — happy and productive.

He crossed his legs and tipped the chair back slightly. Although he had the air of confidence and cool, his heart beat rapidly inside and his palms were sweaty. Ephraim didn't even try for the cool. His only thoughts were: *Hashem, help!*

He cleared his throat. "I'm so glad you joined us tonight, Avrumie."

"Yeah, it was nice."

A silence.

"It's been a long time." Ephraim's voice trailed off, leaving him with that stand-alone statement whose five words spoke volumes. A strange expression swept Avrumie's features, but he quickly composed himself.

"Yes, it has," he replied, but his voice was softer, less assured.

"I hope you'll...come often."

"I'll try." Avrumie took a deep breath. Out with it — Abba had to know what he was up against. "But I'm pretty busy."

"On Shabbos?" Ephraim had to ask. *Baruch Hashem*, his voice came out in a nonthreatening way, quite casual, shocking himself more than Avrumie.

"Yes, even on Shabbos." Avrumie eyed him levelly. "I'm not the kid I used to be, Dad. I want you to know that. I'm not...observant of everything, and I hang out and do things that would probably make you really upset."

He was testing, and Ephraim knew it. He felt the heat rise in him, but he willed himself to play it cool.

"I can imagine," he said neutrally, keeping his face impassive. The next question he asked took Avrumie's breath away. "Is it making you happier?"

Avrumie felt as if he'd been punched in the stomach. His face grew flushed, his eyes watered, and his heart began to pound with the force of that question and the screaming of his conscience. *No! No!* his entire being yelled. *I am not happier. I am miserable and depressed. I feel alone in the world, and as unfulfilled as a human being can be!*

It was time to get to the heart of it all, and Ephraim dug in.

"We never talked about our parting, Avrumie. I know that our last conversation together — before you walked out — was like the straw that broke the camel's back. There was a lot of resentment, a lot of inadequacy and false expectations boiling up inside of us, and we never discussed it like two mature adults. Don't think I can't remember being a teenager, Avrumie. I'm old, but not that old." He permitted himself a smile. "I'm going to say something that will shock you, but I hope you'll take it the way it's meant. Your leaving was a real gift, Avrumie. It was a gift because it forced me to evaluate myself and see where I was wrong. It was the biggest wake-up call I'd ever gotten. Since you've left, Ima and I have been to a counselor who has helped us see where we went wrong in raising you and the other children. All parents make mistakes, but *baruch Hashem* we had the good fortune of being shown how we can grow together to create a happier home. Don't you notice the difference, Avrumie?"

Avrumie sat staring at the man before him. *So this is what an out-of-body experience feels like*, was all he could think. Was this really his father? "Grow together to create a happier home"? Abba, recognizing that there was "a lot of inadequacy and false expections"? And yet it was true. The home was different. The kids were calmer, happier, more...content. He realized that his father was waiting for a response.

"Uh, yeah, I do," he said, hating himself as the words came out disjointed and insincere. *Oh, why can't you just speak to him from the heart*, he berated himself. *Why not let go and let everything become water under the bridge? He's different now, and things will be different*, his inner self cried out furiously.

"I mean, I really do see a difference," he added. "Everyone seems much, like, happier, and you, I mean, you're much calmer and less...." His voice trailed off.

"Less what, Avrumie? You can tell me everything, and I will not interrupt."

Abba's eyes were sincere and honest. Avrumie took a deep breath, and all the words, held in for so long like a festering wound, hurtled from his lips.

"You're less fake about things. You don't pretend all of us are going to be holy tzaddikim and you don't only care about your own glory. You're more patient with the kids, and you're not criticizing the whole time and putting on this whole phony-baloney 'who can make me prouder' act. It was so hard for me, always having to keep up the show for you, being afraid to disappoint you until I couldn't handle it anymore. The yeshivah wasn't right for me, but it was right for you, and that was all that mattered. I was living a fake life, and I hated every second of it, but I had to be the *'talmid chacham,'* can't let on that I'm going to a movie instead of to my *chavrusa* tonight, otherwise all your hopes will be dashed and I'll burn for having no *kibbud av.*

"And then there's the whole business about dress: as long as the yarmulke's big and black, and the shirt is white, and you've got the hat, you're a *tzaddik gamur.* But ditch the hat or put on some stripes, and you're a write-off! How fake can you possibly get? Some of the worst kids I've ever met dressed the part, and looked the part, but inside they were even...even worse than me. Yes, worse than me, and I've been pretty low. It got so that I couldn't even keep up the game anymore. That's all it is, you know — a game. You start out by trying to look the frummest, and you end off by seeing who can act the most goyish. The one who goes the farthest wins.

"Don't think I'm kidding — I've seen guys and girls from the 'best homes,' quote unquote, do some pretty sad things. I know what everybody thinks: they have no dignity; they're plain crazy; they're too mixed up to know anything, blah, blah, blah. The sad truth is, though, that they're not pushing themselves for anything more than this: proving to themselves that they are worthy people. That they can amount to something, even if that something is shooting a perfect game of pool! The thing that connects all of us in this shady group is that we all share the same kinds of experiences. We call it the three F's: *frumkeit*, family, and fakeness. We were all taught lists and lists of *aveiros* and punishments, without ever being taught anything beautiful about this religion. It was always 'don't say that!' and 'don't do this!' What kind of life is that?

"And then there are the questions that don't get answered. 'It's *kefirah*! I don't want to hear another word!' is a favorite cop-out. Or the rebbe will just tell you that you have to have *emunah* and that we can't understand everything when you try to ask. What kind of religion is it anyway if you can't get straight answers to your questions? I know you and Ima don't hate me, but you've really made my life a living nightmare."

Ephraim sat helplessly, riding the wave of pathetic rage, knowing that it emanated from a heart full of pain and emptiness. He reminded himself of Rabbi Woolf's words: *He is not mad at you; he is mad at himself.* It helped deflect the hurt. The old Ephraim would have had a sharp retort ready or would have left the room with a disgusted comment, but the new Ephraim listened to his son and simply sat there, absorbing his words.

Avrumie's instinct was to leave after he had said his piece, but something in him forced him to stay in his seat. He couldn't meet his father's eyes and instead put his head down on his arms, ashamed of the tears that came suddenly but thankful to have finally let them out of his heart.

If he had only looked up he would have seen his tears mirrored in Ephraim's eyes. "Avrumie, Avrumie, your pain is so real, so raw," Ephraim said slowly. He pushed the box of tissues toward his son gently. "My eyes have been opened to a new way of living, a new outlook on life, on Torah, on *Yiddishkeit*. The things that I once held dear have now become devalued, and I have you to thank for it. I mean it sincerely when I say that you have been a real blessing to me and to Ima. Together, we have really taken a close look at the way we have been living and evalu-

ated it. We are now working on experiencing the joy of Torah life —
and there is an unbelievable amount of joy.

"I don't want to say that previously we did not enjoy *Yiddishkeit*, but I
think we were approaching it from a different angle. The questions that
went unanswered — I now humbly admit to fear. Yes, Avrumie, I was
afraid. When you asked me about Hashem, I was afraid that you were
bordering on *kefirah*. I was afraid that by answering you I would be encouraging you in your path to rebellion. Little did I know, at the time,
that my attitude only increased your resentment and poisoned your feelings about *Yiddishkeit*.

"And I want to say something else, Avrumie. I think it was hard for
me to relate to you. When I grew up, I never had the burning questions
that you have. I accepted everything simply. I never looked beyond what
my rebbeim told me. So tonight, I admit to you, that I never understood
'*Chanoch le'na'ar al pi darko*' until I looked clearly at my relationship with
you. You have different needs, Avrumie. Now I recognize that. In my
desire to raise you in a Torah way, I was trying to squeeze my 'square'
son into a round peg, determined that he should fit the mold at all costs.
It didn't occur to me that perhaps it was the wrong peg."

Avrumie cradled his head in his hands, not meeting his father's eyes,
but his eyes were bright and hopeful. His spirit soared. This was more
amazing than he could ever have dreamed. This was nothing short of a
miracle.

Sixty-three

"Get down, Yosef, she sees you!"

"You be quiet, Chanan."

"That's it — I don't want to play with you anymore. You're like a babboon — you can't move quietly."

"Oh yeah? Well, you're like an — an ostrich."

"Oh, good one. Will you keep your voice down? If she sees us, it's over."

"Okay. What's she doing now?"

"Talking to her dolls."

Stifled giggles.

"I can't wait to see her fly into the air when we boo her."

"She'll probably jump ten miles."

"Twenty!"

"Shhhhhhh."

"I'm shhhhhhhing."

"What's that noise?"

"My stomach."

"Why is it making funny noises?"

"It's all the food in there. Didn't Ima make great stuff?"

"Yeah. She made it for Avrumie."

"I'm glad that he's back."

"He's not really back. Just for Shabbos."

"How do you know?"

"I just know, okay?"

"Why doesn't he want to live here anymore?"

"I dunno. Maybe because it's so boring."

"Yeah, it really is."

"Or maybe because he doesn't like us anymore."

"Well, he looked like he liked us. He even brought us chocolate."

"Yeah — who needs chocolate?"

"Yeah. Maybe next time he'll bring us a wrench."

"I want a Swiss Army knife."

"I want a telescope."

"Why?"

"So that I can see if there are really people living on Mars."

"Oh, come on!"

"Now you're being loud — look, I'll bet she saw us!"

"Oh, who cares about her?! She's such a baby; talking to her dollies!"

"Why are you in such a bad mood?"

"Who says I'm in a bad mood?"

"Me."

"Well, I don't have to tell you."

"It's because of Avrumie, right?"

"Don't be such a nosy-nose."

"Why are you upset about Avrumie?"

"I hate when he's not here."

"Me, too."

"And Ima and Abba tried extra hard to be nice to him."

"Yeah — Abba didn't even yell when I pulled Shira's hair."

"You think we could make him stay?"

"How?"

"We could also be extra nice to him."

"We could buy him a present."

"Like what?"

"Like...like a short-wave radio."

"They're really expensive."

"Oh, then maybe...a pocket flashlight."

"Nah — he probably has tons of those."

"You think so?"

"Yeah. But maybe we could do something else."

"Like what?"

"I dunno."

"We could kidnap him, maybe."

A scornful look.

"How in the world would we kidnap him? He's much stronger than us. And anyway.... Forget it — it's a dumb idea."

"I don't think so."

"You never think your ideas are dumb, but they all are."

"Maybe after Shabbos we could write him a letter."

"Maybe."

"See — that idea wasn't dumb."

"Fine — most of your ideas are dumb."

"Moishie beat me up yesterday 'cuz of Avrumie."

"Why?"

"He said I'm a goy."

"Why does he think you're a goy?"

"He said 'cuz Avrumie dresses like a goy so that means our whole family is goyim."

"Did you beat him back up?"

"I tried, but he's stronger. Do you think he's right?"

"Come on, of course not!"

"I thought so. Moishie's just mean."

"Maybe he's a goy himself."

"Yeah."

"The kids in your class are so stupid."

Sixty-four

The phone rang.

Avrumie put the pillow over his head and scrunched back into his dreams, but the ringing was incessant. He grabbed the offending object and held it to his ear.

"Hello?" he grunted through a sleepy haze.

Across the line, he could hear weeping. A girl crying, sobbing.

"Who is this?" he asked, suddenly awake.

"Abe! Abe!" It was Monica's voice.

"What is it, Monica? What happened?"

Monica continued to sob; she could not speak.

"Meet me at the pizza shop and we'll take a walk," he said, and he jumped into his clothes. A quick glance at the clock told him it was four o'clock. He silently slipped out the door and made his way through the shadowy streets to one of their favorite hangouts. In a few mintues he saw Monica walking toward him, her eyes red-rimmed and wet with tears.

"Sherry...attempted suicide," she whispered, and her sobs began anew.

Avrumie felt the world spin around him as he absorbed Monica's words.

"What? How?" he asked blankly, feeling numb.

"Let's walk," Monica said, and they set off into the approaching dawn. Slowly, brokenly, Monica told Avrumie about the call she'd received. Sherry's parents had canceled her phone line and her credit card and had purchased a ticket to send her off to a seminary in Israel. It was the last straw. She'd left a note.... Her parents had found her, called the police, now they were working on her, hoping against hope.... It was too much to fathom.

"What are we doing to ourselves?" Monica asked dully, and Avrumie knew exactly what she meant. There was no meaning in the life they were living, only pain.

"If it happened to Sherry, it could happen to any of us," continued Monica. "Abe, I'm so scared."

"I know," said Avrumie, his thoughts racing. "Does anyone else know?"

"I didn't feel like telling anyone else," said Monica. "I thought...I thought you would be more helpful than they would. I don't know...."

Avrumie was touched, in an odd way. "I'm so sorry, Monica," he began. "This is such a shock. But I think it might be a message to all of us." He took a deep breath and looked at her. "There's no happiness in the life we're living now. We ran away from our homes, from our religion, looking to make a better life for ourselves. But are we? We're all just as depressed as Sherry, and you're right — it could have happened to any one of us. We all are nothing but losers, hanging around, smoking, drinking. It's not fun, it's a waste of time. Where are we really going? Nowhere. It's about time we made a decision to get going and accomplish something in life. We need to really sit and think about where and how everything falls into place. We've all been raised with Torah values, and we've all rejected them, but maybe, just maybe, we've been wrong...." He trailed off, looking down at his shoes.

"I just had a really revealing conversation with my dad. I sort of squared off with him about everything that has happened between us, and it feels really good to get it off my chest. I know that not everyone is as lucky as me — most of us couldn't have that kind of conversation with their parents in a million years. But it really got me thinking, because he asked me if I'm happier now. And what could I say? What could any of us say? If someone asked us if now, after we rejected all the falseness, co-ercion, and restrictions, are we happier people? What would we answer? If we were being completely honest, not a single one of us could have said yes. Not Mark, or Joe, or you, or any of us. At least when we were *frum*, we had some sort of purpose in life, but now we have nothing. We have emptiness.

"It's really a tragedy about Sherry, and I pray that she'll be all right, but I think this might be the wake-up call our gang needs. Things aren't getting any rosier, and they're only going downhill. Sherry reached rock bottom, and the rest of us, unless we change our direction, are also headed for the point of no return." Avrumie took a deep breath.

"I, for one, am leaving. I've sworn off the pool hall, the drinking, the 'scene.' It's too empty for me. I'm sick of the loneliness, the fake glitz, and the emptiness that comes from laughing too much and trying too hard to have fun. I'm thinking of going back to school and getting my-self a decent career. I'm even getting back into Torah learning, but for the right reasons this time. I'm taking things one step at a time, but at least I'm trying to stay on the Up escalator. I just hope that the rest of us will reevaluate things and kind of see the light."

Avrumie broke off abruptly. How had he let himself get so carried away, speaking from his heart, oblivious to the girl listening to him? He suddenly felt ashamed, embarrassed at revealing his true self. But Monica was open-mouthed, looking at him in awe.

"You've given me a lot to think about," was all she could say.

"I think I'd better say good-bye now," Avrumie returned gruffly, and he turned on his heel and strode away. He never even looked behind him.

Epilogue

ina was crying, and she had never felt happier in her entire life. Ephraim stood next to her, tall and straight, with his cheeks bursting in a smile bigger than she'd ever seen. The whole family was there — Chavie, wiping away her own tears, Dovid looking a little wet around the eyes himself, Yosef and Chanan grinning with excitement. Sima was smiling broadly, her shyness a thing of the past, and Shira had her own impish grin plastered across her minus-two-teeth smile. Bracha was, of course, in Avrumie's arms. The tears and the smiles washed away the grief and the pain, replaced it with a glowing love that could withstand the test of challenges and tension. Hashem had truly blessed them, guided them, and yes, He had spared them from things that could have been a lot worse.

Standing in the golden sunlight, Dina felt her soul would burst with happiness and gratitude. They, as a family, had come full circle and emerged, as a butterfly from a stifling cocoon, to soar to new heights. It had demanded a lot of effort and hardship from each of them, but then again, those who sow with tears will reap with joy. It was too soon to relax and breathe easy, but they could take things one step at a time. The important thing was that Avrumie was back, and that was a gift.

Avrumie looked into the shining faces of his family, and he fought back the tears. An unbidden thought rose up inside him, filled his whole insides, and reverberated through the depths of his being: *Thank You,*

God, for making this happen, he shouted inwardly. *I don't yet know You, and I've strayed from Your ways, but I know You will welcome me with open arms, and that You are good and just and true. Thank You, Hashem!*

He lingered for one moment against the brilliant sky, and then he gave himself up to the newfound happiness of his wonderful, special family.

Recommended Reading

The following books answer many questions teenagers may have:

Bulka, Reuven P. *Best-kept Secrets of Judaism*. Southfield, MI: Targum Press, 2000.

Kaplan, Rabbi Aryeh. *If You Were G-d*. Orthodox Union, 1993.

Kaplan, Rabbi Aryeh. *The Infinite Light: A Book about G-d*. Orthodox Union, 1993.

Kelemen, Lawrence. *Permission to Believe*. Southfield, MI: Targum Press, 1990.

Kelemen, Lawrence. *Permission to Receive*. Southfield, MI: Targum Press, 1996.

Speiser, Moshe. *Questions You Thought We Were Afraid You Would Ask*. Southfield, MI: Targum Press, 2004.

Waldman, Shmuel. *Beyond a Reasonable Doubt*. Feldheim Publishers, 2003.

Yossi. *Straightalk*. Southfield, MI: Targum Press, 2004.

A Partial Resource List

Kav Baruch Crisis Hotline
Helping Parents and Teenagers Get Through the Difficult Times
Jerusalem, Israel
(9722) 586-9279

MASK (Mothers and Fathers Aligned Saving Kids)
A Hotline, Referral, and Support Group for Parents of Children in
  Conflict
An international organization: London, Israel, and America
(718) 758-0400
www.maskparents.org

Ohel
A Multi-Faceted Jewish Social Services Agency
(718) 851-6300

Our Place
Teen Drop-In Center
1815 Avenue M, Brooklyn, NY
(718) 692-4058
Open every evening

Project Y.E.S.
A division of Agudath Israel of America
1404 Coney Island Avenue
Brooklyn, NY 11230
Phone: (718) 258-3131
Fax: (718) 504-7887
projectyes@pyes.org
www.rabbihorowitz.com

TOVA
A Teen Mentoring Program in the Five Towns
(516) 295-0550

The Yitti Leibel Helpline
An anonymous hotline staffed by *frum* therapists
(718) HELP-NOW, (718) 435-7669
With branches in Baltimore, Chicago, Cleveland, Detroit, Lakewood,
San Diego, and Toronto